Summer on Porgy

M. L. Johnson

3WAVE PRESS

DEDICATION

To Susan, Dane, Jenni, and Louis

CONTENTS

ACKNOWLEDGMENTS

There were too many helpful people for me to list them all, but there are three who can't go unnamed: Mike Scott for his unstinting cheerleading; David Halvorsen for suggestions, demands, and a beautiful cover design; and Susan, for her patience and unfailing encouragement.

Author's Note

Those of you wondering why I didn't represent the Bahamian dialect with phonetic spelling are owed an explanation; first, it's too slippery a slope for anyone short of a Kipling or a Twain.

Take the word 'boy', the most common interjection in the Bahamas. How difficult can it be to represent the pronunciation of three letters? Well, phonetic crusaders wrestling with the Bahamian version spell it variously bui, boi, buee, and doubtless other ways I haven't seen, but none of these capture the explosive 'b' and clipped upward ending that make it so distinctly Bahamian.

Another difficulty is the variation between islands and even settlement to settlement. Man-O-War, Red Bay, and Matthew Town aren't just three points of the compass separated by vast stretches of water, they have distinctive accents and vocabularies as well.

For these reasons I've stuck to Standard U.K. spelling, as would the speakers themselves if asked to write their dialogue. If the reader has spent time in the Bahamas, they will impose the correct pronunciation naturally. Porgy Island happens to hew closer to the Queen's English than any other Bahamian Island, so my standard spelling isn't as far out of line with the common speech there as it would be if I were writing about another island. As an authority on this, I can tell you why as well: One is the Moxey Scholarship Fund that allows Porgy students to go to Great Britain for a year or more of their schooling if they so desire. The other is the stringent standards imposed by Porgy school teachers, none of whom will abide what they call 'a lazy tongue'.

I can't close without mentioning the transposition of Ws and Vs, a common practice throughout the Bahamas, and never more delightful than when you hear someone mention 'the Bahamian Vomen's Wolleyball team'

TUESDAY

A squat wooden ferryboat, the inaptly named *Porgy Express*, ploughed a wide furrow through the sea on its way to Porgy Island. It was the only commercial link between that sandy dot in the southern Bahamas and Great Exuma Island, and though it was scheduled to arrive at ten-thirty a.m., it was a half hour late; an improvement on the average. The crowded lower deck of the boat was a mix of vacationers and native Porgians, most of the latter returning home from shopping trips to Miami or from visiting family elsewhere in the island chain.

The top deck of the ferry was open to the clear blue sky, and normally most of the tourists would be found there getting a head start on their sunburns and enjoying fresh ocean air untainted by diesel fumes. This Tuesday, however, most of the visitors on board were below enjoying conversation with the local crowd who were in an unusually lively mood. This left the upper deck to a group of youths doing their best to maintain a respectful presence as they watched a well-built man of thirty performing his morning callisthenics. This tall, ruddy fellow was Stewart Moxey, a proud son of Porgy Island, and he was returning home after a decade of globetrotting.

The members of the upper-deck peanut gallery were all young enough to show unabashed interest in a grown man hopping and leaping around. The group sat in two rows facing backwards on the bench seats, swinging their legs and smacking bubble gum as they took in the spectacle. Stewart surveyed his audience with a stern eye as he huffed and puffed his way through the routine, noting that the youngest looked to be about four years old, the oldest not more than twelve. There were a few tourist kids in the mix, but most were Bahamian and these were typical of Porgy's population, ranging from a deep chocolate brown to pink and freckled.

This fascinated group managed to remain quiet through the warm-up stretching, through the push-ups, the sit-ups, and even the fast-forward crunches, with only the odd giggle or punch in the ribs. The jumping-jacks, though, proved too silly for discipline to hold and snickers escalated to laughter and finally, as Stewart stopped to seize a small, chubby boy and hoist him over his head, to high-pitched shrieks. The chatter on the lower deck faltered and then died at the shrill interruption and the pilot stuck his head out and called up.

'Everything all right there, boss? You want those little heathens to come down here?'

'We're doing fine,' Stewart said loudly, 'but I'm going to feed…' Here he directed a questioning look at a pigtailed girl with thick glasses, indicating the boy over his head with a nod.

'Clive Knowles,' she whispered.

'But I'm afraid,' he called down, 'I'm going to have to feed young Knowles to the fish.'

'A Knowles, you say? Not an Anderson?'

'No.'

'Not a Pinder?'

'No.'

'Not a Rolles?'

'No sir, Knowles with a K.'

'Carry on then.'

'Aye aye, Captain,' he said, and the screaming resumed as Stewart swung the boy around. He was then obliged to swing each of them in turn, and by the time he'd finished, he reckoned his workout was done. Taking a seat in the middle of the kids, he laced his fingers behind his head and leaned back, drinking in the expanse of unbroken sea and sky as they steamed ahead.

It was this fitness fanatic that was responsible for the buzz of excitement on the lower deck, for he was a celebrity. Only a moderately famous one, it's true, due to the fact that competitive sailing, his area of expertise, isn't one of the world's more celebrated sports, but his good looks and the media's delight at linking him to a succession of glamorous women served to keep him in the news.

The rumour-mill on Porgy, that island's most efficiently run enterprise by a wide margin, had been churning out speculation as to the date of his return for weeks, and now, by sheer good fortune, these ferry passengers found themselves on the same boat as Stewart Moxey. The Bahamians were working out how to break the news to their fellow islanders for maximum effect and the tourists were composing emails and text messages to friends and family back home with the same general aim. Stewart was a big fish in the small pond of the southern Bahamas.

Water is fundamentally the same everywhere, we're told. Scientists can be tedious on this point, maintaining that H2O is H2O, whether it's the Baltic Sea, the river Nile, or the Pacific Ocean. The same recipe holds everywhere, they stubbornly insist. It was obvious to Stewart that none of these experts had found themselves on the ocean in the Bahamas on such a fine summer morning. If so, they'd have realized that the liquid whatsit supporting the boat was too bright, too crystalline; altogether too ethereal to be confused with the common substance covering so much of the earth's surface. This was knowledge gained first-hand; in his travels as a professional sailor, Stewart had seen the world's oceans and each in its turn was found wanting when compared with this gin-clear (copyright, Bahamas Dept. of Tourism) water. He'd seen the Mediterranean at its best as well as the pristine waters surrounding the Maldive Islands and nowhere attained to the eye-rubbing beauty he was now absorbing. It was here as nowhere else on earth that the colour turquoise really stretched and showed its range.

Stewart was returning home after unprecedented success as a professional sailor and his departure from competition hadn't gone unnoticed. A piece in the International Sailing News was headlined 'Say It Ain't So, Stewart!' and it read as follows:

"Sailing wunderkind and unparalleled race strategist Stewart Moxey, reportedly exhausted after a successful campaign he spearheaded for the Ricardo Syndicate's super-maxi, Cindy's Choice, is taking his first sabbatical from racing since he first exploded on the scene almost ten years ago. His rise from the humble world of Bahamian smack sailing to that of the most skilled skipper in the rarefied world of super-maxi racing is undoubtedly our sport's most compelling Cinderella story. Stewart is said to be returning to his home on Porgy Island in the southern Bahamas to rest for an unspecified period. Don't stay away too long, Stew, sailing won't be the same without you!"

In attributing his break from competition to fatigue, the story was typical of the press coverage, but Stewart himself wasn't so sure. Exhaustion was as good a description as any other, he reckoned, but a waning competitive drive and general malaise were more accurate. Perhaps those stemmed from some form of exhaustion, perhaps not. What was undeniable was the steady decline of his formerly relentless drive to win. Some experts pointed to a lack of serious competition to challenge him, others to the fact that he'd been at it solidly for a decade, stressing that such an uninterrupted stretch would wear down any athlete.

He'd run a gauntlet of psychological tests to please his corporate sponsors, but the lack of any consensus among the medical men led to Stewart's own decision to retire from the field for a while. He wasn't going to wait until the lethargy affected his performance and tarnished his record.

He was fortunate in having the luxury to stop, having amassed a tidy heap of gold due to a large income and modest habits; the only thing that had kept him away from Porgy Island and his family and friends had been his obsession with racing, and with that fading, returning home was the obvious choice.

As the sun climbed and started to bake the upper deck in earnest, the kids began filtering below and Stewart followed the last of them down the stairs. He was met by a wall of smiling passengers armed with cameras and phones, holding items to be signed. Twenty minutes later he emerged forward from the press of people and nodded to the pilot at the wheel.

'Mr. Stewart, welcome home!' the young black man said. 'You don't know me, I wager.'

Stewart had studied him as he boarded and had already narrowed him down to one of two families.

'Where do you live?'

'The Upper Broad.'

'Anderson. Mr. Anderson,' he ventured.

The man laughed. 'You're guessing, but that's fine. It's Ezra. Ezra Anderson.'

He turned to face Stewart and pulled on his protruding ears. 'The jug handles give me away?'

'Well, you Andersons are thick in the Broad,' Stewart said.

'You're being kind,' he said, grinning.

'Aren't many of you young bucks I recognise anymore, I've been away for a good while, you know.'

'I've seen you a few times.'

'Yeah, I usually managed to get back every Christmas, but that's about all these past twelve or fourteen years.'

'You been sailing those big boats that long?'

'No, no, I was in England going to school for a while and then I quit to race full time when I was about your age.'

'But you raced the smacks 'round here, I know that.'

'Sure, since I was a kid. But even when I was in middle school in England, I was home for the big races like Georgetown, and of course back then I was here every summer.'

'And now You made it back for the tournament.'

'I might be back for a while this time.'

'You're not here to fish in it, though?'

'You know, my dad doesn't even enter anymore, much as he loves to fish.'

'Yeah, why is that? Didn't you folks start the whole thing?'

'Well, my great-grandfather. The first one was back in the '30s.'

'Way back.' He whistled, shaking his head.

The tournament they referred to was the PIB, the Porgy Island Billfish Meet, a fishing tournament that swelled the island's population of 1,500 to twice that number. It drew avid fishermen from around the world.

'Well, thank God for it,' he added. 'The shillings from these next couple of weeks are what keep this island going.'

'You ever work the sportfishers?' Stewart asked. Local mariners were in high demand to crew the tournament boats.

'Naww. I run this old tub all week. Not complaining, mind you, I get the first shot at every pretty thing coming from California, Miami, Europe. If they don't come in a yacht or seaplane, they come on my boat.'

Stewart nodded.

'Yes sir. It's the closest I get to this,' Ezra said, pulling out a Nassau tabloid and turning it toward Stewart. It was a photo of Stewart on a sleek speedboat with a Scandinavian princess, a notably attractive young woman.

'Don't believe everything you read.'

'That's a fact. They've had you engaged to about half a dozen different beauties but I don't see a ring.'

Stewart laughed. 'The problem is, the truth would put people to sleep. I'm hardly in one place long enough to see the same girl twice.'

'Is that so?' he said, wincing at this depressing disclosure.

'You're some relation to Missy, aren't you?' Stewart said, shifting the subject. 'Missy Rolles.' He referred to the formidable manager of the Moxey Arms, the resort hotel owned by Stewart's family.

Ezra nodded.

'Your aunt?'

'No, my mum's cousin.' He cocked his head at Stewart. 'How is it she came to run your hotel, anyhow?'

'Back when my folks managed it...'

'Your folks did?'

'Yeah, when I was young. You didn't know?'

'I thought Missy was born to it.'

'I know, hard to imagine. But Dad handled the staff and my mum did everything else. Then when she passed...'

'In a car mash-up in Nassau, I...' He caught himself and looked sympathetically at Stewart. 'Pardon, I wasn't thinking.'

'Nothing to be sorry for, that's how it happened. She and my auntie both.'

'Leonard's mum.'

'That's right, they were sisters. So after that, my dad promoted Missy from head maid to assistant manager to help him out. It was going to be temporary, but it wasn't long before he handed the whole thing to her. Or maybe I should say, until she took it.'

They laughed nervously.

'But however it went,' Stewart added, 'he's never regretted it.'

'No, no, I 'spect not. That Gussie Mae runs a tight ship.'

Stewart nodded. 'We might have the best-run resort hotel in the Caribbean.'

'Y'know,' the pilot said hesitantly, 'Missy was at our house the other night and she was a little vexed. Well, plenty vexed. Some trouble getting in touch with you.'

Stewart creased his lips and gave a slight nod.

'She was planning a homecoming,' the pilot continued, looking at him out of the corner of his eye. 'But said she couldn't learn when you'd reach.'

'I hardly knew myself,' he said, looking away evasively. 'I've been chasing my own tail lately.'

'Tired y'say?'

'Something like that.'

'Well, that's what all the sip-sip's on about,' the young captain said, 'so could be she'll forgive you,' but his quick sidelong glance was sceptical.

'Here we are!' he said loudly, as the tip of the island appeared on the horizon. 'Welcome home, Mr. Stewart.'

As the Porgy Express rounded the east point of Willstown Harbour, Stewart surveyed the sleepy town as it rolled into sight; the busy wharf, the familiar green-and-yellow schoolhouse, and the cluster of pink government buildings on the low hill behind. Ezra interrupted the rush of memories by pointing out a crowd gathered expectantly on the wharf front.

'Looks like you have a little greeting party,' Ezra said and he smiled at Stewart's alarm. 'I didn't call anyone you were coming, for true.'

Stewart shook his head. 'No, I didn't think you did. Probably not for me anyway.'

He turned and found a seat, but he'd been spotted. He heard a chant of 'Stewart Moxey, Stewart Moxey' coming from the wharf as a number of small Bahamian flags appeared above the crowd, waving wildly. The passengers laughed and took up the chant.

Despite the enthusiastic welcome, the group didn't keep Stewart long in the midday heat and fifteen minutes later a golf-cart taxi dropped him at an entranceway framed by two towering ficus trees. Putting his bags down on the cut-coral walk, he took a moment to gaze out over the grounds of the Moxey Arms, the hotel founded in 1928 by his great-grandfather. The hotel's property started at his feet and extended down a terraced hillside to the sandy beach forming a half-moon arc known as Ambergris Bay. In the centre of the grounds stood an imposing old colonial house ringed with broad porches, a rambling, two-story giant known as "The Hall", and scattered around it guest cottages could be seen poking up through the thick greenery. A young black boy in livery a size too large for him came officiously up the walk pulling a baggage cart.

'Good morning, sir, can I take your bags?'

'Yes, thanks. You're very timely.'

'Yes sir, Mr. Moxey, we got a call you reached.'

'Call me Stewart.'

'Yes sir, Mr. Stewart.'

'You're Missy's nephew, aren't you?'

'Yes sir, I'm Myron, second assistant to the concierge, sir. Aunt Missy said to tell you that she'd like to see you directly you reach, sir.' He looked at Stewart meaningfully, adding, 'And Mr. Scoonie too. He said he'll be at the Mutt'n'Fish.'

'Who should I see first?' Stewart mused.

'If you don't mind me saying, sir, if you're hungry they'll be serving lunch at the Mutt'n'Fish.'

'So Missy can wait, you think?'

'Please sir, I didn't say that.'

'No, and you can trust me not to repeat anything you didn't say.'

'Thank you,' Myron said, adding rather more than a perfunctory 'sir.'

'And thank you,' Stewart said, tipping him. 'Would you drop the bags at my apartment? It's upstairs at The Hall next to--'

'Next to Leonard's place, I know it, sir,' he said, adding sheepishly, 'pardon my interrupting.'

'No, that's right.'

Stewart followed him until the path split and, heeding the boy's thoughtful advice, he took the left fork into an arching canopy of mango trees heavy with fruit. The sweet aroma was the strongest assurance yet that he was home. Exiting the grove into bright sunlight, he stopped and shielded his eyes, surveying the narrow arm of land that enclosed the south side of the bay.

Perched on the ridgeline halfway out to the point sat the Mutt'n'Fish Pub & Restaurant. Though not owned by the

Moxeys, it served as the resort's de facto restaurant and watering hole. The unpainted wooden siding ranged from bleached grey to silver and it wasn't unusual for distracted visitors to mistake it for a heap of driftwood, but if anything on Porgy Island could be said to constitute its essence, its heart and soul, the popular choice would be the Mutt'n'Fish.

Despite the building's rough outer crust, the interior was appointed with a collection of wood, bronze, brass, and iron salvaged from obliging ships wrecked on the reefs surrounding the island; massive blocks, ballast stones, tackle, hand-forged chain, a couple of ship's wheels, and the rusting fluke of an anchor were all featured.

A few minutes later Stewart climbed the porch steps and entered the coolness of the restaurant. He might have been six or twelve or twenty years old for all the evident change inside. The Bermuda shutters were propped low on the windows to cut the harsh midsummer sun, and it was dim after the glare outside. A scarred bar of polished mahogany stretched along the left side and as Stewart's eyes adjusted, he noted a middle-aged black woman leaning against it at the kitchen pass-through, singing quietly as she wiped glasses. Two younger girls waited tables as a few scattered groups of customers enjoyed pre-lunch cocktails.

Sitting alone at a round table in the back was a brooding, dark presence. It was a rotund black man and he was reviewing invoices with a critical eye and an occasional groan. The woman at the bar spotted Stewart and, in her surprise, dropped the glass she was holding. 'Gladys,' the man growled, without bothering to look. 'Is that my retirement I hear breaking?'

'As if you will ever retire,' Stewart called back.

'Mudda sic!' the big man said, turning quickly. The woman cried 'Stewart!' and hurried to hug him. After a warm greeting from her and the two waitresses, Stewart walked back to join him.

The man was Maximillian J. Sawyer, the latest in his line to take over the Mutt'n'Fish Pub & Restaurant. He wore a green fez complete with a gold tassel, and even more oddly, it didn't seem out of place on him.

'See what you cost me when you show up unannounced,' the large, bespectacled man said, rising to greet Stewart. He moved with a curious combination of nimbleness and dignity.

'I'm pretty sure that glass was already chipped,' Stewart said.

'You know that, do you?'

'Aren't they all? It's good to see you, Max.' Stewart wrapped both his hands around the massive one extended by Maximillian, barely enclosing it.

'Very sweet to see you, my boy. All is well?'

'Between Thank God and Oh Lord,' Stewart answered, slipping into the local idiom like a pair of comfortable slippers. 'It's awfully good to reach.'

'Yes, isn't it always, but, ah, what do you have against giving us some advance notice?'

'My schedule's been so hectic, I didn't want to commit to a date I couldn't keep. Well, that and...'

'And what?'

'Mainly that,' Stewart said.

'Yes, well, Missy thinks you were trying to foil your own homecoming celebration.'

Stewart winced.

'Ah, she was right, was she?' Maximillian said, chuckling. He motioned for Stewart to sit as he did so himself. 'She usually is.'

'I couldn't face a big jump-up and all the hubbub.' He glanced around, looking for a change of subject. 'I thought the pater would be here.'

'He's running late, let me hail him,' Maximillian said, reaching for his phone.

At that moment the door burst open and a tall, rangy man with a shock of thick white hair and an equally impressive moustache rushed in. He looked at Gladys.

'I hear Stewart's back, have y--' He stopped and slowly followed her pointing finger to the table in the back. Seeing Stewart, he broke into a broad smile. He leaped forward and then just as suddenly caught himself, like a gearbox lurching and then freezing. He'd just remembered his intention to temper his enthusiasm in an effort to impress on his son the trouble his thoughtlessness had caused. He walked back at a slow, measured pace and Stewart easily interpreted the message, never having seen his father move with such a show of injured dignity.

'Great to see you. I'm sorry I've been out of touch lately,' Stewart said as the two embraced, 'but it's good to be home. How have you been?'

His father, realizing he wouldn't be able to keep up the facade of coolness for long, was glad that his son had opened with the very topic he wanted to address.

'Fine. Fine for the most part, I'd say. And you?'

'I'm well,' Stewart said, taking a deep breath. 'What part hasn't been fine?'

This time Scoonie bit his lip to stop himself from answering quickly. The reply needed weight. Gravitas. After a few moments of dramatic silence, he spoke. 'Missy has been somewhat testy lately.'

'Oh yes?'

'Oh yes. Yes, yes.'

'Did she say why?'

'Apparently her emails weren't getting through to you. It was unfortunate, but she refused to believe that I was as much in the dark as she was herself.'

'I was just telling Max I didn't know myself exactly when I'd reach,' Stewart said.

'Well, I wish you great good luck explaining that to her,' Scoonie said ominously, a quaver in his raspy baritone. 'She's been in rare bad humour the past few weeks...she thought we were in league, you and I, withholding the date and she made it extremely uncomfortable around here. Very uncomfortable. You know how she can be.' His moustache and eyebrows quivered, dependable indicators of his deeper emotions.

Stewart winced. He'd known Missy would be peeved and there would be a price to pay, but he hadn't imagined she'd implicate his father.

Voicing the thought, Stewart said, 'I didn't dream she'd blame you. Why didn't you mention it to me?'

'Exactly what I said a dozen times,' Maximillian said.

'I knew you must have your reasons,' Scoonie said to his son. 'And I reckoned I could deal with it.'

Maximillian snorted.

'Are you suggesting I wasn't rowed by that woman?' Scoonie said, turning on Maximillian. 'Rowed as never before,' he added with feeling, wounded by this attack from his flank.

Maximillian shook his head. 'No, you were, you surely were. I was just mystified that you thought you could stand up to it. I recall giving you the odds of a soap bubble in a hurricane.'

Stewart suppressed a smile at this and turned to his father. 'Honestly, if I'd known--'

Scoonie raised his hand, stopping him. A double twitch animated his moustache and the tips gave a final quiver before coming to rest, a sign the matter was closed. He smiled broadly at his son as Gladys approached with a tray holding three bowls of conch salad and mugs of beer. With these distributed, some time was devoted to small talk as they ate. Scoonie, free to express himself now, reached over and shook his son's shoulder.

'Billy is anxious to see you. And Leonard, of course,' he said, referring to Stewart's younger brother and cousin, respectively. 'I couldn't be happier to have you home, my boy. And now,' he said, pausing a moment to wipe the foam from his moustache, 'the matter of cookbooks.'

This inquiry wasn't idle chatter. It had nothing to do with the latest book of trendy salads, a fondue revival, or the self-absorbed biography of some celebrity chef; he referred to the ruling passion of his existence: Chili-con-carne. He was a man of fierce enthusiasms and chief among them was chili, its lore, techniques, and recipes.

'Yes,' Stewart said. 'Well, I checked the second-hand bookstore in the Grove and that one you mentioned in South Miami off Sunset.' He shook his head with pursed lips. 'Nothing.'

'You'll have to try our new recipe,' Scoonie said, passing quickly over the bad news. 'It's very good. Absolutely sound. Not ground-breaking perhaps, but we have the highest hopes for it.'

'Your cookbook request sounded urgent. I thought you might be in a last-minute panic.'

'No, no. No. But as you know, you can't rest in this game. You've got to be alert, exploring every avenue, no stone unturned. That's why I particularly appreciate your taking the trouble.'

'I've been telling your father,' Maximillian said, 'I think we've about exhausted the published material. We must have every chili cookbook in print.'

'There you put your finger on it; every cookbook *in print*,' Scoonie said. 'That's exactly why I'm focused on used bookshops now. Who knows what old gem is sitting on a dusty bookshelf with some forgotten magic ingredient. The internet has been alive, absolutely buzzing, with speculation on a legendary--'

'Mythical, more like,' Maximillian interjected.

Knocked off rhythm for a moment, Scoonie pressed on, '-- a legendary lost manuscript by Frank X. Tolbert. They say it begins where *A Bowl of Red* leaves off.' At his own mention of that revered book, his hand went reflexively to his heart and he nodded knowingly to his son.

Maximillian caught Stewart's eye, shaking his head at Scoonie's speculations.

Stewart raised his hands defensively. 'I won't be drawn into this, gentlemen. You were having this same argument--'

'Discussion,' the two said in unison.

'Pardon me—discussion—the last time I was here.' Stewart stood to go. 'But carry on. I'm off to find Billy and Leonard and, if the gods see fit to punish me, Missy.'

'But that was just a warm-up,' his father said. 'Gladys,' he called out, 'what's next?'

'Grouper,' she called back. 'Parmesan Grouper.'

Scoonie raised an eyebrow.

'You might've told me before stuffing me to the gills with conch,' Stewart said.

'Your appetite has atrophied, being away,' Maximillian said, shaking his head. He and Scoonie were both trenchermen, though Maximillian cursed his friend's ability to cheat the weigh scale.

'I want to see Billy and Leonard,' Stewart said. 'I'll be back for supper if not before.'

The two men nodded, and he hadn't turned to go before they'd resumed their squabbling.

Stewart exited the front door and crossed the porch in a couple of bounds, fairly flying down the worn steps. He was in rare good temper and the anticipation of seeing his brother Billy and cousin Leonard buoyed him further still. He hadn't felt this good in recent memory.

Dropping off the last step, he stopped in his tracks with the surprised abruptness of a woolly mammoth landing in a tar pit; a dozen steps ahead a short black woman stood in his path with arms akimbo. The ominous ticking Stewart heard wasn't a time bomb but rather the tapping of her high-heeled shoe on the coral walkway—though at the moment it was a toss-up which he'd prefer. Missy Rolle had an air of bemused disapproval, an ambiguous expression typical of her. On Stewart's side, his face was pale and drawn. The blood that normally lent his complexion its reddish vigour had retreated to parts unknown.

'That,' she said, 'is the face of a guilty man.'

He smiled sheepishly in confirmation as she approached, for Missy had the singular ability of making this grown man and international celebrity instantly shed twenty years and revert to a gibbering fifth-year schoolboy.

'You are looking,' she continued, 'at the humiliated chairman of the Stewart Moxey homecoming celebration. What do you have to say for yourself?'

The tip of his tongue found his lower lip and travelled left to right, and pausing at the corner, retraced its path. Though he wasn't feeling it this particular moment, Stewart was a favourite of this sturdy female firebrand, trailing only her immediate family and his cousin Leonard in her heart's esteem.

When Scoonie had shown no interest in remarrying after his wife's death, Missy had taken on the task of providing the civilizing female influence she considered so essential to the development of Stewart, Billy, and their cousin Leonard. None of the three motherless boys welcomed this, for Missy was a strict disciplinarian, but as they grew to adulthood she'd mercifully shifted to a more neutral role, something approximating a doting aunt. Unscheduled reappearances of the former despot, however, were all the more jarring for their rarity.

He bent down and hugged her, and the taut set of her lips relaxed. One of Missy's more disconcerting qualities was the remarkable agility of her emotions. She could transition from a giggle to hurling thunderbolts and back again in the time it took most people to work up a healthy indignation. Some observers maintain this capricious nature is a defining characteristic of Bahamian women-hood, but even if that's true, Missy had raised it to an artistic level far above the norm. Such nimbleness of mood kept everyone on their toes in her presence, which is just how she liked it.

'Lovely to see you, Missy,' he said gingerly.

She shook her head and sighed. 'I'm glad you finally reached, child, because I could not get ahold of you. How is it your email and phone were both confuddled up?'

'I was just trying to avoid a lot of fuss--'

'I wanted a lot of fuss.'

'I'm sorry,' he said, 'it was all my doing, you know. I take full--'

Missy's hand came around in a whistling arc and he pulled his head back just in time to see it stop in front of his nose. His vision was blocked, but he could hear the hiss of teeth being sucked, the time-honoured method by which Bahamian women register disapproval.

She lowered her hand and her eyes narrowed to slits. 'What did your daddy say!' It wasn't a request.

'He--'

'He said I rowed him, didn't he?'

'He just--'

'I know he did,' she said. 'I know it. But if you knew what I've put up with between him and Max and that brother of yours and all their chili foolishness. This year has been the worst I can remember and that is saying something.'

She caught herself.

'Listen to me carry on,' she said, suddenly cheerful again. 'You ignoring my texts and emails and making me look a fool aren't a bit important right now. Right now I want you to satisfy my curiosity, Stewart Jacob: Are you back here for a while, a good long while?'

'I hope so,' he said, noting her use of his middle name, never a good sign. He exhaled in an overwrought gesture of exhaustion, a transparent plea for leniency.

'That answer does me no good, no good at all,' she said, heating up and shifting into the rolling cadence of an evangelist at a tent revival. 'I want the truth, the honest truth and nothing but. Are you hearing me?'

Her eyes burned into his.

'Missy, I...

'Are you planning to leave?' she said.

'No pl--'

'A return ticket? To anywhere?'

'No, I--'

'Gladys showed me in some sailing magazine where somebody or other said you'd be back to playing in those boats within a month. Do they know something?'

'It's not--'

'Yes or no.'

She directed a steely gaze at him that any celebrity attorney would trade for their crack publicist. Stewart swallowed, collecting himself.

'No. Word of honour, it's one day at a time, Missy. I wouldn't have the energy to plan a thing right now.'

Stewart froze as she searched his features for any trace of insincerity. Apparently satisfied, the mother hen returned.

'Stewie, we just missed you so, that's why all the fuss. You take your rest and I'll badger you when you're stronger.' She patted his arm. 'And you know this didn't stop your homecoming party. Just delayed it a little. It'll have to be after the tournament now, but that will just give us time to really do it up.'

She beamed a loving smile up at him.

WEDNESDAY

It was unfortunate that on Stewart's first morning back on Porgy, he was awakened by a painful throbbing just aft of his forehead. It had been years since he'd had to contend with a truly foul hangover, but he was fast remembering the price of taking on such an excess of spirits. He lay still with his eyes closed as memories of the previous evening filled in; on the screen in his suffering head a jerky newsreel flickered, showing Billy, his cousin Leonard, and a half-dozen friends welcoming him home with an impromptu celebration that had run into the wee hours. The other attendees were seasoned campaigners on the rum-and-gin-swilling circuit and his mistake had been trying to draft in the tailwind of these veterans.

As his senses gained their footing, he realized the uproar wasn't just in his head. Outside, a summer squall was moving in, complete with high winds and menacing clouds. Palm fronds lashed wildly and he realized the incessant pounding in his head was abetted by a shutter that had rattled loose. When not suffering a significant hangover, Stewart enjoyed a sharp turn in the weather as much as the next person, but this assault on his ears—ears currently sensitive to the rustle of a bedsheet—seemed like spiteful overreach.

Easing upright, he pulled on a pair of shorts and went out on the porch in search of the offending shutter. Securing it, he made his way unsteadily to the railing and grasped it with both hands. Bravely meeting the day, he relaxed his squint and gazed seaward. He suffered a few false starts trying to focus for distance until finally the panorama of Ambergris Bay began to arrange itself. The black sky made the bay, typically a bright turquoise, glow with an eerie green that seemed to emanate from the seafloor itself.

A movement on the beach caught his eye. It almost looked as if someone (a hotel guest?) was pulling one of the Arm's small sailboats down to the water. It was foolhardy to take a boat out in such conditions and, judging by the size of the fool in question—a large child or possibly a small woman—it bordered on lunacy. The winds were howling from the northeast, leaving the inshore waters smooth in the immediate lee of the hill on which the resort perched, but a mere thirty yards out it was another story. There, the backs of the chop being pushed out to sea were streaked white by the force of the winds, and scudding foam filled the air.

He tightened his grip on the porch rail and shouted, putting his all into it, but his voice was swallowed by the overwrought shrieking of the wind. All his effort accomplished was a ratcheting up of the pain in his head. He scanned the beach from end to end, praying for the intervention of some good Samaritan out for a stroll, but it was sensibly deserted. It appeared that he alone was witnessing this suicidal attempt at a morning sail.

He swallowed gamely, accepting his duty. Looking below and picking his target, he sprang over the second-story railing feet first, aiming for a thick sea-lettuce hedge that childhood experience suggested was just the thing to break a fall: it was asking too much of any bush, however, to absorb his current two-hundred-plus pounds, and the landing brought up a loud grunt from his recesses. It's a tribute to the reflexive dependability of Bahamian manners that he mumbled an apology to the plant as he jumped to his feet. A split-second later he was running down the winding path at breakneck speed. The rain held off until he reached the beach, when large drops began to dot the sand behind him. The density of the raindrops in a Bahamian summer squall is such that the deluge overtaking him wouldn't appear to the casual observer so very different from a waterfall. It was the equivalent of a month's rainfall in the Pacific Northwest of the United States dumped in a matter of minutes.

Stewart had hoped to catch both boat and nitwit foundering in the shallows, allowing him to pull them back to safety without getting in over his waist, but this nitwit proved surprisingly nimble, hopping into the boat just as the wind filled the sail. Sprinting into the water, Stewart was up to his armpits before he gave up the chase. He watched helplessly as the boat pulled out of reach, and in his frustration, he cupped his hands and shouted, 'Hey you!' as loudly as he could.

It felt like he'd turned his lungs inside out. While his choice of words might have lacked a tough, authoritative tone, he'd shouted at the perfect moment between gusts and the interim wind carried them lightly seaward. The dark-haired figure turned and waved and she—he could see now the fiendish imp was a woman—smiled brightly. That she was so cheerful under the blackening sky and gale-force winds sent a chill through him. It might not be a case of bad judgement at all. It might be genuine madness.

He mustered his darkest look and motioned her back with a dramatic wave of his arm; it was difficult to see through the downpour, but it almost looked as if she laughed. The one thing he could clearly make out—and it instantly brought his blood to a boil—was the dismissive wave of her hand.

When such moments are reported in the press, the hero is often credited with having but a single, selfless thought of concern for the victim. In this instance that assumption would be wrong. In this case the thought at the forefront of Stewart's mind was the desire to wring the neck of the defiant homunculus managing, incredibly, to sail away.

He ran back and pulled a small catamaran into the water, and was soon underway in pursuit of the daft girl. He'd taken a couple of precious seconds to dunk his head, but that had done nothing to ease the pain. With a hand now on the tiller and the other holding the sheet, what he resented most was the lack of a third to cradle his forehead.

The other boat had a considerable lead and was already out in the raging chop when the optimistic thought occurred to him that if the girl possessed a sliver of sanity, the increasingly fearsome conditions might bring her to her senses. Crazy doesn't necessarily mean suicidal.

While the better part of his attention was dedicated to catching up to the girl, he couldn't stop himself from speculating on the psychological springs of such loony behaviour. If she turned out to be insolent and not stark raving mad, so much the worse for her, for then she'd get a dressing down like she'd never known. This thought was the first bright note of the morning for Stewart. He resolved to let neither youth nor sex moderate the severity of his scolding and he began mentally drafting a blistering tirade. If only, in the few seconds he'd seen her, she hadn't appeared so fresh and full of life.

The other boat had a considerable lead, but the catamaran was faster than her monohull and he'd be able to overtake her in a matter of minutes. She was on a very broad reach, almost downwind, a daft thing to do in these conditions. He'd have to catch her before she was too far offshore or it would be a hellish trip tacking back. Suddenly the other boat swung to port, aiming at the south arm of the bay. Finally a development in his favour on this cursed morning. Now he'd be able to cut across and intercept her. Maybe she wasn't so crazy after all. Perhaps realizing her mistake, she was putting herself into a position to be rescued. In spite of himself, he felt some sympathy for this plucky girl, who, having gotten herself into an embarrassing and dangerous situation, refused to yield to panic. While there was no excuse for such impudence, he had to admit she was putting a brave face on it.

Her new course was aimed back at the limestone point, setting herself up for a relatively easy tack that would send her back toward him. It looked like he'd have her in hand in no time.

But she didn't tack. She maintained her manic beeline for the ragged and flinty ironshore with no sign of stopping. Was this a planned suicide after all? He urged the catamaran on, wringing every bit of speed from the little boat.

As the gap between them closed, his subconscious worked away busily at its sums, estimating wind, speed, angle, and other complexities second nature to a professional sailor. The paths of the two boats were converging and it was increasingly important that he track her movements. Catching glimpses of her through the cloudy window of his sail, he watched closely for signs of panic. He smiled grimly as the little boat skittered along, all but out of control. The poor thing had no idea, but she was probably setting some sort of speed record in this squall.

Though the bulk of the storm was mercifully shifting south and moderating, a rogue gust of wind sent a shower of spray between them and he lost sight of the other boat. Turning slightly downwind to get a fix on her position, he suddenly realized his mistake. Though he was ahead on their intersecting paths, the other boat had accelerated faster than he'd thought possible and the small jog put him directly in its path.

Stewart's mind was experiencing one of those moments when many strains of thought that have been working away behind the scenes come together in an instant. It was an epiphany of resentment toward his brother, his cousin, and his half-dozen friends at the party the previous evening; toward Harold, the boat-shed boy who hadn't been at his post; and most of all, toward the girl herself. If the little miscreant hadn't defied his direct command, she wouldn't now be a millisecond from cutting him in half. He set his teeth and jammed the tiller on the tiny chance he could scoot past.

This would've worked if, at that moment, a gust hadn't come from behind. He threw all his weight back but there was no saving it and the port bow buried itself and the catamaran pitchpoled. The violence of it Stewart launched into the air and he traced an impressive arc, catching a bright flash of white as he entered the water. This, he realized, was the glare from the other boat's bottom and he braced for impact and the crunch of hulls meeting.

It was a near thing, but there was no collision. No bone-shaking crash. No shattering fibreglass. Instead, the other boat traced an impossibly tight arc to starboard, executing a perfect carving gybe. It was a thing of rare beauty, guaranteed to raise the eyebrow of the most jaded sailing aficionado and it was receiving the attention it deserved on the porch of the Mutt'n'Fish Pub & Restaurant. Watching from under its protection were Maximillian, Stewart's brother Billy, and his father, Scoonie. These three, the Mutt'n'Fish chili team, were not just world-class chili experts; they were also competent sailors and they fully appreciated the boat handling required for such a move. The sail popped with such violence that, even at that distance, it caused Scoonie to jump. The little sailboat continued around until it slowed in the eye of the wind. Maximillian's large, leonine head shook in amazement at the manoeuvre and he gave a low whistle of appreciation as Billy nodded agreement.

Stewart, of course, hadn't enjoyed the luxury of such a disinterested view. Surfacing from his dunking, he looked around frantically, nursing the hope that the girl was still in one piece. Rather than injury and wreckage, however, he was met by a stunningly lovely face suppressing a giggle. Giggling was so out of place in the morning's grim drama that Stewart shook his head in an effort to reset his senses.

'I'm sorry, I didn't expect you to turn downwind like that,' he heard a solicitous voice say.

He realized with a start that the giggling and the statement both came from the girl sitting calmly in the boat. And contrary to all reason, the boat was upright and pointed into the wind while the girl damped the snapping sail with the most delicate and skilful touch. Questions clamoured for Stewart's attention, but he couldn't take his focus off the enchanting creature addressing him. It suddenly occurred to him she was waiting for a response; as he started to speak a bouncing chop splashed him in the face and he caught a mouthful of water.

'Are you all right?' she called as he sputtered.

'I'm fine.' He said, regaining his dignity. 'Are you all right?'

She laughed and nodded. 'Can I help you right it?'

The goddess spoke in riddles. 'Write what?'

'Right the boat.' She illustrated with her hand, her eyebrows raised in amusement.

In spite of the fact circumstances were clearly mocking him, he found himself wanting to speak volumes to this girl.

'No, I'm fine, it flips easily' he said, wisely confining himself to essentials for the moment. 'I'm with the hotel. I was concerned for your safety.'

She nodded, considering this. 'I'm sorry I worried you. That wind was fun while it lasted, though, wasn't it?' she said, indicating the clouds and subsiding conditions with a nod.

'I can escort you back,' he said. 'Just give me a second to flip this thing.'

She flashed another devastating smile. 'That's all right, I can manage.' She gave him a quick wave and sheeted in. 'Oh, my name's Natalie,' she called back as the boat sheered smoothly away.

Nothing that had passed through Stewart's mind in the previous minute could properly be described as rational thought. He was overcome with emotion as he capsized, and he was overcome with it now. The chief emotion at the moment, however, was a feeling of loss at the girl's departure and an overwhelming desire to catch up to her, to talk to her; in short, to begin their life together. Following closely, though, was a sense of contentment and the assurance that what had just occurred was the unfolding of destiny. Nothing so propitious could be anything less than fate.

As the wind and chop settled, Stewart leaned back in the water and relaxed, a six-foot-plus overcooked noodle. Idly watching the other boat tack back to the beach, he realized his headache had disappeared. This was puzzling but somehow it failed to grip and he turned his attention to the clearing sky, the crystalline water, and the sunlit patterns dancing on the sandy bottom.

Though he'd always recognised the natural beauty of his home, he couldn't remember it ever displaying such a range of transcendent qualities. Like a goldbricking worker suddenly smiling and industrious when the boss shows up, all of creation seemed to have shaped up in this stimulating girl's presence. The sun cast its choicest rays on the bleached sail and the old weathered hull, setting them off with the crispness of a Winslow Homer painting. The Colours fairly glowed. It was dawning on Stewart that Cupid had pierced him with rare accuracy. He did fail, however, to note the irony that what now prevented him from seeing the irony he'd always mocked the concept of love-at-first-sight, was the very thing itself; love-at-first-sight.

Wheels within wheels.

The chili team trio was still on the restaurant's porch watching Stewart as he sprawled comfortably in the water. They shared a single pair of binoculars and Maximillian was using them at the moment.

'Any change?' Scoonie ask.

Maximillian shook his head.

'Then what are you so intent on?' he said peevishly.

'Nothing, have a look yourself.'

Handing them to Scoonie, he turned to Billy. 'What's he doing out there, do you think?

Scoonie spoke. 'Well, he's not doing much. I wonder if he didn't put his back out. We'd better call Harold to check on him.'

Billy shook his head at the obtuseness of his two elders. 'Isn't it obvious?'

'That he's injured himself?' his father asked, adjusting the binoculars.

Billy shook his head again. 'He's not hurt, not physically. He's embarrassed. Humiliated.'

'Where do you get that?' Maximillian said.

'He was just bested at his own game out there. That girl clearly out-sailed him.'

'In those little boats?' Maximillian chuckled at the youngster's ignorance. 'That's not his game.'

'No indeed, that's child's play,' said Scoonie, studying Stewart carefully. 'I think he's smiling now, so maybe it isn't his back.'

Billy snorted. 'If he's smiling, it's purely from embarrassment. Take my word, he's in no hurry to come in. He's taking time to lick his wounds and rationalize losing.'

Maximillian shook his head at the young man's poor judgement.

'What is undeniable,' Billy persisted, 'is that female out-admiraled him in a clear sailing contest. Tell me, is that his area of expertise or is it not his area of expertise?' He looked pointedly from his father to Maximillian.

'Darling,' Maximillian said, 'if Kingston Butterwort crowed about making a sheep's-tongue souse more outstanding than mine (not that he could), I would laugh and remind him that chili is the preeminent test of culinary expertise and in that area, we've trumped him threefold. He could protest until the whelks uncurl that a souse is the equal of chili but imagine such a claim. It's laughable. This is the same.'

Scoonie flared an eyebrow at Maximillian, impressed with his friend's impromptu analogy. When Billy didn't respond, his father felt obliged to clarify: 'Souse equals skiff, chili equals supermaxi.'

'Yes, yes, I got it,' Billy said irritably, shaking his head at the two laughing men. Scoonie stopped and pointed.

'Looks like he's moving now,' he said.

Sure enough, Stewart had popped the boat upright and was pulling himself aboard. In the distance behind him the storm was moving quickly on its way to annoy Cuba.

The morning's high drama had been thirsty business for the three men and they'd just settled in comfortably with drinks when they heard the clatter of heels on the porch steps. A large, handsome, and undeniably imposing black woman approached their table. It was the foremost mover-and-shaker of the island's social life and noted blister of the first rank, Pamela Pims Pinder. She was flanked on the right by a short stout woman who so resembled her in all aspects but height, they might have been sisters. In fact they were cousins and this shorter woman was Ida Thompson, nee Sawyer, and she was Maximillian's sister. Trailing in their wake was a toothy blond woman with the bad luck to have been christened Nellie.

Pamela Pims Pinder was proud and dignified, her standard mien. The normally effervescent Ida was doing a strained imitation of her larger dour cousin, while Nellie twitched her nose rabbit-like and stared at the floor, pulling down the trio's gravitas and paining Mrs. Pinder, a perfectionist in matters of presentation.

The women were impeccably dressed, with Mrs. Pinder and Mrs. Thompson wearing shoes, handbags, and hats that perfectly complemented their dresses. Even Nellie, not recognised on Porgy as having the least bit of fashion sense, wore a flattering pantsuit.

The three men rose, all properly raised Bahamian gentlemen, and greeted the women with a polite nod and a 'Good morning'. Pamela Pims Pinder saw their courtesies and raised them an air with a subtly ironic curtsy, clearly implying the men must have been raised by wolves. Few, even in the bastion of tradition that is the southern Bahamas, could match manners with her and not suffer some measure of humiliation.

'You ladies are stunning,' Maximillian said, the formalities concluded. 'Is it Sunday?'

Mrs. Pinder directed a scathing eye at the drinks on the table. 'For the sake of your immortal soul, Cousin Maximillian, I certainly hope not. And yours also, gentlemen,' she added brightly, not wanting to slight anyone.

'Please have a seat, won't you?' Maximillian said, motioning to the chairs.

As the men resumed their seats, Nellie also sat, but she lurched back to her feet when she saw that the other two women remained standing. Pamela Pims Pinder cleared her throat with the regal authority that was her hallmark.

'What I have to say won't take long,' she said. 'We stand before you as representatives of the Porgy Island Museum and Historical Foundation. As you certainly know, the Society has purchased the old Thompson house on the back of the dune, a stone's throw from here.'

The men mumbled in the affirmative.

'We have come about your Friday and Saturday music nights. We're here in a spirit of neighbourliness to request that all such raucousness end by nine-thirty p.m. Might that be possible, gentlemen?

There was silence as the men considered this.

'By "raucousness", you mean the musical entertainment?' Maximillian said.

'Normally I wouldn't do the term that disservice,' she sniffed, 'but, for purposes of this discussion, yes, that is precisely what I mean.'

Maximillian was stirred.

'The Mutt'n'Fish's "raucousness" brings more attention and acclaim to this island than anything short of the tournament. It's about the best press Porgy gets.'

'If that's the sort of element one desires,' she said, raising an eyebrow. 'We at the Foundation hope to develop the museum itself into a larger cultural draw and attract a more discriminating visitor.'

'No offense to you gentlemen," Maximillian said, giving a quick nod to Scoonie and Billy before turning back to the women. 'But the day those crusty old artefacts equal the draw of Eddie Minnis or Mr. Jimmy Buffett will be a cold day in…well, let's just say Inagua.'

Maximillian's pre-apology to Scoonie and Billy was in reference to the fact most of the museum's contents were historical items once owned by the Moxey family.

'I take it that your answer is a categorical no, is it not,' Pamela Pims Pinder said primly.

'Indeed it is no and you can put that in your preferred category, my dear Threepea.'

He meant the 'Threepea' to sting. Much of the friction between Maximillian and Pamela Pims Pinder could be traced to her wedding day thirty-eight years earlier when he'd applied the sobriquet 'Threepea' to her in honour of her married initials. To her horror it stuck, largely due to the inordinate love Bahamians have of nicknames. In spite of her protests it was the name used by even her closest friends. It was the only area of her life she couldn't control with her formidable personality. Even her late husband, Leon, had used it, a cherished bit of rebellion to a rigid totalitarian regime.

Maximillian wasn't finished. 'I would as soon shut down the Mutt'n'Fish entirely as stop the music. Have you forgotten it was our mutual great-uncle who started music nights here in the year 1953? Pardon me if I decline your invitation to dance on his grave.'

'You shutting down the Mutt'n'Fish is neither here nor there to me, Maximillian Sawyer. As for the history of our mutual antecedents, I'm certainly not proud of everything they were up to.' She smiled subtly. 'Concerning this issue, though, you've made your position clear. I can't say I'm...We're,' she corrected herself with a glance at her compatriots on each side, 'surprised by this attitude, either.'

'What I don't understand is what this has to do with the museum. Don't you close at five o'clock or so?' Maximillian said.

'Our hours are ten a.m. to five-thirty p.m., closed twelve-thirty to two for lunch. However, the museum board has been good enough to allow me to establish living quarters on the top floor of the Thompson house.'

He nodded slowly, his faced screwed into a question mark.

'Obviously,' she said with a flash of exasperation, 'the noise would be impossible.'

'You're well behind the dune over there. I can't imagine you'll hear anything much except maybe on a couple of tournament nights.'

'Quite impossible. You are doubtless unaware of it, but I have an extreme sensitivity to noise,' she said brusquely. 'Well, thank you, gentlemen, for your time. I'd like it noted that the Porgy Island Museum and Historical Foundation's highest-ranking officer made an overture of friendship to the proprietor of the Mutt'n'Fish Pub & Restaurant, hoping for cooperation concerning this important matter, and was rebuffed. Roundly rebuffed. Witnesses?'

She looked to each side and each woman raised her hand in turn.

'You'll be hearing from our attorney forthwith,' she said. 'Mr. Sawyer, Mr. Moxey, and Mr. Moxey, good day.' As the women filed off the porch, the three men sat in silence exchanging puzzled glances. Maximillian took off his glasses and wiped them with the hem of his shirt. He looked every bit the Long Islander his mother was, with bright green eyes set in a dark face and freckles ranging faintly across a broad nose. He held his glasses up to the light, alert to smudges.

' "Your answer is a categorical no," ' he quoted mockingly, and snorted. 'This is what comes of my uncle marrying a Nassau girl.'

Scoonie and Billy raised their drinks in silent agreement. Nassau, that distant Babylon, was widely viewed as the fount of most of the world's ills.

Meantime Stewart had sailed back to the beach, marinating happily in the general wonderfulness of life. Once again the impulse possessed him to immediately find this Natalie and sweep her up in his arms, and once again he exercised what he deemed admirable restraint in honour of the momentous proceedings fate had decreed. He was determined to take each step in its ordained order. Considering this was a once-in-a-lifetime event, he'd prefer that it unfold at a natural, measured pace, the better to savour it.

That the girl might not be experiencing the same emotions didn't enter his mind. Stewart didn't see this as arrogance on his part, it was simply common sense: The girl's smile had pierced him to his depths and no girl of that calibre dispensed such a captivating and inviting smile to just anyone.

After Harold helped him get the boat out of the water, Stewart sprinted to the Mutt'n'Fish taking the steps three at a time all the way up and he entered the restaurant with the air of a lottery winner. It was starting to fill up with lunch patrons and Stewart threaded his way through the crowd to the back of the restaurant where Scoonie sat alone at the captain's table. He dropped into a chair next to his father, who, though he smiled at his oldest son and clamped a hand on his knee, merely nodded in greeting. Scoonie was occupied with deep thoughts and his son's recent sailing mishap had already slipped from his mind. The strange melodrama with Threepea had crowded out all other considerations. Moments later Maximillian walked out of the kitchen wiping his hands, followed by Billy. Stewart smiled at them, still breathing hard from his sprint up the hill.

'You looked pleased with yourself for someone just humiliated by a slip of a girl,' Billy said.

'You saw that?' he said good-naturedly.

'We were out on the porch watching the squall pass,' Maximillian said.

'She must be staying here,' Stewart said, looking from Maximillian to Billy and back.

'The girl out there in the boat?' Maximillian said.

'And it just occurred to me who she is,' Stewart said brightly.

Billy and Maximillian looked at each other. This was an unusual Stewart.

'That's got to be Natalie Jones. That girl got an Olympic gold. I think she won the U.S. Nationals a couple of times too. You've seen her picture, it was everywhere last year.'

They looked at Stewart blankly.

'In sailing magazines, you barbarians. She's a crack Laser sailor. Something of a phenomenon.'

'Well, whoever she is, you're right about her staying here,' Billy said. 'She and a friend are in the Upper Pink Cottage.'

'What sort of friend?'

'Blondish. Younger than you…'

'Yes…'

'Tall, nice looking.'

Stewart nodded impatiently. 'Yes?'

'Athletic,' Billy said. 'Very fit.'

Stewart nodded again.

'And from all appearances, charming,' Billy continued thoughtfully.

'This person's sex is…' Stewart said, edging up on his seat.

'I'm sorry, what was that?'

'Sex?' he repeated. He spoke evenly but with obvious tension.

'What is it you're needing to know?' Billy said, looking at him innocently.

'Male—or—female?' Stewart said through clenched teeth, bringing to Billy's mind harsh lessons from their childhood.

'Oh, gender, you mean?' he answered quickly. 'Female. The roommate is definitely female.'

Stewart exhaled and smiled, gazing into the distance. 'I'll see you gentlemen later,' he said, and bolting up and out of the chair, he crossed the restaurant and was out the door in a few bounds.

Billy and Maximillian looked at each other.

'Is the lad smitten?' Maximillian said.

'Smote.' Billy said, 'Out of the park.'

Scoonie surfaced from his private musings. 'Who's smitten?'

'Stewart; with that girl who just whipped him out there, apparently.'

'I know who you mean, I spoke with her yesterday. Charming girl. Absolutely natural he'd be taken with her. Strange if he weren't, really.'

'Have you ever seen that kind of intensity in him before? Other than competing?' Billy said to Maximillian.

'Sailing, you mean? Racing?'

Billy nodded.

'He did seem strangely focused behind that grin, didn't he?' Maximillian said.

'Where's he off to?' Scoonie asked absently.

No one answered, and he turned to Maximillian, voicing the concern that had been dominating his thoughts.

'What is most chilling is the fact that seconds after you— consider this carefully—you, Maximillian J. Sawyer, called her Threepea, she managed a smile.' He shook his head as he looked at his large friend. 'These are deep waters.'

'Yes indeed,' Maximillian agreed. 'That didn't escape me.'

Maximillian's use of the word 'focused' to describe Stewart's state of mind was spot on. The young man had gone straight to his room from the Mutt'n'Fish, where he shaved, showered and put on a favourite shirt.

He'd always wondered why he had never felt compelled to chain himself to a particular female for life as so many of his friends had done, but now it couldn't be more obvious. It was a case of never before encountering Natalie Jones. Natalie. Gnat. He'd seen her called that in numerous articles. Gnat Moxey. It was a cute name.

He burst out the door and ran down the stairs, the epic hangover of earlier a fading memory already filed away between the croup and measles. Moments later he knocked on the door of the Upper Pink Cottage and a tall, voluptuous girl with strawberry-blond hair opened it.

'Well, hello,' she said with an accent like Tupelo honey, which coincidentally, comes from near her childhood home. This curvaceous amazon's voice invoked a world of mint juleps, Greek porches, and spreading oaks draped in Spanish moss. Though Billy had described her appearance, she was so much the antithesis of the petite brunette Stewart was expecting that speech deserted him. They stood looking at one another, she smiling comfortably, and Stewart, awkwardly. Finally his voice gained traction.

'Hello, I'm with the hotel, my name is Stew--'

'Stewart Moxey!' she said, her drawl soaring to the upper registers. 'I just knew that was you. I didn't dream I'd get to meet you. Of course I'd heard your family owned this...'

She stopped herself with a hand on her breastbone, and taking a deep breath, held out the other. 'I'm Ginger Hobbs.'

Stewart reached out and took her hand. Her ardent manner had taken him by surprise, and before he could speak, she was off again.

'I must sound like a stalker, but I'm not. I promise you I'm not. I know you from your pictures in the sailing mags. I'm a snipe sailor myself.'

'That's great...' was all that Stewart could come up with.

'I've followed your career since I was in junior high school,' she said, going on with enough conversation for the two of them. 'Come on in why don't you, it's warm out there,' she said, tugging him forward. 'How 'bout something to drink?'

Stewart hesitantly followed her in.

'I was looking for Miss Jones,' he finally managed to say. 'Is she staying here?'

A faint flicker of disappointment crossed the girl's features.

'She just went out a few minutes ago. Oh!' she said, regaining her poise. 'Is this about what happened this morning? With the boats? Was that you! She told me all about it. She's not in any trouble, I hope.'

'No, nothing like that. Not at--'

'It wasn't intentional, of course. I heard the whole thing. She tells me everything, we're ancient friends. Anyhoo, she said she didn't anticipate you changing course like you did. Natalie's not a troublemaker,' she said, laughing. 'At least not usually on purpose.'

'No, no, I didn't think so. I just stopped by to see that she's all right.' Stewart said, feeling positively articulate now, 'I hope you're enjoying yourself. How long will you be staying with us?'

'I'm leaving the day after the wedding,' she said, working it out on her fingers. 'So I'm here another…well, over two weeks.'

'Oh, you're getting married here. Congratulations!'

She laughed heartily.

'No, not me, silly. I'm the bridesmaid. Gnat, that's Natalie, is marrying…' She stood stiffly and adopted a grand manner with a booming French accent. 'Le Baron Rouge.'

Stewart's expression at hearing this was so odd that the girl gave a nervous laugh. 'I'm not really mocking him, of course,' she said. 'I'm thrilled for her.'

The colour drained from his face and as his expression froze, he looked like nothing so much as an ice sculpture. The only sign of life was the rise and fall of his Adam's apple as he swallowed.

'They call him The Red Baron in the news sometimes,' she added hesitantly, watching Stewart with increasing concern. 'I'm sure you've heard of him.'

Stewart had heard of him, but it wasn't The Baron's celebrity that had brought on his paroxysm. What was having such a marked effect on him was the instantaneous reordering of his future. Despite it having been revealed to him less than two hours earlier, he'd accepted this future as a settled matter. In his confusion Stewart's gaze drifted downward and his mind, searching for a mooring, fastened its attention on the cottage floor. He noted that it was the attractive Abaco heart pine, select wood from the Bahamas' north-eastern-most island, and the grain was undulating like a Junkanoo dancer. The flooring was famously fine stuff, but it occurred to him that such movement was unusual for even such a celebrated wood. A moment later his vision faded to black and he felt himself pitching forward.

Coming to, he found his face nestled against something soft and fresh smelling, and cautiously raising his head, he found he'd fallen into his hostess. She didn't seem at all upset to find him in her arms. Apparently his momentum had pushed the two of them back and onto the bed. She sat leaning against the pillows and comfortably cradling him, as if catching collapsing men was part of every modern girl's routine.

'Oh praise Jesus, you're back,' she drawled as Stewart silently struggled to free himself. 'Gracious, you're in as bad a shape as the magazines say. You just relax right where you are for a while, Mr. Stewart Moxey, you just had yourself a little fainting spell.'

Stewart's head was swimming, but none too well. He wasn't sure of the protocol in a situation of this sort and decided the safest course would be to follow her instructions, at least until his head cleared a bit. At the moment his mental state was such that he couldn't have recalled his mother's maiden name or a password based on a family pet if the fate of the earth depended on it.

Lying sprawled on the bed with this girl's arms holding him, he looked for all the world like a glassy-eyed grouper on ice. He shuddered to think how this would appear to Natalie if she walked in and it was this thought that prompted him to act. Moving carefully, he worked his arms down to the bed on each side of the girl as she cooed comforting words. When he judged the time was right, he began pushing himself up.

While this was going on he struggled to offer an explanation, but his vocal cords weren't having it. The grim silence on his part added to the awkwardness of the proceedings as his push-up began to lift the two of them off the bed. With the greatest reluctance the girl released her hold on him and as he regained his feet she jumped up and wrapped an arm around his waist. Manoeuvring him to take a seat on the bed, she continued chatting away merrily. The strangeness of the situation seemed to be entirely lost on her.

'You sit and rest while I get a damp cloth on your head. You know something, sweetie, I don't think you should be exerting yourself like this. I'd better call a doctor.'

In a moment of supreme effort, Stewart forced breath over the obstinate vocal cords and his voice returned as a honk, like a suddenly uncorked clarinet. 'No, no.' He hooted, and wrenching his voice down to its customary register, added, 'No doctor please, that was just a…a temporary…something. Or, nothing. More likely nothing.'

Though the hardware was finally functioning, coherent speech wasn't following.

'I'll take that wet cloth, though,' he finally managed to say. If he could keep her busy it might forestall other helpful impulses. He stood hesitantly as she went to get it.

'Here you are, you poor darling,' she said, putting a hand on his shoulder and forcing him back down on the bed. The girl was surprisingly strong. She laid the washcloth tenderly across his forehead.

'You're going to need to relax a little bit more. I insist,' she said with mock severity and cocked a flashing eye at him. 'Do you know you're a frightfully bad patient?'

Stewart smiled weakly. With every passing minute the likelihood of Natalie Jones returning increased and he was horrified at the prospect of being discovered in his present convalescent state attended by this smothering nursemaid. It was essential that he obtain a private conference with this Natalie and he couldn't help but think the party now attending him wouldn't be supportive of his aims. This Ginger Hobbs had gotten entirely the wrong idea.

She went on chattering happily as Stewart contemplated the news of Natalie Jones' betrothal and a fresh wave of unreality swept over him. When she paused for a breath, he spoke quickly.

'Where did Miss Jones go?' He said it as offhandedly as he could manage.

'Gnat said she'd heard the phone reception was better up the hill, but I think what she really wanted was some privacy. I can't blame her, she knows what a horrible snoop I am. After all, she went to call The Baron. He's expected tomorrow and she's very excited. They say he's coming in an enormous yacht.'

'She was excited?'

'You should have heard her, she sounded like a schoolgirl. And I should know,' she laughed, 'we were best friends and roommates at boarding school.'

'She was excited?' he repeated. 'What I mean is, she was still anxious to call him after...'

Stewart paused, at a loss how to continue. She screwed up her face, puzzled.

'After the accident and everything this morning,' he finally managed to finish.

'After the accident?' she said. 'Yes. But why...'

'I thought it might've shaken her up. Upset her, you know.' He pasted on a smile.

'Oh, no. Not at all. After she told me about it, she laughed and that was the end of it. I think it went right out of her head because she was worrying about the flowers for the ceremony as she went out the door.'

'Well, I'm relieved.'

'Oh,' she said, brightening. 'You were worried for her sake. That's so sweet, but don't be, she's perfectly fine.'

'I'm feeling fine myself now,' Stewart said, speaking the most bald-faced lie of his life if you didn't count his previous three-word statement. He stood up carefully.

'It was so nice meeting you,' she said, standing and taking his hands in hers. 'I hope I see you again soon. Maybe I can save you again!' she said, laughing.

'I hope so too.'

'On second thought, I'm not letting you go,' she said, tightening her grip. His eyes widened, and he gulped.

'Until you promise me,' she continued, 'that you'll call a doctor as soon as you get home. Promise?'

'Yes, that's exactly what I'll do. I'm going to go do that now,' he said, thereby making a clean sweep of it: Every one of his last four statements to this sweet girl were lies as brazen as any he'd ever uttered in his life, although, he rationalized in his own defence, in a decreasing order of severity.

He tottered down the walkway, making for his apartment and a comfortable chair in which to collapse. Ginger watched him from the window, concerned with his shaky progress. It was all she could do to restrain herself from running to his aid. A burgeoning love-light shone in her eyes.

THURSDAY

The next morning Stewart walked into the Mutt'n'Fish just as his father was digging into his breakfast. Waving a slice of forked bacon over his head, he motioned his oldest to the back.

'Just the man I wanted to see,' he said as Stewart approached. 'There's a new doctor in Georgetown and I'm going to check him out. Or rather, he's going to check me out. How about coming along? I had Leonard lined up, but he's changed his mind. Something about a girl.'

Stewart sat down with a curt 'good morning' and winced. Scoonie sensed the need to sweeten the pot.

'Did I mention we'll be lunching at Jen & Bill's? My treat.'

Scoonie had a horror of doing anything alone. He was a social animal who relished companionship, and none delighted him more than that of his sons.

'I'll get back to you after a cup of coffee,' Stewart said listlessly.

His father eyed him critically. 'You look like a beached jellyfish and yesterday you were springing out of chairs like you were rocket-propelled.'

'I didn't sleep particularly well.'

'No? Sorry to hear it. Lumpy mattress? Loud neighbours?' he said, smiling.

Stewart half-closed his eyes, not appreciating the levity.

'Lorraine!' Scoonie raised his arm to get the waitress's attention. He directed a downward-pointing finger to indicate Stewart. 'Boiled fish, please ma'am!'

It was his prescription for all ailments. He looked to Stewart for confirmation, who nodded faintly.

'Grits?'

With his eyes closed the suffering young man nodded again.

'And,' Scoonie added, 'coffee with an inch of Appleton dark--'

'What? No!'

'You prefer the light? That's fine, but it's very mild, you know. Max's coffee simply steamrolls—'

'No, what I mean is, eight a.m. is a bit early for rum, thanks very much,' Stewart said.

'Purely medicinal,' his father said, looking at the restaurant clock. 'But perhaps you're right. Just a couple of tablespoons of the light, Lorraine,' he amended.

As Stewart ate breakfast, Scoonie outlined the day for them, with special emphasis on lunch at Jen & Bill's.

'The menu is as masterful as ever,' he said. 'You do remember the food?'

Stewart nodded.

'Of course you do. Well, it's hardly changed at all except in one important particular: Duff is now served every day. I don't know if you recall, but it was only available weekends and holidays. And you recall their duff.'

Stewart did. The thought of that light, doughy goodness smothered in guava sauce awoke mouth-watering memories.

Scoonie's eyes sparkled and he lowered his voice reverently. 'And mark this: Guava and coconut. Six days a week.'

'Coconut duff. I've never had that.'

'No, I hadn't either until recently, but it is equal to the guava.' His father was lost in thought for a moment. 'Don't hold me to that. In any case, either one alone is well worth the trip.'

By the time Stewart finished his breakfast it was understood that he would accompany his father to George Town. He couldn't muster the will to resist and the trip would be a welcome distraction.

Though the news the previous day that the girl Natalie Jones was engaged to be married had shaken Stewart to his foundations, by evening he was convinced that the outsized effect she'd had on him was due to his hangover. Starting with a psyche not in the best of shape and then foolishly trying to keep pace with a group of such practiced drinkers, what did he expect? This sensible explanation had sent him to bed content that the matter was resolved, but in the wee hours a renegade emotion in the form of a small, striking brunette had awakened him, playing havoc with his sleep. The result was a fitful night and he was feeling it.

'Should we take one of the flats boats,' Scoonie said, interrupting Stewart's thoughts. 'Or the ferry? It's on the reverse schedule today. Which do you prefer? Leonard claims twenty-four minutes across in that little Hell's Bay skiff on a morning very like this.'

The thought of speeding anywhere sounded exhausting and Stewart gave a low moan.

'My thoughts exactly,' his father said, correctly interpreting his response. 'A slow and relaxing trip has its appeal on a fine summer day like this, doesn't it? I anticipate a nap on the return run.'

In honour of the fine morning they set out on foot, and as they came in sight of the harbour, a large yellow yacht with voluptuous curves trimmed with chrome was just docking. A sleek sportfishing boat in the same mustard colour pulled in behind it.

'Who is that?' Stewart asked, realizing as he spoke it must be The Baron le Rouge. The girl Ginger had said he'd be arriving today in a yacht.

'Oh yes,' his father said. 'Your absence these past years has mercifully shielded you from this. We're witnessing the Butterwort carnival pull into town. You won't see a more garish spectacle anywhere.'

So it wasn't The Baron. In spite of the fact that it was his father's nemesis arriving, an inexplicable wave of relief passed through Stewart.

'I like that Viking sportfisher,' he said, referring to the boat trailing the larger yacht.

'Yes,' Scoonie conceded. 'Somehow, by accident as likely as not, he did get a rather nice fishing boat. Of course then he defaced it with that hideous mustard colour.'

'I always liked their old Hatteras,' Stewart said, turning his attention to the yacht. 'I suppose that's gone.'

'Oh, years ago. Kingston goes through yachts like prunes through a parrot. As you see, he likes these vulgar Italian things now. That Hatteras you remember was a relic from an era when the Butterworts were a civilized people with taste. Discreet. Understated. I'm sure that would seem very common to Kingston now. These new Mediterranean horrors mirror his ghastly soul. Look at those inflated curves. It's a clown's idea of a yacht, designed with twisty balloons.'

'Yes,' Stewart agreed, laughing. 'Scaled up a bit.'

'Exactly!' his father said. 'To obscene proportions.'

They made their way down the mild slope to the streets of Willstown and as they approached the ferry dock, they could hear the booming voice of Kingston Butterwort, reigning head of the Butterwort Department Store empire, as he and his entourage descended the gleaming gangway and made their way into town. It was Kingston's practice to announce his presence on the island immediately upon arrival by making an ostentatious walking circuit of Willstown, renewing acquaintance and distributing largess from Butterwort department stores. The gifts enabled the townspeople to overlook his patronizing manner, normally so distasteful to Bahamian citizenry. He also benefited from his family's long association with the Island. The old folks recalled the gracious and unpretentious Butterworts of an earlier era and tended to view young Kingston with a forgiving eye.

The Butterworts had first wintered on Porgy in 1928, when J.M. Butterwort, the family's ageing patriarch and founder of the department store chain, sailed east to the Bahamas to escape the upstart barbarians besieging Palm Beach.

At about the same time, the Moxeys were forced to face the sad reality of their declining fortune and turned the jewel of the family property holdings, Ambergris Bay, into a commercial venture. Among the hotel's first guests were the Butterwort clan, and the first cottage that Scoonie's grandfather, W. Thaddeus Moxey, added to the property was christened 'Butter' and painted pastel yellow in recognition of it being that family's unfailing winter retreat.

As a toddler, Kingston, like his father before him, was splashed in the surf of Ambergris Bay before he could walk. All the various Butterworts and Moxeys had been as intertwined as friendly families can be until the second Chili Cook-off. That year the culinary rivalry erupted that broke the bonds of friendship between Scoonie and Kingston Butterwort, a relationship formed in the tender years of early childhood. The rift was largely ignored by the older members of both families, but as the old-timers passed on and Kingston was left as the reigning adult male of the Butterworts, the two families drew apart. Scoonie silently reflected on this history as they took their seats on the ferry.

A light wind made a herringbone pattern on the ocean's surface, and distant clouds sailed the perimeter of the horizon, leaving a clear canopy of blue overhead. It was the sort of morning this corner of the world was famous for. As they pulled out of the harbour, Stewart realized his mood had improved markedly since breakfast. It seemed that he'd only needed to get out on the water in the fresh light of day to put the whole confused question of this Natalie Jones behind him and he was already looking back on the previous night as an isolated unpleasantness. Inhaling deeply and turning to his father, he found his formerly jovial companion staring blankly at the deck with a sour expression, his moustache twitching furiously.

'Not to quibble,' Stewart said, 'but I was led to believe I'd enjoy stimulating company today.'

Scoonie shook himself.

'Sorry, just momentarily lost in the past.'

'You look like you lost your lucky shilling,' Stewart said. 'You aren't thinking of Rocco, are you?' He referred to Maximillian's beloved basset hound that had passed the previous month.

'No,' he said bitterly. 'A creature lower than the scaliest dog, never mind dear old Rocco. No, I was thinking of the devious Kingston Butterwort.'

'Seeing him reach brought all this back?'

'Maybe; but this close to the Chili Cook-off I'm sorry to say he's never far from my thoughts. I was just thinking about how the rivalry started. But of course, you remember.'

'Ah, no,' Stewart said. 'You're forgetting when I was born. I have heard bits and pieces of the saga over the years, of course. It all started when he stole your recipe, didn't it?'

'Goodness, what was I thinking? I hadn't even married your mother at that point; how would you remember when you were still a couple of years in the future. Yes, it was the year of the second Chili Cook-off, but my first year as captain. The team was made up of Maximillian, your uncle Sydney, me of course, and Kingston.'

'Kingston Butterwort was on the team? The Mutt'n'Fish chili team?!' Stewart looked at his father in disbelief. 'I knew you were friends, but...' He trailed off, speechless.

'Yes, hard to believe now, although completely natural at the time. The two of us had known each other from infancy, you know; we were as close as brothers. Kingston would come down every Christmas, every Easter, spend most of the summer here. He'd show up and melt into the gang like he'd never left. None of us in the pure air of childhood had an inkling of his true villainous nature. He'd always had an outsized sense of his own importance; for instance, he'd pout a bit when he didn't spear the biggest fish. But nothing, really, to suggest a truly black heart. That he kept hidden until the critical hour.'

'The critical hour?'

'I'll come to that. In those early days the Chili Cook-off was very simple and straightforward.' He turned and gazed out to sea with a faraway look in his eyes. 'What a refreshing and innocent time it was. That second year, Maximillian had come up with adding goat peppers pickled in lime juice and Worcestershire sauce...'

'Isn't that King's Scotch Bonnet chili?'

'That's right, that was the birth of KSB. It seems almost primitive now, but at the time it was a sensation. We knew we had something. We were celebrating with a batch about a week before the Cook-off and Sydney and I were praising Maximillian to high heaven for the genius of it. Kingston was sour and sort of brooding, but like I say, he was like that now and then and we didn't think much of it. After we'd all had a few too many beers, he stood up in front of us and in the grandest manner proclaimed the chili definitely sub-par. He announced he was leaving the team and said that he might even form a syndicate of his own. I was sure it was all a joke and that he'd pull a face and laugh it all off, but he threw that nose of his up and walked out without another word. We were astonished! I mean, just floored. At least Sydney and I were. Somehow Maximillian had taken that blackguard's measure early on.'

'But didn't Kingston know the KSB recipe?'

'Exactly. You see right to the crux of it, don't you? Yes, that was our worry all week. Oh, we agonized over it, trying to predict his course. Would he act honourably and come up with his own recipe or take the low and winding serpent's path. He had a mysterious package flown in by sea-plane the day before the competition. Even then, with his father still at the helm of the Butterwort empire, Kingston had enormous resources available to him. He's the only son, you know, and his father doted on the blister. I was sure he'd outdo us with some exotic spice. After all, everything for KSB was available on the island, so what could he be bringing in? It turned out to be premium-grade meat from the Powell Ranch of South Dakota, "The

World's Premier Purveyor of Gourmet Beef", as their motto goes.'

'The same brand that you use.'

'Yes, now of course, but in those early days it was unknown to us. Kingston had reasoned that copying our recipe, he could only beat us by improving on the key ingredient. Ingenious in his trademarked diabolical way. But here is where Maximillian distinguished himself. With what I can only attribute to supernatural intuition, he'd somehow sensed the coming betrayal and when mixing that batch of peppers in front of us he'd flourished an inferior Worcestershire sauce for us all to see, when in actuality he was using Crosse & Blackwell's.'

'There's a big difference?'

'A very key difference. And coming from the States, Kingston was unacquainted with C&B, so we rushed out and bought up all there was on the island. Sydney even got word to your Aunt Clara in Georgetown to do the same, on the small chance he might inadvertently pick up a bottle there. Well, it turned out it didn't matter; he was oblivious to the distinction. Even so, it was a near thing, battling the clearly superior beef. We won by a mere three points, a close decision.'

Scoonie leaned back and stretched out his long legs.

'As you know, I've led the team to eight more victories since that first chili-pot, two of those by a full thirty-point sweep, but not one was sweeter than that blessed day. It was so clearly a victory of right over might and of transparent decency over the inkiest treachery.'

Scoonie's moustache bristled like a rudely awakened porcupine and he turned to see if his story was making a sufficient impression on his listener. He needn't have worried. Strict early moral training, de rigueur in the Commonwealth of the Bahamas, had not been wasted and his son was appalled.

'You reported him to the tournament board, of course.'

'No, and I'm proud to say we arrived at that decision before our victory. Taking into account our long association with the Butterworts and not willing to sully the family name and punish the other fine and guiltless family members, we did not.

We trotted along the high road, thinking that having to live with the ignominy of his actions would be punishment enough. We thought Kingston possessed enough honour to feel dishonour. Ha! Youth and naiveté.'

The stirring account finished, the two sat in silent contemplation, Stewart absently watching two circling frigate birds while Scoonie puzzled over the inexplicable dark turns of human nature, from Caligula to Kingston Butterwort.

The ferry docked and Scoonie hurried off to his doctor's appointment after arranging to meet Stewart in the early afternoon for lunch. Stewart had just enough time to catch up with a couple of old friends before it was time to meet his father, and when he got to Jen & Bill's, the waitress was clearing away a glass and handing Scoonie his second beer.

'Been here long?' Stewart asked.

'Just long enough to finish a Kalik.'

'And now, I see, a Strongback,' Stewart said, nodding at the rival brand. 'Very ecumenical of you.'

The lunch lived up to Scoonie's advance billing. Conch salad to start, then grouper fingers fried in a goat-pepper batter, pigeon peas, cocoanut rice, and finally, lime-marinated hogfish sautéed in butter, a simple favourite of Stewart's since childhood. They closed out the campaign with the celebrated guava duff and coffee.

They boarded the ferry in an overstuffed condition, and the ride home for Scoonie was a quiet meditation on lunch and the relative merits of guava versus coconut duff. Stewart's restless night caught up with him and conspired with the easy motion of the boat to put him to sleep. His nap was mercifully free of the diminutive sailor that had been the disturbing fixture in his dreams.

As the soporific effects of lunch began to ease, Stewart stirred and sat up. Scoonie was gazing at the passing clouds with a philosophical air, still musing happily on the nuances of duff. He was recalling a pineapple duff he'd had on the island of Eleuthera in his youth and wondering about its current availability. It might be worth a trip to Gregory Town.

'You haven't mentioned your check-up,' Stewart said, straightening and stretching. 'I assume it went well.'

His father turned, waking from his revelry.

'Oh, no bad news, of course not. No, no. No, this new fellow is competent enough, I guess. He noted my excellent health…'

He paused thoughtfully before continuing.

'…And I won't question his abilities on such short association, but I wonder if he's suited to a medical career.'

'Why do you say that?'

'Oh, just a passing feeling. Hardly worth mentioning.'

'A feeling?'

'Oh, nothing really, a very slight premonition.'

Stewart waited for the other shoe to fall. Scoonie could no more keep a discussion of his health under several hundred words than he could curb a conversation about chili.

'Well,' his father finally said, as if weighing the appropriate degree of candour, 'the gifted physicians I've known have had an eye, a sort of intuitive feel for the extraordinary. It's an aptitude like any other.' He turned and looked at Stewart. 'Genetic I wouldn't doubt, although experience certainly sharpens it.'

'And you don't think this new man has it?'

'It wasn't at all apparent. As you know, every first-rate medical man that has checked me out for the past twenty-five or thirty years has been dazzled by my uncanny health.'

'How can you tell which ones are first-rate?'

'It's mainly a measure of how highly they rate my fitness. If they're sufficiently impressed, a high level of competence can be assumed, I think. What could be a better test?' he said with a knowing look.

'That logic is a bit circular,' Stewart pointed out.

'Well-rounded, you mean? Well, of course.'

Delighted with his son's sagacity, he became more animated.

'Yes, well, you remember old Doc Fishbein. Small fellow, reminded me of Woody Allen, if Woody Allen were lucky enough to be a certified medical genius, ha-ha. The first time the nurse showed him my numbers, blood pressure, heart rate, cholesterol, etc., his jaw just fell. I mean really dropped. I can still picture him standing there with his jaw down around his wingtips and his eyes swivelling from the machine's readout, to my chart, to me and then around the horn again. He had the nurse take my blood pressure a second time, and I'd been resting, so it came out even lower.' Scoonie laughed merrily. 'He was an astute fellow, that one was. A natural physician.'

'But you said this new doctor found your health excellent.'

'Excellent, that was the word he used, yes, but what I'm trying to get across is his unnatural reserve, a complete lack of surprise. As if I were a routine case! And here I am, older and more fit than ever. But this fellow's young,' he said, 'likely he lacks the experience to appreciate something really noteworthy. He might not even recognise it at his age. Nothing to compare it to, probably.' He laughed indulgently and shrugged. 'I'll keep an eye on him, he may yet develop.'

The ferry's diesel engine died abruptly as Ezra throttled back, his eyes wide. 'Mudda sic, would you look at that!'

As they eased around the point, a colossal yacht came into view; it was nearly three times the length of Kingston Butterwort's boat and four decks high. It had more the aspect of a cruise ship than a yacht and it appeared to be sitting in the approach to Willstown Harbour, awaiting admittance.

'Looks like they're going to have to move Mr. Butterwort's boats. That ship's gonna take up the whole front of the wharf,' Ezra said.

'Who in the world can that be?' Scoonie said, bubbling with delight. 'It can't be making Kingston happy.'

Scoonie couldn't have been more correct in assessing his former friend's state of mind. When the harbourmaster— always mindful of departure tips—respectfully asked that Mr. Butterwort move his boat to the east dock, he ignited a firestorm of temper in that easily combustible man.

Yes, the harbourmaster nodded in agreement with the red-faced, sputtering autocrat, it was true the Butterworts had always had their place at the centre of the wharf front, and yes, the east dock did pick up a bit of wake from passing boats, but no, there was unfortunately no choice.

'How long will this monstrosity be here?' Kingston said, motioning toward the gleaming superyacht.

The harbourmaster looked at his clipboard. 'Our printer ran out of ink, so I don't have that information, but I'll have Amy check the computer.' He talked quickly as he fished a cell phone out of his pocket. 'Likely they're not here for the Tournament. Monsters this size are usually on their way to St. Barts or down that way, but I'll find out pronto.'

'The prime minister had lunch on my boat last year, you know,' Kingston said meaningfully. 'I'd hate to see anyone lose their job over this.'

'I'm in a bind here, Mr. Butterwort. When this bunch booked,' he said, while motioning for the megayacht to wait, 'our girl misunderstood and set down its length at seventy-four feet when it should have been seventy-four meters. It was our mistake and I can't throw them out on the roadstead, sir. There's no mooring for a boat that size and if that thing swung at anchor, it would sweep thirty boats. They'll have to be accommodated inside. Yes sir, it is unfortunate, but it will be an inconvenience for everyone, not just you.'

Kingston snorted. 'And who else, exactly, will it inconvenience?'

'The mailboat will have to use the east dock. They don't like that. And everyone will have to go around my office to load and unload, meaning dust and trucks driving over my toes the second I step out my door.'

The harbourmaster's tone of shared suffering had no effect on Kingston.

'So there'll be mailboat traffic too? What a nightmare!' Kingston bellowed. 'At least put me in that little west slip so I won't have to deal with that.'

'Sorry again, Mr. Butterwort, but it's too tight a squeeze. With all due respect, sir, if this won't suit you, you'll just have to look elsewhere.'

Spoken to like a common tourist! His blood pressure shot to the upper regions and his eyes bulged. Kingston's seams were stretched to the limit and only his fear that the pressure would pop his carefully nurtured hair-plugs stopped him from abusing the harbourmaster further. He turned away in disgust.

The Butterchurn VIII, Kingston's yacht, was standing off, waiting for instructions, and he caught their attention. Swinging his arms like a game-show presenter, he indicated their new berth with bitter sarcasm. The yellow yacht moved dutifully into its humble home, followed by the sportfisher.

Minutes later the mighty behemoth steamed in and moved into the vacated space with the delicacy of a large woman easing into a fragile chair. Kingston had repaired to his salon and ordered a generous cocktail, but before the steward could return with the soothing emotional balm, agitation propelled him up and out and before he knew it his Top-Siders were carrying him toward the Superyacht. He had a vague notion of embarrassing the usurper by direct application of his trademarked withering stare, but as he approached the yacht and its massive bulk loomed over him, he was overcome with the humility that every boat owner feels toward a more impressive vessel.

Coming to a halt in front of the craft, his ego swayed for a moment before buckling under the weight of its towering majesty. He stood open-mouthed with a feverish brow and protruding eyes, exhibiting the classic symptoms of Advanced Marine Envy. He was obsessed with all things seagoing and this magnificent beast surpassed his most extravagant dreams.

Lost for some time imagining himself at the helm of the colossus, his daydream came to an abrupt end when he noticed the crew smirking at him as they worked to secure the boat. Snapping his mouth shut and putting on a dignified frown, he straightened and challenged their stares with his most imposing board-room demeanour. They looked away with wry smiles and went on with their duties. On the top deck a small group of continental sophisticates looked down on him in Gallic bemusement and, though they were too far away for him to hear it, there was clearly some snickering going on. Damnable frogs! Turning his attention to these beautiful people with their cigarettes and drinks, he watched each of them casually turn and drift away from the railing as he met their eyes. Everyone, that is, but a thin, elegant, redheaded man. The brazen carrot-topped chump continued staring mildly, as if observing an interesting specimen of the local fauna. Smiling suddenly, he gave Kingston a smart salute. What an ass. Kingston turned and stalked back to his own boat.

The arrival of the massive yacht carrying Natalie Jones's intended had also rattled Stewart, returning him to the same unsettled state of mind that had interfered with his sleep the night before. He headed for The Hall and some solitude in which to make sense of these mercurial moods afflicting him. As he reached his apartment, a low moan of agony issued from the open door beyond his; Leonard's apartment. Creeping forward, he peered in. His enormous cousin was sitting on the edge of the bed in his underwear with his elbows on his knees, and if his hands hadn't been holding his ears in a death-grip, he would have resembled Rodin's Thinker to a detail. Hearing the floor creak, he turned and looked at Stewart, his large, honest face trying to mask undeniable anguish. He straightened and put on a pathetic smile.

'Oh, hi Stew. H-how was the run to Georgetown?'

'Was that you I heard groaning?' Stewart said.

'Ah, possibly...yeah, it could've been me.'

'What in the world is the matter?'

'Nothing much.' He was flushed with embarrassment.

'Leonard, it's me,' he said, entering the room. 'That was a soul in torment if I've ever heard one.'

The two men had been raised more like brothers than cousins and Leonard's emotions were an open book to Stewart. He expected honesty from his cousin.

'I appreciate the concern, but there's nothing you can do,' Leonard said. 'And I mean especially you. Thanks for looking in, though. Close the door on your way out, would you?'

'No, I won't. Not after that cryptic crack about me. What's going on?'

Leonard lay back on the bed and spoke at the ceiling.

'It's a girl. That's all.'

'What girl?'

He motioned with a tired arm toward the Upper Pink Cottage. Natalie Jone's cottage. The hair on Stewart's neck stood on end.

'I don't blame you, though,' Leonard said.

'Glad to hear it. What is it you aren't blaming me for?'

'Her thinking you're so wonderful,' Leonard said with a mirthless laugh. 'It's not your fault.'

'But she doesn't...does she?' Stewart said, hope stirring despite his best effort to suppress it. 'I've hardly said ten words to her.'

'Well, whatever you said, it was enough.'

'Where did you get this idea?' Stewart said.

'I spoke to her myself, this morning. She was full of questions about you.' Stewart's spirits continued their rise despite Leonard's fractured features. 'I'm feeling lower than hell's cellar at the moment, and I wouldn't mind some privacy...'

'You do know she's engaged to be married?'

'You're thinking of her friend Natalie,' Leonard said, irritably waving the notion away. 'Ginger's here as her bridesmaid.'

'Yes...Ginger,' Stewart said slowly as the mists cleared, taking with it the faint hope that Leonard's words had sparked in him. It was shamefully apparent that he was fine with the shattering of his cousin's dream if it meant fulfilment of his own.

'Well,' he said slowly, 'I've got some good news for you.'

Leonard looked at his cousin sceptically.

'What?'

'Nothing will come of it.'

'What?'

'Just what I said.'

'What does that mean, though?'

'Ginger and I will not be an item.'

'What?'

'The field is clear. Knock yourself out.'

'Wait!' Leonard said, puzzling the matter out. 'Then why did you run up there yesterday in "a fit of infatuation"? Those were Billy's very words. And Ginger said something about a fit too.'

'Erroneously drawn conclusions all around. Take my word for it. You might find you're wrong about her feelings too.'

Leonard fidgeted for some moments before speaking.

'But what about the fit?'

'What?' Stewart said, lost in his own thoughts. His attention had already shifted back to Natalie Jones.

'Why would they both mention it? Billy and Ginger.' He shook his head impatiently at Stewart. 'This fit you had, explain that.'

'I'd rather not go into it. Long story. But concerning this Ginger, if nominated I will not run, if elected I will not serve. Isn't that enough for you to be going ahead with? I'm—not—interested—in—Ginger.'

Leonard's eyes narrowed. 'Why not? She's a wonderful girl.'

Stewart stared at his cousin in disbelief.

Noting his expression, Leonard came to his senses and shook his head. 'Sorry, I guess I'm a little wound up. God bless you, Stewie!' He jumped up and put on shorts and a shirt. Patting his bleached and woolly hair into place, he slapped his cousin on the shoulder with a grin and ran out the door.

As Stewart made his way to his own apartment in a cloud of gloom, he remembered a yellowed quote pinned to the wall of Porgy's All-Age School twenty years earlier. "The best way to cheer yourself up is to cheer someone else up." What rot! It was no wonder Sam Clemens wrote under a pseudonym.

At the same moment that Leonard bolted for the door, the diminutive gold medallist Natalie Jones was pushing her way into the cool interior of the Mutt'n'Fish Pub & Restaurant. The dining room was dim and empty, but she could hear a spirited duet issuing from the double kitchen doors. She recognised one voice as that of Frank Sinatra, but the other vocalist was new to her. They were singing 'That's Life.'

'Hello, are you open?' she called out. The fact that they obviously weren't would have dissuaded many people, but Natalie, in addition to being intrepid by nature, was in a particularly determined frame of mind. When there was no response she walked behind the bar and peered through the glass in the swinging doors. The kitchen was brightly lit, and though she couldn't see anyone, the singing continued. She pushed one of the doors open a few inches and called again. The voice of the amateur vocalist stopped abruptly and an instant later Frank, along with Nelson Riddle and his orchestra, was silenced.

'Hello?' a voice called. 'Show yourself.'

Hesitating only a moment, she stepped through the swinging door and a movement to her left caught her attention. A well-built young man in a white apron was standing behind a stainless-steel table with a jumbled pile of shells heaped on it. He held a small hammer in one hand and one of the large pink shells in the other. Natalie's curiosity overcame her surprise and she said, 'What in the world are you doing?'

'I recognise you,' Billy said. 'You're the girl that humiliated Stewart Moxey.'

She looked at him critically for a few moments before replying.

'Don't say that. It was all a misunderstanding. Are you a friend of his?'

'No.'

'If I'd known it was him, I'd have been more respectful. My father and my brother both worship him; if they ever found out, I'd probably be drummed out of the family. He is, as I'm sure you must know, a sailing legend.'

'Please, stop, you're making me a little sick. Not while I'm handling food.'

'Why? Don't you like him?'

'On the contrary, you might say I love him like a brother, but that doesn't mean I can stomach blather like that.'

Natalie studied him.

'You are his brother, aren't you? A somewhat abbreviated version.' She continued despite a harsh glance from Billy. 'You haven't answered my question.'

'I'll bet you're not five four in three-inch heels?' Billy said, sizing her up. He'd been stung by the height crack. 'I've got at least seven, maybe seven and a quarter, inches on you.'

'I apologize. It was a tactless observation, not a cut.'

'If I weren't so pleased with you dunking Stewart, I might ask you to explain your presence in my kitchen, but I do feel somewhat indebted...'

'Is this your kitchen?'

This girl was exceedingly cheeky. 'Good afternoon,' he said stiffly, in an effort to bring the conversation to order. 'And you are?'

'I'm sorry, you're perfectly right. My manners seem to have deserted me. My name is Natalie Jones.'

'Pleased to meet you, Miss Jones,' he said, returning to his warm manner. 'I am W. F. B. Moxey, but feel free to call me Billy. Now, is this my kitchen? Not strictly speaking, but I am the head chef and kitchen manager, so yes, in so far as you're concerned--'

'Oh? Where did you go to school?'

He squinted at the imperious tone.

'Though the relevance of the question escapes me, I'll indulge you.' He put the hammer and shell down and began to count off on his fingers. 'Starting at age four, Willstown kindergarten and nurs--'

'Cooking school!' she interrupted, with a flicker of impatience.

'Yes, right. I see.' He cleared his throat and started again. 'London School of Cooking, two years. Three semesters at Paris Cul, what you might call graduate level. And then some specialized training at the SAUCI. That's the--'

'San Antonio Ungulate Culinary Institute,' she finished for him.

'You're well informed.'

'I like to cook. Why did you go there?'

'The SAUCI?'

She nodded.

'Chili-con-carne. Exclusively for chili.'

'Really?' She giggled. 'Why?'

'Why?'

'Yes. Can't I wonder why?'

'You disappoint me, grasshopper.'

'Why?'

'Well, you don't strike me as the sort of hayseed that would visit India, ignorant of the Taj Mahal. Or Paris, unaware of the Eiffel Tower and rude waiters. And yet here you are in the southern Bahamas with no apparent knowledge of the celebrated Porgy Island Chili Cook-off.'

He looked at her censoriously as she shook her head.

'PICCO?'

'I've never heard of it.'

'I vacillate between outrage and astonishment,' Billy said, throwing up his hands like a teacher despairing of the class dunce. 'No, worse; hurt, outrage, and astonishment.'

She laughed musically and clapped to applaud his performance. Billy was beginning to understand his brother's attraction to this girl.

'I've always considered myself a sophisticated traveller,' she said. 'But apparently I'm not. I thought the Billfish Tournament was the big event here.'

'It's a common enough mistake, but please, let's not be common. The Porgy Island Billfish Tournament is merely a hook on which to hang, a frame to showcase, a pedestal, so to speak, on which to mount the pre-eminent event in our island Commonwealth, the Porgy Island Chili Cook-off.'

'So the fishing tournament serves mainly in a supportive role,' she said, playing the straight man.

'Precisely. Though not all of the fishermen are aware of the fact. I wouldn't mention it.'

'I'll be sure not to.'

'Now, before we stray too far from your original question asking what I'm doing, I'm cleaning conch for conch salad.'

'Oh, yes! Please explain the role of carpentry tools in food preparation.'

Billy's face went deadpan, and he held up the hammer. 'Used to put a hole in the shell.' He pointed the shell down and knocked a small hole in the end.

He held up a short knife. 'To jook the creature free.' He inserted the knife in the hole and gave it a twist. Then, pulling the unsightly mollusc from the shell, he began cleaning it as he talked. 'Thursday night is very big for conch salad around here and both prep cooks called in sick.' He paused and looked up. 'Do you mind if I work while we chat?'

'Not at all. I hope it's not serious.'

'Our chat? I doubt it.'

'No! Your two cooks taking ill!'

'Oh, yes, that,' he said, nodding quickly. 'No, no. They didn't share details, but it sounded to my practised ear like they're just suffering from an eye problem.'

'Both of them?' she said with concern.

'Yes. They just couldn't see coming to work.'

'Ha ha ha,' she said dryly. 'And they say vaudeville is dead.'

'Now, what brings you here in the middle of the afternoon?'

'I'd hoped the bar might be open. Tonight I'm having dinner with my mother-in-law.'

'And you want to get pickled for the occasion? Is that wise?' Billy paused in thought for a moment. 'You're married?'

'Pending. I should say future mother-in-law; the wedding is the week after next. We're getting married here. My stomach's been in a knot since breakfast and I thought a glass of wine or three would help me relax, but our conversation seems to be doing the trick. I'm feeling better.'

'So you don't get along with this mother-in-law?'

Natalie smiled wanly. 'Believe it or not, I've never met her. Our courtship has been something of a whirlwind.'

'But this mother-in-law's reputation precedes her, does it?'

She nodded grimly. 'I've heard she can be difficult. I talked to my fiancé on the phone yesterday and he told me to expect an aging, ill-tempered French aristocrat with arthritis and gout—'

'Ha ha ha,' Billy laughed, cutting her off, but he stopped abruptly when the girl failed to join in. 'He was joking, I hope. I mean, exaggerating to lessen the blow, so to speak.'

'I'm afraid he wasn't. She's Comtesse Douairière d'Anjou.'

'Pardon your French.'

'The Dowager Countess of Anjou,' she translated.

'Ahh,' Billy said sympathetically. 'Sounds formidable.'

'Yes,' she said. 'That's an understatement, I'm told.'

Her expression was resolute and set off her beauty nicely. She reminded him of Joan of Arc in a Hollywood epic being led to the stake, her large brown eyes shining bravely.

Without a word, Billy wiped his hands on a towel and pulled two frosted glasses from a freezer, filling them with milk. He massaged a small yellow lime on the table, and slicing it, squeezed half into each glass. In contrast to the fast and flamboyant cleaning of the conch, his movements were deliberate and performed with ceremonial care.

'Won't that curdle the milk?' Natalie asked as he finished with the lime.

'Yes, and providentially, that's just what we want.'

'We do?'

She looked at him sceptically.

Billy winked. 'Bahamian buttermilk.'

He went to a corner of the kitchen and bent down, reaching back into the recesses of an old cabinet, and pulled out a dark bottle. Wiping off the dust, he held the hand-lettered label up where she could see it.

She read aloud, 'William's Unblended Rum.'

He poured a modest dose in each mug.

'Is that all?' Natalie said.

Billy nodded, indicating the bottle. 'In the neighbourhood of 160, 165 proof.'

'That sounds like moonshine's neighbourhood,' she said, taken aback. 'That can't be legal.'

He cocked his head in thought. 'I'm not sure.'

Billy pointed to the faded lettering at the bottom of the label.

'Bottled 1958,' she read. 'Where did you get it?'

'My grandfather made this. First produced by my great-great-great-grandfather—give or take a great—and namesake, the original William Moxey. Never a smashing commercial success, though. Sugar cane needs regular water throughout the year and we get most of our rain in about five months. Most batches didn't amount to more than a few hundred bottles. This one is from the last time it was made.'

'Very special, then.'

Billy nodded. 'Less than thirty bottles left. Priceless. At least to us. Kept under strict lock and key over at the Arms. I managed to spirit this one away, so to speak, last year, and it only comes out for special occasions.' He handed her the drink and passed his own under his nose, closing his eyes and swooning.

'Well then,' she said, 'I'm flattered. Thank you very much.'

'Of course,' he said. 'You don't meet a grumpy French mother-in-law every day, do you? Cheers.'

'Cheers,' she said, and they toasted.

'To family,' he added.

'Family,' she echoed, and her nose, wrinkled in trepidation, relaxed as she drank. 'Mmmm,' she said, surprised. 'Tasty.'

'Of course,' he said, eyeing her. 'You'll learn to trust your uncle Billy. He motioned for her glass with the bottle and added a little more. 'If it follows form, any moment now you should be steeped in tranquillity.'

'You know, you're right,' Natalie said a short time later, noting with satisfaction that her psyche was already stretching out with its hands behind its head.

They enjoyed the drinks in thoughtful silence, and just as they were finishing, they heard someone call from the dining room. Billy went to see who it was, trailed by Natalie, and they were met by a breathless Ginger Hobbs.

'Hello. I'm looking--' she said, and seeing Natalie, she blurted out, 'There you are, we've been trying to find you! He was worried sick.'

'Who, what happened?' Natalie said.

'The Baron arrived early, over half an hour ago. I called and called but no answer. He seems a little put out.'

Gnat pulled her phone out.

'Out of power, sorry, Gin. Thanks so much, Billy, you've been a lifesaver. I'll introduce you two when we have more time.'

The two girls rushed out, Natalie with the steady eye of St. George off to slay a dragon, and Billy wasn't at all pessimistic of her chances with a crabby French dowager.

Following Leonard's high-spirited departure, Stewart's mood had continued its slide south. His heart's spontaneous leap when he thought Leonard referred to Natalie exposed the grim truth that he had in no way mastered his emotions concerning this girl. His psyche was ignoring all orders from headquarters.

He went out and took a seat on his porch, gazing out over the sweep of green gardens edging the white sand, which in turn slipped under turquoise water. Happy couples strolled the manicured paths, and on the beach squealing children with bright plastic shovels pitched sand while beachcombers, giving them a sensible berth, collected shells. Fragments of conversation and laughter drifted up the slope.

In short, a blissful atmosphere, which in no degree assuaged Stewart's spirit. Anyone viewing the handsome young man on the veranda, blessed with health, a bulging bank account, and the certainty that he stood to inherit all that he surveyed, would find it difficult to feel sympathy for him. Brooding under such circumstances points to a dangerously self-indulgent nature. Count your blessings, one would say. It was to Stewart's credit that he was thinking that very thing himself and his shame at the helpless state of his emotions only added to his misery.

This agitated state of mind drove him outside and he began briskly walking the resort's convoluted walkways in an effort to exhaust whatever energy was powering his ungovernable moodiness. After a mindless circuit of the grounds, he headed out to the south point where he performed a punishing workout and then repeated it. Soaked with sweat, he took the ridge-top path back and found himself turning in to the Mutt'n'Fish.

While the needle on Stewart's emotions remained pinned to wretched, Billy was buoyant. The effect of an invigorating chat with a clever and attractive audience was still operating, as was that of his namesake rum, and he was elevated to regions uncommon to even such a temperamentally upbeat personality. The girl's heartfelt thanks and her smile as she waved goodbye had been a final boost and he could be heard whistling "New York, New York" with rare spirit as Stewart entered the restaurant. Billy, just finishing his task, looked up as his older brother entered the kitchen.

'Don't you have someone else to clean conch?' Stewart said crossly by way of greeting.

'And a good afternoon to you too, Brother.'

'It is, is it?'

'Did you meet young Jones and her friend on your way in?' Billy asked, ignoring his foul mood. He had, however, touched on the single topic sure to engage Stewart's attention.

'Natalie Jones! Was she here?'

'None other. Just left with her buddy Ginger. I'm surprised you didn't run into them.'

'I came from the south point.'

'That would explain it. What were you doing out there?'

'Just out walking, getting some exercise. What was she doing here?'

'We chatted a while. She came in for a drink.'

'Oh,' Stewart said, affecting a bored tone. 'What did she have to say?'

'Well, she seemed embarrassed about that business with the boat capsizing. She was horrified to have caused the whole thing. She also said that you were a legend—her very words.'

'I see.'

'And she said her brother and father are big fans of yours.'

'Her brother and father?'

'That's what she said.'

'I see. That's all?'

'Also…' Billy hesitated.

'What?'

'Well, she's here to marry some Frenchman.'

'Yes, I heard that,' he said simply.

'I thought you might be disappointed,' Billy said.

Stewart forced a laugh. 'Well, yesterday, maybe. I was in a strange state of mind. But that kind of girl, with that sort of superficial appeal--'

'Superficial?'

'Well most of it, obviously, being her appearance.'

'You mean beautiful?'

'Yeah, skin deep and all that…'

'Have you talked to her since that business in the boats?' Billy said, eyeing him.

'Mmmm,' Stewart said, musing as if she hadn't crossed his mind. 'I don't think I have.'

'In our conversation she didn't strike me as shallow. I would have said charming.'

'But then, you've always been more susceptible to feminine wiles than me.'

Billy nodded thoughtfully.

Stewart raised his eyebrows. 'So, did she say anything else?'

Billy creased his lips at his brother's embarrassing transparency.

'Nothing?' Stewart said, mistaking the expression for a no.

'Oh, we discussed a few other things: cooking schools, the Chili Cook-off, her future mother-in-law…'

'Her mother-in-law?'

'Yeah, she meets her today for the first time.'

'I see. No mention of anything her roommate said, or…well, anything…'

'Anything about you, for instance?'

'Yeah,' he said, not succeeding in the least at hiding the note of hopefulness in his voice.

Billy shook his head. 'I'm afraid not.'

'Well, no matter,' Stewart said, forcing another laugh. 'But I wouldn't want her to think I was still upset about the boat or anything.'

'No, I think she's fine on that score.'

'Wonderful,' he said dully.

FRIDAY

The sun hadn't yet reached its peak, yet such is its muscular influence in this southerly clime, it managed to roast several unwary sunbathers without straining a golden ray. The beach was quiet except for the muffled breaking of tiny rollers on the sand. Higher up on the lush grounds of the Moxey Arms, silence was even more complete with two notable exceptions: one was the hum of honeybees at work on the blossoms that spilled down the terraced hillside; the other was the business-like clack of Missy's heels on the cut-coral walkway as she approached the Mutt'n'Fish on an errand that was a waste of her valuable time.

The restaurant was having a new walk-in refrigerator installed and it was closed for lunch. Taking advantage of this rare interruption of business, its namesake chili team sat around the captain's table in the rear of the empty dining room enjoying the chili that they were reasonably confident would sweep the field in nine days' time. The new recipe was profoundly toothsome, and though aware of the dangers of over-confidence, they were allowing themselves a small celebration at the very likely prospect of victory.

The last time the Mutt'n'Fish team had won the Chili Cook-off had been four years ago, and though Kingston had only three championship pots to the Mutt'n'Fish's nine, he had won the most recent two contests; his chiding that their dominance was over, and the Butterwort team represented the new face of chili expertise had stung them deeply. It must be granted that a bit of premature celebration was understandable given the unremitting effort they'd put in the past few months.

The three men heard Missy's heels on the porch and they turned as she bustled in from the harsh glare, making straight for the back carrying a small white bowl. She held up a hand to interrupt them as they greeted her.

'I don't have time for your niceties. I'm late as it is and I'm just making this delivery as a favour.'

'A favour for who?' Scoonie asked.

'A favour for *whom*,' she said.

'Yes, exactly. Who sent it?'

She gave Scoonie a dismissive shake of the head and put the covered bowl down in the centre of the table. As Maximillian lifted the foil for a look, it gave off the odour of cold chili, faint but unmistakable to the onlooking experts. The three looked at her as one, each wearing the same dumb and puzzled expression.

'Kingston,' she said. 'This is his newest chili.'

If she'd pulled a snapping barracuda from her purse and dropped it on the table, it wouldn't have pulled the three pairs of eyes any further from their sockets.

'Is that your chili?' she asked, ignoring their shock. She nodded at Maximillian's bowl.

'Won't you sit down and have some?' Maximillian said with reflexive hospitality, but his eyes, like those of his teammates, were fastened on the bowl in the centre of the table.

'Thank you.' She sniffed. 'But unlike you three, I can't squander my time mooning over recipes. And in fact I had a taste of Kingston's chili earlier when he treated me to a delightful brunch.'

She turned and headed back the way she'd come, but all eyes remained fixed on the Butterwort chili. Scoonie finally found his voice as she reached the door.

'Missy!' he bleated brokenly, a lamb that had lost its lunch money. The pathetic tone in his voice stopped her and she turned, a hand on her hip.

'Where did you get this?' he asked.

'I just told you. From Kingston.'

'Kingston Butterwort?'

Missy rolled her eyes.

'He just handed this to you and you walked out with it?' Billy said.

'Not that I have time for this, William, but when I complimented Kingston on his chili this morning, he suggested I bring a bowl back for Maximillian to try. I suspect he sent it as a sort of peace offering. I think he might want to move beyond the juvenile rivalry that you three seem to glory in.' She waved dismissively and continued out the door.

This obviously loopy analysis would normally have prompted snorts and an exchange of incredulous looks, but no one could pry their attention from the bowl in the centre of the table.

'Think it's genuine?' Billy said.

Maximillian waved the aroma toward him.

'Mmm boy, could be.'

'Poisoned?' Scoonie ventured.

Maximillian snatched it up and went into the kitchen. A couple of minutes later they heard the chime of a microwave oven and he reappeared with three steaming ramekins. His face was grim.

Scoonie leaned forward. 'Did you try it?' he said quietly, concern straining his features.

Maximillian shook his head.

'No darling, but I gotta say it smells good enough.' He pushed his Fez back on his head, a gesture reserved for only the most portentous moments.

Scoonie closed his eyes as if to give thanks, but his silent petition was that the food of which he was about to partake would choke a dog. He opened his eyes, facing it like a man, and took a spoonful.

As the writer of Job so succinctly put it, that which he feared most had come upon him. It was clearly better than Kingston's winning chili of the year before and likely better than their own current contender in which they'd had, until scant moments earlier, such confidence.

A black cloud of despair descended on the little band. With the cook-off mere days away, this spoke disaster. To best understand the reason for such despair, consider this short excerpt from Billy's thesis at the San Antonio Ungulate Culinary Institute:

The science and art of chili research requires long, tedious periods of careful tasting and testing, testing and adjusting, adjusting and refining, all of which lead, under favourable conditions, to incremental improvements for which the questing culinary artist is pitifully grateful. Breath-taking breakthroughs in this mature field are almost unknown.

Inventive genius was pithily summed up by Thomas Edison as consisting of one part inspiration to ninety-nine parts perspiration, and he could have included chili innovation in his statement with little loss of accuracy.

Maximillian and Scoonie were, of course, equally aware of this, and how Butterwort could have produced the wonder tickling their taste buds was as dismaying as it was demoralizing.

'Is this as good as I think it is?' Billy asked.

Maximillian looked at the young man sternly. 'Don't get carried away.'

'Max, it might be better than ours,' Scoonie said, his voice climbing. 'It scares me.'

'Could be is all I'm granting at the moment. What we need is an independent opinion.'

'Yes,' Scoonie agreed, though without conviction.

Kingston's advantage lay with the Butterwort chili team, the best his large fortune could buy: a group comprised of two classically trained chefs backed by a team of supporting staff and, it was rumoured, at least one full-time agent scouring the globe for the finest spices.

In addition, Kingston had allied with a group in Arizona and another in Calgary, Canada. The three merged into a group known as The Chili Collective, sharing secrets and expertise. They'd divided up the various chili competitions between them, never competing in the same contest. The past successes of the Mutt'n'Fish team over this formidable and secretive group had only been possible because of the obsessive commitment of its three members, and in the two recent years of Butterwort's dominance, even that hadn't been enough. They were facing the frightening possibility that the days when the efforts of a small group of amateurs could triumph over ruthless machines pooling knowledge and resources, were over. The trend of large, well-financed collectives strangling independents had extended its tentacles to southern Bahamian chili contests, and for the third year in a row, it appeared the appalling bunch had the title well within their grasp. The three men sat contemplating these depressing developments in silence, a trio of death row inmates on execution's eve. The front door of the restaurant creaked like the entrance to a tomb and a head poked in.

'Hello?' a voice called.

'I'm sorry, we're closed for kitchen repairs,' Maximillian answered gruffly, without turning. 'As the sign says, we should be open for dinner.'

It suddenly occurred to Billy whose voice it was.

'Come in, young Natalie,' he called out.

Her head bent in further and she studied the men in the distance for a moment, sensing the funk hanging in the air.

'I'll come back later,' she said and, giving a little wave, ducked out.

'No!' Billy shouted, causing Maximillian and Scoonie to jump. 'Come in, please.'

The door reopened a crack and the hand holding it hesitated. Scoonie called out in a broken tone, 'Yes, dear. Please do come in.'

This last poignant plea touched her heart and she slipped in the door as Maximillian's massive bulk disappeared into the kitchen. As she approached the table, Billy pulled out a chair and Maximillian reappeared shortly, carrying a tray with two small ramekins, a glass of ice water, and a slice of johnnycake on a saucer. Putting it on the table, he introduced himself and took a seat.

'I don't mean to disturb your...' She stalled and was silent. The funereal pall hanging over the men had unnerved even this intrepid girl. It was as if she had crashed a black mass halfway into the human sacrifice.

'Would you do us the favour of trying a bite of…' Maximillian stopped suddenly. 'You're not a vegetarian, are you?' he said. From the tone, he might have been asking if she collected shrunken heads.

'No.'

'Do you like chili-con-carne?'

She nodded.

'How about heat, can you take some spice?'

She nodded again.

'Then try a bite, if you please,' he said, pushing one of the ramekins in front of her.

As she did so, the men did their best not to stare. She gave it a moment's consideration and was relieved to be able to give a positive report.

'Oh, that is good. Simply wonderful,' she said, fanning her mouth. 'It is spicy.'

Scoonie and Billy each forced a smile to put her at ease, but Maximillian, though polite, was all business as he handed her a glass of ice water and the johnnycake.

'The bread works best to relieve the heat.'

When she was ready, he gave her the second ramekin. She took a bite and closed her eyes in quiet contemplation.

'Oh, very good,' she said, and continued in a meditative vein. 'Even better, in fact. The first one might be a little more balanced, but this one has pizzazz.' She smiled with her eyes still shut, blessedly unable to see their stricken faces. 'Yes, it's brighter somehow. Delicious!'

'How did I do?' she said, opening her eyes to three pained expressions. Taking in Billy first, she was struck by his resemblance to a pallbearer. Maximillian, sitting next to him, was much the same though his mourning seemed to have a deeper, more spiritual aspect.

She turned to Scoonie last, as she'd seen at a glance that he was in the worst shape of all; he seemed to be in the grip of actual physical anguish. This wasn't just a pallbearer suffering the loss of a close friend, this was a broken-hearted pallbearer with advanced lumbago. As Natalie studied him, he gazed back, staring through her as if she were the clear Bahamian sea itself.

'You did perfectly well,' Maximillian said grimly. 'We'd reached the same conclusion just before you came in.'

Scoonie emerged from his trance, remembering his manners.

'Yes, yes, you were splendid, my dear. Regrettably accurate.'

'You have two wonderful chilies,' she said. 'Why is everyone so glum?'

'The second chili you tasted is from Kingston Butterwort.' Scoonie invested the name with all the loathsomeness at his command.

Natalie stared blankly.

'Our perennial rival,' Billy explained.

She pondered this before speaking.

'Your recipe is fine, though. It's...solid. If the judges value a sound, classic version over a...' She searched for a disparaging comparison. '...a glitzy one, it could win.'

She gazed around at the trio, but no one was buying it. 'You're not giving up, I hope,' she said. 'I think you stand a very good chance.'

They smiled politely, all wearing the mask now. Trying to convey to this young innocent the supreme importance of a victory over the vile Butterwort was beyond any of their powers. She probably viewed it as a mere contest of flavours, a kind of good-natured game. Like most civilians, she hadn't the faintest inkling of the existential battle between good and evil masquerading as a Bahamian chili competition.

After an uncomfortably quiet spell, Maximillian broke the silence.

'Thank you for your help, Miss Natalie. Very perceptive. As I said, it confirms what we ourselves thought.'

She took another quick bite of the Butterwort chili followed by a bite of the bread.

'Yes, I have to be going, but let me just try this one again,' she said, pointing to the team's chili.

'Certainly, darling. Take your time,' Maximillian said.

'Do you detect anything…significant?' Billy asked.

'Yes, anything?' Scoonie said, his attention suddenly alive.

'I almost wonder if you might bring out the flavour of the beef a little more. Your sauce is wonderful, but I think it might be smothering the meat a bit. That could be what's holding it back.'

'Of course,' she added apologetically, 'I don't pretend to know chili like you…'

'No, please,' Maximillian said. 'We welcome a fresh perspective. Please go on.'

'Well,' she said, 'I make a beef stroganoff and there is one essential ingredient that brightens the flavour of the meat without diluting the spices. Well, really two.'

Scoonie slid forward in his seat and all three men stared so intently that she was momentarily taken aback. She looked down at her hands on the table, gathering her courage. The simple ingredients she was about to suggest seemed very ordinary in light of such serious purpose.

She raised her head and met Scoonie's stare.

'Coffee,' she said, 'a cup or two of coffee and a touch of cinnamon. The cinnamon's important, but not too much, not enough to really taste. I'm just guessing, of course, but you might try it.'

'We will, my dear, we will,' Scoonie said, trying to show enthusiasm while Maximillian nodded thoughtfully.

She stood to go. 'I apologize for the interruption. I only meant to stop and thank Billy for his help the other day. The Bahamian buttermilk was a salvation. And thank you for the chili. Best of luck.'

By the time the men finished their goodbyes, she was out the door and gone.

'Very sweet of her to try and help,' Scoonie said.

'Odd, the cinnamon thing,' Billy said.

'Yes, indeed,' Maximillian said, 'but I believe that girl just might have an astute palate.'

They heard a voice and Natalie reappeared, walking toward them.

'I forgot to ask,' she said. 'Do you know where Stewart is now?'

'I do,' Billy said.

At that moment, Stewart was stooping with both hands in a hole, mixing compost into the soil. Sweat poured off him in rivulets and his face was streaked with dirt, but his mind was enjoying a peace it hadn't experienced for days. The simple but arduous task of transplanting banana plants was responsible for this. Following the disturbing pattern of previous nights, his dreams had been interrupted repeatedly with the troublesome spectre of the petite brunette. Unable to shake it off on waking, he settled on a solution that answered most of life's emotional quandaries for him; physical exercise.

He'd noted that the bananas next to the front office steps needed thinning, and he was moving half of the patch's strength down the hill to a bare spot recently vacated by ageing papaya plants. It would be just the thing to occupy a beautiful summer morning. What had been among the least favourite chores of his youth now attracted him with its demand of mindless physical effort.

He put on work clothes and pulled an old straw hat down from the rafters that he hadn't worn since high school. Collecting the necessary tools, he went to work with a vengeance. Wrangling with the shovel and hoe, he felt a baseline sense of well-being returning. No longer working to corral his own thoughts, the girl slipped from his mind as his attention zeroed in on chicken manure and earthworms. He whistled.

The sun had climbed overhead, warming things up considerably, and Stewart exuded a pungent combination of compost and sweat. He was stooping with a hose to water a final small transplant and contemplating a swim when a cheery voice behind him spoke.

'Excuse me, sir, can you tell where I can find the hotel's director of sailing?'

Hearing Natalie's voice emanate from the void after he'd finally banished it from his consciousness startled him to his depths. He leaped and came down heavily on the unfortunate young plant.

Natalie herself jumped back and began to apologize, but her sincerity was compromised a good deal by giggles. She struggled to stifle it as Stewart stood and composed himself.

'Let me start over,' she said, holding out her hand. 'Natalie Jones.'

He quickly hosed off his hand and dried it on his pants. Shaking her hand, he received a decidedly electric tingle.

'Stewart Moxey.'

'I'm sorry for that,' she said, pointing at the bent banana plant. 'I didn't know I'd startle you like that.'

'It's all right. I'm a little jumpy this morning. Haha,' he said, laughing weakly at his own pun.

'Yes, haha,' she said sweetly.

'There's no director of sailing, I'm afraid, but maybe I can help you.' This came out a good deal more stiffly than he intended.

'I knew, I mean, I know that. I'm afraid that was a bad joke. I was just at the Mutt'n'Fish and your brother told me you were here.' She beamed at him. 'I was looking for you.'

His heart jumped. 'So then,' he said, speaking as matter-of-factly as possible, 'you've met Billy.'

'I have,' she said. 'A couple of days ago, actually. He went out of his way to buck me up for a difficult ordeal. And today I met Maximillian. I feel so sorry for him. For all three. They do take the chili contest seriously, don't they?'

Stewart could feel his emotions rolling over for this girl, and the excitement of her being a scant four feet away, well within range of being swept up in one's arms, was pressing on him. All the effort of shoring up his mental and emotional defences against her seemed to have vanished. He suddenly realized she was looking at him expectantly, waiting for a response, and he worked to piece together her last statement.

'Pardon, but why is it you're sorry for them?' he asked.

'That their rival's chili is so good.'

'It is?' he said, putting on a concerned look. 'But how do you know that?'

'They had a sample of it. You didn't know?'

'I didn't. I—I hadn't heard,' he stammered.

'They have some of...Butterfort's, is it?'

'Butterwort, Kingston Butterwort.'

She giggled. 'That's quite a name.'

'It is,' Stewart agreed, smiling. 'Would you like to sit? I'm afraid I've forgotten my manners.' He indicated a garden seat and she sat down.

'This is nice. Aren't you going to sit? You're the one that's earned it.' She nodded, indicating the banana plants.

'Yes and I'm afraid I smell a little ripe.'

'There's no shame in honest sweat, as my dad says far too often. Please, sit down,' she said, patting the seat. 'I won't feel comfortable with you standing.'

Stewart sat, his heart pounding against his ribs.

'Thank you,' she said, smiling sweetly. 'Anyway, they were tasting some of this Butterwort's chili and it's very good. I'm afraid they were devastated. Your father looked like he was in a state of shock.'

'I don't like hearing that,' Stewart said, purely in the interest of providing conversational filler. The fortunes of the Mutt'n'Fish chili team were normally of genuine concern to

Stewart, but at the moment he was wrestling with his own matters. There would be time to worry about the chili contest later.

'No, I expect not,' she said, and after waiting what seemed a suitable period of mourning, continued.

'I wanted to apologize for taking the boat out the other day, and the capsizing, the whole...incident.'

'Oh, that? Don't give it another thought; I was just concerned for you...for your safety. I stopped by the cottage that same afternoon to check on you. Did your roommate tell you?'

'Let me think: Mmmmm,' she said, laughing and putting a finger to her cheek. 'Has she talked about anything else since?'

'It was odd; I had a sort of fainting spell or something when I was there. I hope it didn't scare her too badly.'

'Nothing like that, in fact she was quite taken with you. I think you brought out the nursemaid in her. Of course that isn't hard, she's the nurturing type.'

Stewart could think of no good reply to this. 'Yes, she seemed like it,' he offered up hesitantly.

'You didn't like her?' Natalie said, her eyes narrowing.

'No, no, she was fine. A very caring person.'

'She comes on a little strong, but she's an angel.'

'I don't doubt it a bit, she seemed very nice.'

'I hope I'm not overstepping by saying this, but she liked you very much.'

'Ah, well, that's, ah...flattering.'

'If you knew how particular she can be, you'd mean that.'

'But of course I mean it.'

Stewart's awkwardness looked to Natalie like the crassest insincerity.

'I'm sorry. I can see that I put you on the spot. That was tactless of me.'

'No, not at all,' Stewart babbled. 'It's just...well there's...' he fumbled for a moment and stalled completely.

'There's someone else,' she finished for him.

No, Stewart wasn't willing to grant this. That there was some renegade emotion affecting his psyche at the moment, he could not deny. That that disturbance took the form of the girl sitting next to him was also undeniable. However, he'd set his will against it and he allowed his will the final word in these matters, not his emotions. So there was, in fact, no other girl.

'A particular someone,' she said, probing further.

'No, no one in particular,' he said.

'So, it's many someones, is it?' she said with a teasing smile. 'What I've read about you is true, then.'

'What?'

'Your reputation as a playboy.'

'No,' he said. 'No, not at all. That's just a lot of media hype, aided and abetted by my own sponsors, I'm afraid. You can chalk all that up to PR.'

'So, no basis at all?' she said, tilting her head back. Stewart detected a note of sarcasm and a distinct darkening of her mood.

'I hope you don't believe everything that you read about me.'

'Of course not,' she said. 'I read something in *American Sailor* that made it sound as if you'd lost the will to live, and now you've apparently found a reason to carry on. Perhaps many reasons,' she said stiffly.

Stewart shook his head in resignation.

'I'm sorry, that wasn't fair,' she said. 'Your love life is your own business."

'Apology accepted. And please don't form your opinion of me from the press.'

'Ginger found a couple of articles that said you were a decent guy.'

'What about you, what do you think?'

'That doesn't matter, the issue here is Ginger.'

'I didn't mislead her...'

'No, I believe that. And anyway, you have nothing to apologize for. I warned her you probably have a little black book in multiple volumes.'

'Didn't we just straighten that out?'

'We straightened out the fact that it's your own business how you conduct your life. Let's just leave it there,' she said. 'I'll talk to Ginger, she'll be fine. I'm actually relieved we had this talk. She's the sweetest thing imaginable, and as tough as she might seem, she isn't at all. I'd hate for her to be hurt.'

Stewart's brain circuits were sparking like a lamp cord under a chair leg and he glared at her in frustration. Unfortunately, the result was an expression that looked to Natalie like nothing less than the most brazen arrogance.

What a man! And after she'd found him so attractive a match for her friend. His shallow appeal to Ginger was understandable; she could sense it to some degree even in herself. Why were such awful men so often attractive! Dropping all pretence, she stood abruptly and turned away from him.

'Thank you for your time, Mr. Moxey,' she said, curt as a cat. 'Good day.'

Stewart stood as she walked off, watching her blankly. It was just as well she hadn't waited for a reply because Stewart was nowhere near coming up with one. He sat down again as she disappeared from view, thoroughly baffled as to what had just occurred.

A practice of Stewart's that accounted for much of his success in life thus far was the ability to learn from his mistakes and find an upside to every seeming setback. In this case he was stymied. The only apparent silver lining seemed to be that, having taken Natalie's measure first-hand, the illusion was over and done. She was a blister and no mistake.

SATURDAY

It was another cloudless morning on Porgy. The sun's rays slipped under the wide eves of The Hall's porch and penetrated the curtains and bedsheet pulled over Stewart's head with careless ease. If he'd enjoyed a refreshing night's slumber, as anticipated, he would have welcomed the cheering sunbeams; but he had not. His unpleasant encounter with Natalie Jones the previous day might have revealed her callous and unpleasant character, but it had done nothing to loosen her hold on his dreams and he'd suffered another restless night.

Despite his grogginess, he knew better than to expect any more sleep. He got up and set the coffee-maker going before showering and getting dressed, determined to put the day on a more pleasant trajectory than the previous ten hours. Picking up coffeepot and cup, he decamped to the porch and had just settled into his chair when his bleary-eyed cousin exited his own apartment. This suited Stewart fine; conversation would keep him from brooding on the night's disturbing implications.

'Morning, Leonard.'

'Stewart,' he said. His manner was very clipped.

'You look like you just woke up.'

'Well, I did. So what?' Leonard said. Being a constitutionally early riser, he viewed sleeping past five o'clock as a marked moral failing and the statement struck him as an accusation. He angled a chair away from Stewart and sat down to stare with keen interest at the porch railing.

"I did too,' Stewart said.

Leonard didn't reply, and a glance convinced Stewart that his cousin was determined to maintain his foul mood. Fine, he decided. He was none too thrilled himself and certainly not in a mood to coddle anyone else's tender feelings. If Leonard wanted to stew in whatever silent, corrosive state he was in, welcome to it. The two sat without speaking.

It was a full ten minutes before Stewart broke the silence. 'You're not still vexed with me, are you?

'What about?' Leonard said without turning.

'Come on. The business with that girl Ginger.'

'I'm over all that. In fact, I don't care if I ever see her again,' he said in a tone of manufactured indifference.

'So you're done with her?'

'Completely done. In fact, not even done. There was never anything to finish.'

'No feelings one way or--'

'No, Stew, I'm telling you. I could not care any less!'

'Speak of the devil,' Stewart said quietly, standing. He leaned over the railing and peered down the walk, calling out, 'Ginger! Good morning!'

Leonard leaped up and ran into his room, knocking over a chair on his way. Stewart laughed to himself and took the opportunity to go get another coffee cup. When he returned, Leonard was just sticking his head out of his doorway.

'Was it her?' he whispered.

'No, my mistake,' Stewart said, suppressing a smile. 'Sorry.'

Leonard's face glowed. 'That's not a bit funny, Stewart.' He was rubbing the shin he'd barked on the chair. 'I mean it.'

'Okay. That was rotten,' Stewart said, filling the cup. 'You caught me after another lousy night. I was just testing your sincerity, this is the second time you've lied to me lately. Lying is such an insidious habit and especially to close relations. And both times about this girl.'

Leonard was still bent in the doorway, nursing his leg. Stewart waved the coffee to coax him out.

With a set face impressing that Stewart was not in the least forgiven, not by a long shot, Leonard emerged stiffly and they both sat.

'So what's going on? Have you seen her since we talked?'

'I took her to Waltanique's for lunch yesterday,' Leonard said, his voice flat.

'Ah, plying her with conch fritters. Savvy.' Stewart chuckled.

'Yeah, I know, taking a girl to a conch stand for a first date. Pretty dumb. Even if it does have the world's best conch fritters.' He shifted moodily and turned to face Stewart.

'But, really,' he went on, 'what could put someone in a better mood than beer and Waltanique's fritters.'

Stewart nodded without answering.

'And if she's too high and mighty to appreciate Waltanique's, what would I do with her. A girl like that would never be happy with a Bahamian fisherman. It seemed like a good test.'

'You're taking this girl pretty seriously, aren't you?'

'Stewart, she's...' Words failed him. He stopped and stared at the ocean again. It was an emotional moment for the big man and Stewart waited for his feelings to subside before speaking.

'So she doesn't appreciate the finer things. It's better to find out...'

'Oh, she appreciates, all right,' Leonard said, interrupting him. 'She appreciates plenty. And she didn't fail any Waltanique test, if that's what you mean.' His tone deepened. 'Oh no, not at all.'

'So what is the problem?'

'Problem? No problem,' his voice going high with irony. 'She loved the fritters, said the conch stand was charming. Loves the Bahamas. Loooves Porgy. I'm pretty sure she'd love nuclear waste if it had anything to do with you.' He adopted a singsong southern accent. 'So what was Stewart like in grade school? How about as a teenager? Was he always such a fabulous sailor?' He looked pointedly at his cousin. 'You know how much I love those fritters. I almost couldn't keep them down.'

He turned his head up and stared at the ceiling, moisture pooling in the corners of his eyes.

'You could've just told her the truth.'

'What do you mean?'

'That I'm not the dreamboat she imagines. Tell her what Stewart Moxey was like in school, how I got suspended for cussing out Mrs. Carey; tell her about the time you whipped me in the Minnow's sunfish race. I don't care, tell her anything you like.'

Leonard shook his head. 'Like you strangling puppies...'

'What!'

'No. Not that it would've put her off,' he said, shaking his head. 'You should have heard her.'

Stewart exhaled. 'This is all about celebrity, Leonard,' he said. 'The silly glamour of celebrity. When people see your picture in a magazine, then on the internet, then on TV, they can't even see the real you in person. All they see is this bigger-than-life image. She's just star-struck, but believe me, it won't last. It's completely artificial, but it's real.'

'Oh, that makes sense,' Leonard said bitterly.

'You know what I mean. There's no truth to it, nothing beyond what some reporter wrote or some glossy photo. Take my word for it, it's temp—' Stewart stopped. Leonard was mumbling to himself.

'What?' Stewart said.

'Nothing.'

'It wasn't nothing. What did you say?'

'Just that it's not fair. Forget it.'

'I caught that, but what was the first bit?'

'It's nothing you haven't heard your whole life. She just went on about you being so handsome.'

Stewart turned away, shaking his head.

'Don't go playing dumb, Stewart, that just insults my intelligence. The fact is you favour Grandpa Clarence and I—I look more like Grandma.'

'It that what this is all about?' Stewart laughed. 'You think you look...womanly?'

'Good Lord, no!' Leonard said, horrified. 'But then neither did Grandma, get right down to it.'

Stewart nodded thoughtfully. It was an inarguable point.

'It's this nose and these bloody jowls,' Leonard said, grasping them in turn.

Stewart bit his tongue to stifle a smile, but his cousin caught it.

'You can mock a fellow, can't you?' He turned away, hurt.

'I just think that's asinine,' Stewart said. 'You don't look much like her. I mean, there's some superficial resemblance maybe, but...'

'No, thank God, not too much, I guess,' Leonard said, turning to face him, and the look of dumb relief on his face was, for a frozen moment, so exactly like their grandmother that it shook Stewart.

'But,' Leonard went on, 'I know I'm no bally film star by any stretch. And that's fine. People are always going on how you favour old Grandpa Clare and how handsome you both are. Good for you, I always say, but with this girl, the thing stings.'

He added something under his breath.

'What was that?'

'Nothing,' Leonard said. 'I wasn't talking to you.'

'I'm trying to help you here. You said something about a crab.'

'You can't help.'

Stewart glared at his cousin. 'How do you know?'

Leonard glared back with such animosity that Stewart stood and turned his chair to face his big, brooding cousin.

'What's this all about?' Stewart said, more heatedly than he intended. 'I see something's really eating you. Let's hear it.'

'Well then,' Leonard said, his manner that of someone taking off the gloves. 'If you just have to know, Stewart, then I'll just tell you. You, Cousin, just got the lucky toss of the genetic dice. And you getting the glad eye from Ginger, rather than me…'

'You'd give me the glad eye? Awww…'

'Har har.'

'Yeah, sorry. So go on.'

'It's all on account of the merest chance. Pure. Luck.' He spread the two words out like butter.

'Don't forget the crab,' Stewart said.

'Yes, and a crab, that's right,' Leonard said. 'Well now. Prepare yourself, you're going to hear it all now. You know how Scoonie's always going on about you being such a good sailor because you were conceived on their honeymoon cruise?'

Stewart nodded. 'To Cozumel.'

'That's right. Well, that's a little bit of a white lie on his part, because you weren't exactly conceived at sea.'

'Huh?'

'Just what I said.'

'How would you know that? And what does it have to do with anything?' Stewart looked at him carefully. 'Have you been drinking?'

Like many hard drinkers Leonard followed an elaborate set of rules, and first and foremost on his list was, aside from a single gin and tonic he allowed himself at lunch on Fridays and weekends, Absolutely No Drinking Before Five p.m. That he would be accused of such a lapse, particularly by Stewart, was a cutting blow and the injustice of it showed on his face.

'It's not even ten, Stew!'

'Sorry. I'm sorry, but it is a little bizarre. How would you know that? Dad would never…'

'No, no,' Leonard said, interrupting. 'No. I know because back in sixth year--'

'Sixth grade!'

'Yeah. I think so. Wasn't that Mrs. Knowles?'

'Yeah, the teacher that moved back to Andros.'

'That's the one.'

'That might've been grade five,' Stewart said. 'I'm thinking of the one that said Billy would be the Bahamas' T.S. Eliot. No, you're right, that was sixth year.'

'I don't remember her saying that. Eliot. Writer fellow, right?'

'Yeah, a poet Billy likes. Nothing I ever cared for,' Stewart said. 'But Billy still brings it up.'

'Anyway,' Leonard continued, sweeping these irrelevant details away with a wave of his hand, 'I was coming home from fishing and I could hear our mums going on like mad. You know how they used to do. They were laughing and having such a fine time that I sat down in the bushes under the window to listen and your mum was talking about that trip, the honeymoon cruise. Well, you know how she was such a bad sailor? She said she was sick for about the whole cruise, so as long as they were at sea there were no'—he cleared his throat—'relations.'

'So,' Stewart said brightly, 'I was virginally conceived?'

'Geez, Stew.' He winced and squirmed in his seat. 'There's no call to be sacrilegious.' Taking a breath and exhaling slowly, he continued. 'Anyway, they had a couple of days in port and your mum said she started to feel human again and that evening she and your dad took a walk to a secluded beach, moonlight, etcetera, and voila!'

He paused and looked sideways at Stewart.

Stewart nodded impatiently. 'Would you get to the point? Does this mean I have Mexican citizenship? Do I have sand in my genes?'

'Ha ha. Go ahead, have your little joke, but actually that's kind of important, the fact that this all happened in the sand.' He slowed theatrically. 'Because, at the climactic moment...'

He stalled again and looked to see if his audience was sufficiently attentive. Stewart rolled his hand to hurry things along.

'Okay, okay—so at the big moment a sand crab pinched your dad. And he jumped.'

'Jumped?'

' "Jumped like billy-oh!" Those were your mom's very words.'

'Pinched by a sand crab?'

'Yeah, you know, a ghost crab. The whitish ones. What do you think the odds of that are? The timing, I mean,' he said, looking meaningfully at Stewart. 'Definitely something crazy.'

'Astronomical,' Stewart said, his voice flat.

'Right! Right! Off the chart unlikely.'

'Get on with it.'

'That's it!'

'That's what?'

'The point I'm making. You don't see?'

'See what?'

'What that means?'

'The significance?'

'Yeah, the significance.'

'No, I don't. It's safe to say I don't see significance from here to Haiti.'

'You remember that science film on conception, don't you?'

'Yeah, in fact that's why they fired that Mrs. Knowles. For showing it. That's why she left, you know?'

'I know that. But do you remember it, the movie?'

'Vaguely, but it's safe to say the concept holds no mystery for me,' Stewart said.

'So you know there is a horde, a mass, a kind of Oklahoma land rush of the male contribution.'

'The sperm.'

Leonard winced again, squinting as he rolled his head side to side.

'This is my sainted aunt and your mother we're talking about. How about a little consideration, some delicacy?' He took another deep breath and continued. 'So, yeah, this mob is surging for the egg and it's a matter of winner take all. You know the saying; second place is the first loser?'

Stewart nodded.

'And you can see how the slightest movement by either of the…the…'

'Participants,' Stewart offered dryly.

'Participants, thank you, can affect the outcome.'

Leonard studied his cousin's face for a hint of understanding, of comprehension.

'For God's sake, Stew, a lurch like that would be like turning a racetrack on end. The one carrying something like Grandma's DNA mugprint could well have been in the lead, straining'—here Leonard leaned his huge frame forward, mimicking a jockey—'about to close the deal, the finish is coming up, he's…right…there…when suddenly the ground shifts underneath them—an earthquake to all intents and purposes—flinging contestant B, carrying Grandpa Clarence's Hollywood gene, to victory.'

The world's largest jockey shook his arms in the air in mock celebration and lowered them slowly, waiting for the sensational implications to sink in. 'You see what an arbitrary thing it is? How much luck is involved?'

'Our sixth year,' Stewart said. 'We were what, eleven years old?'

'Twelve, more like.'

'You've had this in storage since then?'

Leonard was silent for a moment before he spoke. 'That was the year you took Janet Evans to Junkanoo.'

'Why not? I liked her.'

'Yes,' Leonard said, his expression the pained, fleshy embodiment of unrequited love. 'Didn't we all.'

Stewart was stunned, and, not for the first time since returning to the island of his birth, at a loss for words. He stared straight ahead, frozen in thought, and had Billy been present to observe his brother, he might have noted his likeness to a patient etherized upon a table.

Missy entered the Mutt'n'Fish's kitchen as the morning crew was just leaving, having finished clean-up. She saw Billy in the back, whistling happily as he wiped down knives.

'Good morning, Missy,' he called out as she walked back. 'What's the occasion? We see you here so rarely and now, two days in a row.'

'Good morning to you, William. Scoonie said you were here. I didn't know that you were working breakfasts.'

'I just came in to work out a few new dinner items.'

'Really,' she said, absently straightening a stack of napkins. 'You do go the extra mile, don't you? In fact, that's what brought me here. I just overheard a guest telling her friend how accommodating she finds the folks at the Mutt'n'Fish.'

'Glad to hear it.'

'Don't be so glib. She was genuinely touched.'

'Really?' Billy said, stopping his work to look at her. 'Thank you for telling me. I do like to hear the positive reviews.' He assumed a reflective posture, gazing up. 'But, you know, credit where credit is due; nobody can run this place like Max. He's the restaurateur equivalent of you, I reckon. I mean how you're so natural at steering the Arms on a straight course. He's got that same unerring touch with this place.'

Missy nodded agreeably.

'That's sweet of you, Billy.'

'No more than you've earned, both of you,' he said and, lowering his voice, added, 'I shudder to think the shape the Arms would be in if you hadn't taken over.'

'You're very generous.'

Billy couldn't remember the last time that there'd been such a flow of reason and goodwill between Missy and him. Their relations tended to be on the rocky side, but he was feeling positively affectionate toward her. They were two intelligent, reasonable people, why the constant undercurrent of discord between them, he wondered? Why shouldn't respect and harmony be the rule? He smiled warmly, catching her eye and she beamed back.

'It's nice of you to credit Maximillian, but in the conversation I'm referring to,' she said, 'he wasn't mentioned. It was your name that came up.'

'Really?'

'That's right.'

'Well, I try to do my part,' he simpered.

'You're too modest,' she said. 'From what I gathered, you can take all the credit in this instance.'

Billy flashed her a look of gratified surprise.

'Yes, it seems you set all to rights for this girl with a bottle of old and very rare rum. I think the word she used was "priceless". "Priceless and very strong". That had a familiar ring.'

The world didn't exactly go black for Billy, but it was a near thing. For a few seconds he had a sort of bloodless, disembodied experience as images flashed across his mind from a TV nature show of a trusting antelope being ambushed by a tiger at a waterhole. It just went to show, the announcer had pointed out, what a jungle the world can be. Billy shivered as a chill went through him and he seconded the motion.

When Missy had taken over management of the Arms, Scoonie asked her to watch over the last few dozen bottles of William's Unblended Rum, and though Missy was herself a strict teetotalling Baptist, she had done so with the fervour and efficiency with which she assumed any charge.

She turned to face Billy squarely and her gaze pierced him with the ease of an earth-boring laser hitting a stratum of marshmallow. With one hand on her hip, she extended the other palm up, but Billy was already on his way to the cabinet to pull out the bottle. He handed it over with pained resignation and Missy held it up.

'Half empty, I see.'

'Not to be critical, but that's a telling difference in our respective approaches to life, Missy. I was just thinking what a pity it is giving up a bottle that's half full.'

She rolled her eyes and turned toward the door as he gave a wistful wave to the bottle.

'The locks have already been changed,' she called over her shoulder as the door swung closed.

The tournament was only five days away and the island was already brimming with visitors. The Arms had no vacancies and all harbour slips were filled. A few of the more remote moorings were still available, but soon boats would have to find their own anchorage or spend their nights in the Georgetown or Stocking Island marina. A festive atmosphere was evident at every Willstown bar and restaurant.

The Mutt'n'Fish was full at every meal, and when Gladys had to take a reservation for fifteen under the name of Mr. C.C.O. Winner, a name new to her, she suspected a prank.

'The caller sounded nervous,' she said to Maximillian. 'I wish I'd asked for a phone number.'

'So nobody we know?' Maximillian asked.

She shook her head. 'No one I recognised. It was a man's voice, but it sounded like he was trying to disguise it.'

'Disguise it?'

'Like he didn't want me to know who he was,' she said.

He shrugged. 'It's all right. Go ahead and prep for it.'

At the appointed hour, a loud crowd entered the restaurant headed by Kingston Butterwort.

He was in high spirits, and when he spotted Maximillian behind the bar, he walked over. His entourage held back, waiting.

'Mr. Sawyer, how are things with you?'

It was to Kingston's credit that he managed this with such aplomb, for he'd always been intimidated by Maximillian.

'Fine, Mr. Butterwort,' Maximillian replied. 'And you?'

'Couldn't be better, couldn't be better. I guess you were wondering who C.C.O. was?' He smirked over his shoulder and his group snickered.

Maximillian walked over to the reservation book. 'I saw something like that in the book. Here it is, initials C.C.O. You know him?'

'Are you sure those are initials?' Kingston said, playing to his entourage. 'It sounds more like a title of sorts.'

'Is that right. So you do know him.'

'I think I do. That title in full is Chili-Cook-off Winner,' Butterwort said with a wicked smile and his party laughed.

'Is that right?' Maximillian said, and looking in the book, he read in the resonant voice that Kingston had always found irritating. 'Party of fifteen, Mr. C.C.O. Whiner. You say that's Chili-Cook-off Whiner?'

'Winner,' Butterwort blustered, 'Chili-Cook-off Winner.'

'It says Whiner here,' Maximillian said, glancing down at the book again.

'Your girl took it down wrong,' he said, harrumphing.

'I don't know. Gladys is a pretty good speller.'

'I tell you, that's me and she got it wrong,' he said heatedly.

'Well let's not quibble. Either way, you're welcome to the table. Ocillea, seat these folks at the Whiner table.'

Butterwort glared at the back of Maximillian's head as the big man disappeared into the kitchen and then turned to find his group looking at him blankly. 'What are you waiting for,' he said irritably, motioning for them to follow the waiting hostess.

The harried group filed past Natalie and Ginger, who were already enjoying their dinner. The two girls were just forking into perfectly prepared grouper and Ginger made a face caricaturing the dyspeptic gentleman that passed them harrumphing loudly. Natalie tried to muffle her giggle.

'Stop it, I'm trying to eat,' she said to Ginger, who was busy mugging.

'What seems to be the problem here?' Billy said loudly, suddenly appearing at their table. Both girls flinched and when Natalie saw it was Billy, she shook her head.

'Not you too,' she said. 'I'm trying to enjoy this wonderful fish and can't get a bite down.'

'Pardon me, did I startle you?'

'Yes, you did,' Ginger said, holding out her hand. 'I'm Ginger Hobbs.'

'William Moxey,' Billy said, giving a half-bow as he took it. 'Pleased to meet you. I don't like to scare strangers, so consider me a friend.'

'That's right, I said I'd introduce you two the next time we met, didn't I,' Natalie said.

'And we're already fast friends,' Billy said.

'Who was that man with the unpleasant face who passed us a moment ago?' Ginger asked. 'Did you see him?'

'I'm not sure,' Billy said, 'but your description is sufficient to hazard a guess. Was he shortish? Fattish? Walking with the grace of a donkey on its hind legs?'

The girls laughed.

'I think that's the one,' Ginger said.

'In that case, you've just seen the Mutt'n'Fish chili team's arch nemesis, Kingston Butterwort.'

'So that's him,' Natalie said.

Billy nodded. 'I'm sorry you had to see that while you're eating. He didn't put you off the grouper, I hope.'

'It's delicious. But I do have a question.'

'Oh, don't, Gnat. I told you it's fine,' Ginger said, and turned to Billy. 'Someone warned us about fish poisoning and now she's worried--what did he call it, Gnat?'

'Ciguatera,' Billy said, answering for her. 'Do you mind if I sit?'

'That was it! Oh yes, please do, if you can spare the time.'

'Happy to,' Billy said, pulling up a chair and resting his elbows on the back.

'Now,' he continued, 'who did you hear this from?'

'It was a customer leaving just as we were served. He said to be careful eating any reef fish here--'

'Did he seem blissful?' Billy said, interrupting.

The two girls looked at each other, puzzled.

'I don't know,' Natalie said.

'Why in the world...'Ginger added.

'I only ask because that's said to be the happy result of ignorance,' he said.

Ginger rolled her eyes. 'You're very snide, aren't you.' She turned to her friend. 'Like I said, Gnat, it isn't true.'

'Concerning the fish that we serve, it is true you needn't worry,' he said. 'But ciguatera can be a problem wherever there are fish dining over coral reefs. Are you familiar with the stupendous novelist Saul Bellow?'

Both girls nodded.

'He was poisoned by a fish dinner while on vacation south of here. He was rushed to the States for treatment and, even so, nearly died. I believe it was grouper, too.'

'Grouper!' the girls chorused, and both dropped their forks.

Billy held his hands up. 'Relax, the danger is confined to large fish and we don't serve anything over twelve pounds. Since I've worked here, the Mutt'n'Fish has only had a single case of ciguatera poisoning and that was due to a customer insisting I cook an overlarge black grouper that he'd caught himself.'

'And he died?' Ginger said, wide-eyed.

'No, no. Folks very rarely die from it; in fact I've never known it to happen.'

The girls picked up their forks, breathing a sigh of relief.

'Although,' he added, 'many do say that death would be preferable. It's reportedly very uncomfortable.'

'So no one eats big grouper, I guess,' Ginger said.

'Oh, plenty of people still do. And barracuda, horse-eye jack and other fish even more prone to be poisonous than grouper. There is occasionally a case here on Porgy, but as I say, nothing fatal. The danger with Saul Bellow was due to his age. He was roundabout eighty, I believe.'

'There must be a way to test the fish,' Natalie said.

'There are dozens of methods,' Billy said.

'Such as?' Ginger asked.

'A fish is said to be safe, if,' Billy said, ticking them off on his fingers.

'Number one: Flies will land on it.

(#2) Ants will eat it.

(#3) Dogs or cats partake without ill effect. [A very cold and heartless method, that one.]

(#4) Pammy Cartwright gives the thumbs up.'

'Who is that?' Natalie asked.

'Local savant. Will assess your fish for a minimal fee. She reads the vibrations or something,' Billy said, raising an eyebrow sceptically. 'And my favourite: (#5) A silver coin tucked into the flesh fails to turn black.'

'That is bizarre.'

'Yes, and so inconvenient. How many silver coins do you run across nowadays?'

'No, good point,' Ginger said. 'But still, it sounds almost strange enough to work.'

'Sadly, it doesn't. In fact, none of them do.'

'None?'

Billy shook his head.

'So a fish dinner is a sort of tableside Russian roulette.' Ginger laughed uneasily.

'No, like I say, avoid the big ones and you'll be fine. Fish under a couple of feet long are ninety-nine and forty-four one-hundredths safe, pure as Ivory Soap. I have enjoyed a lifelong diet rich in seafood, as evidenced by my overdeveloped cranium, and I've never been poisoned.'

He rapped lightly on the top of Natalie's head.

'It's a pity there's no way to be one hundred percent sure, with fish so plentiful here. I have a horror of food poisoning, but I love seafood.'

'One hundred percent? Tell me what in this life is one hundred percent,' Billy said, creasing his brow. 'However...'

'What?'

'Well, there is "Stanley's Saturday Surety".'

'What's that?' Natalie said, brightening.

'It's a procedure peculiar to a certain Stanley Pinder of Willstown. The method got its name because he only keeps a large reef fish if he catches it on a Friday or Saturday.'

'I hope you don't expect me to believe that. As Ginger says, do I look like I fell off the turnip truck?'

'That's very colourful, the expression is new to me,' Billy said, always appreciative of a vivid turn of phrase. 'But I haven't finished. The method is genius; despite his being particularly fond of both barracuda and amberjack, two of the most shameless offenders, he has never been poisoned. His neighbour is an elderly woman and the church organist. When he catches a fish on the biggish side, he cuts off a portion for her Saturday supper. He then cocks his ear the following morning when the Sunday service begins and if he hears organ music coming from the chapel, he sharpens up the fillet knife and enjoys a carefree Sunday brunch. If the choir is a cappella, the fish goes straight in the rubbish. Stanley says when he wakes up with a good appetite and doesn't hear the swell of that organ, it simply breaks his heart.'

'But that is monstrous!' Ginger said, and Natalie nodded agreement with a stricken face.

'Before you judge him too harshly,' Billy said, 'the organist is his mother-in-law and a nasty piece of work.'

SUNDAY

A panting crewman pushed open the door to the lounge of the Butterchurn VIII and caught his breath.

'Speak up, man. Cat got your tongue?' Kingston said.

'Sorry sir, I was at the bow. That redheaded Frenchman is coming this way, sir.' Kingston jumped up and looked out the window. Sure enough, the arrogant Continental was strutting down the quay toward the Butterchurn with a small attractive brunette by his side.

Earlier in the morning when Kingston instructed his crew to keep a lookout for The Baron, he hadn't definitely decided to force a confrontation with him but having put away two double espressos with a touch of Goslings in each, he was feeling up to the challenge. Timing his exit carefully, he opened the door just as they were passing the gangway. The woman turned and gave him a friendly smile and her companion pulled his nose down a degree or two and nodded.

'Good morning,' Kingston said. 'Beautiful morning.'

'Yes, isn't it?' the girl said, and the Frenchman's expression warmed slightly as he nodded agreement.

'I was just going to have some coffee,' Kingston said. 'Care to join me in the lounge?'

'We were just on our way to get some,' the girl said. 'Could we?' she added, looking at her companion.

'We can stop for a few minutes if you like,' he said, followed by a frozen smile, but Kingston caught a fleeting look of distaste.

'Yes, please, come in and relax. Have an espresso, latte, whatever you'd like. I have a couple of questions about your boat.'

The Baron nodded with a tired air.

'If you come this way, you can see a bit of this one,' Kingston said, holding the door. Once in the lounge, introductions were made all around and a crewman was dispatched with the coffee order.

'This is very nice,' Natalie said as they were seated. She turned to The Baron for confirmation.

He nodded with an indulgent air. 'Yes, a nice little boat.'

Kingston ground his teeth at the diminutive, but swallowing his ire, he forged ahead.

'It's a custom Brillare, the Italian builder. Just got it last year; this is the first time I've brought it to Porgy.'

'Oh, do you come here often?'

'Every year. I've been coming since I was an infant.'

'Really! What a wonderful island. This is my first time. Antoine's also.'

'I'm afraid you're thirty years too late. You should have been here back in the day.'

'It seems to be like that everywhere, so many places are being overrun with tourists,' The Baron said. 'My country is being ruined in the same manner.'

'Oh, but France is still charming,' Natalie said. 'And I think here is as well. How can it have changed so much when it's not crowded or built up?'

'Well yes, the island itself is still relatively pristine. And other than this time of year, tournament week, it isn't overrun with tourists. No, the problem is the bunch running it now.'

'The local government, you mean?'

'I mean the Moxey family, the ones that own the resort and generally run things. Those degenerates have far too much influence. The tragedy of it is, the Moxeys used to be a fine family. The current lot aren't a patch on those of the past.'

'What is that, a patch...?' the Frenchman asked.

The girl jumped in to explain. 'Not worth much. Sorry to interrupt,' she said to Kingston. 'Antoine struggles with some of our expressions.'

'No, no, thank you,' Kingston said. 'Yes, that's just what I meant. It's shocking to those of us that have watched it happen. Those early Moxeys were good people but the two generations in control now don't have any idea what they're doing. Not just them, either, their hangers-on and employees are equally lousy. I can only think of a single exception: the manager, Missy Rolles. In fact, in my opinion, she's the only reason the resort continues to function at all. Count yourselves lucky that you have your yacht and aren't bunking at the Arms-_'

'But I am,' Natalie said. 'And I've found them to be very pleasant.'

Kingston saw The Baron raise an eyebrow at this.

'Well,' she added, 'with the exception of Stewart Moxey, perhaps.'

Kingston scowled, his head giving an involuntary shake. 'He's the least of it. Wait until you get to know his brother. His father!'

Natalie started to voice another objection when the clock in the lounge chimed ten o'clock. 'Oh, I'm supposed to be meeting Ginger right now, the time got away from me,' she said, jumping to her feet. 'My girlfriend and I are going to the Sunday service. Pardon me, I have to run.'

As The Baron stood, she said, 'Stay and finish your coffee, dear. You don't need to walk us there.'

'No, I should go as well,' The Baron said.

'I have a couple of questions about your boat if you could spare a few more minutes of your time,' Kingston said, wincing inwardly. Having to beg this arrogant Frenchman was wounding.

'The service ends at eleven, Antoine,' Natalie said, 'if you'd like to meet us in front of the church.' He made a longsuffering face but sat back down. Thanking Kingston for the coffee, Natalie left.

'Your question about the boat?' The Baron said hurriedly, making it clear that his attention, like a premium sale item, was only available for a limited time.

'Have you had it long?' Kingston asked, hiding his pique at the man's arrogance.

'The Papillon isn't mine,' he said simply.

'So, you're jus…you're leasing it?' Kingston said, barely disguising his glee as he felt himself gain the upper hand. Now he was getting somewhere. If the man was a mere renter, an adjustment in their relative standing was in the offing. This was delightful news. It was exactly the chink in the man's armour he'd hoped to find. Let him try to play the superior European now.

Normally The Baron wouldn't deign to reply to such a question from the likes of this glorified shopkeeper, but the man's smirk was insufferable.

'I have one, nearly a twin of the Papillon, on order at a yard in Belgium,' he said. 'With some improvements, of course. I'm still debating a small increase in the waterline.'

As The Baron intended, this blow had his host reeling. Kingston had a rough idea what the massive vessel cost, and try as he might, he couldn't help but feel awe and not a little envy for anyone batting in that league. And that the man was in a position to consider upgrading such a vessel was even more crushing to the stalwart titan of industry. As a sour Kingston sat digesting this one-upmanship, Natalie re-entered the lounge.

'Pardon me,' she said, and turned to the Baron. 'Ginger says the service ends at eleven-thirty. Is that all right?'

'Fine, fine,' he said, irritated that she'd interrupted his moment of triumph over the vulgar American.

'What do you have on order in Belgium?' she said, having overheard his statement.

'Nothing, nothing,' he said, waving dismissively. 'I'll see you after your church.'

'We're just talking boats,' Kingston said with a valiant attempt at cheerfulness. 'You know men and their toys.'

Natalie smiled—a little crookedly, he thought—and left.

Kingston couldn't hide the continuing downward spiral of his mood and this brought an undeniable rosiness to The Baron's cheeks. All that Kingston could manage in his deflated condition was a couple of trivial questions that The Baron effortlessly spiked before excusing himself with a thin smile.

When the church service ended an hour later, among the first to shake the pastor's hand on his way out the door was Billy, followed closely by Natalie and Ginger. He turned and smiled broadly at the two girls.

'I didn't see you in there!' Ginger said.

'I was sitting behind you.'

'Are your father and brother here? Maximillian?' Natalie asked.

'No, I'm the only regular church-goer in my little circle.'

'And the only one that needs it, I imagine,' Ginger said, and the two girls laughed.

'What!' Billy said, feigning outrage. 'I don't think we've known each other twenty four hours and already you feel free to attack me?'

'I'm a quick study,' she drawled.

Natalie took Billy's arm. 'Come and meet my fiancé,' she said, pulling him to a corner of the churchyard where The Baron stood studying a bronze plaque mounted on a stone pulpit. The Baron turned at her voice and Natalie introduced the two of them.

'I was reading the history of this church,' The Baron said to Billy. 'Established 1785. And the founder was also a William Moxey. An ancestor of yours, no doubt.'

'Yes, my ancient namesake, though there've been a few Williams between us.'

'Fascinating. It says your family were Loyalists that fled the Revolutionary War of the United States.' Billy nodded as The Baron continued. 'Do you know of that period?'

'A little,' Billy said. 'On account of our family history.'

'Do you know of "The Treaty of Paris"?'

Billy nodded. 'Yes, it officially tied up things between Britain and the U.S.'

'Yes, it was the peace treaty that ended the American Revolutionary War.'

'Matter of fact,' Billy said, pointing to the inscription, 'that fellow, the first William Moxey, was the Loyalist representative at the signing.'

'Incredible. Do you know of Charles Gravier Vergennes?'

'No,' Billy said. 'Who's he?'

'He was the French Foreign Minister that arranged the signing. And a direct ancestor of mine through my mother's side.'

Billy raised his eyebrows. 'That's quite a coincidence.'

'Yes, isn't it?' The Baron said.

'So then this Vergennes was working against Britain's interests in the negotiations. I guess that means our ancestors didn't see eye to eye on the matter.'

The Baron looked at him narrowly. 'Yes, the Americans, naïve as always, succumbed to the base mercantile incentives of the English and betrayed us, their loyal allies. A lamentable chapter in their history.'

'Maybe so, but a happy one for my family. The Moxeys were granted this island by King George the Third in recognition of my namesake's small contribution to the effort,' Billy said modestly.

'And, as you say, in direct opposition to the noble Vergennes,' The Baron said darkly, glaring down his nose at Billy.

'Did I say noble?' Billy said innocently. 'But don't take it personally, that wasn't the last time the French lined up on the wrong side.'

The Baron snorted. 'Pleased to have met you, Monsieur Moxey,' he said, turning abruptly to Natalie. 'Shall we go.' She nodded and gave Ginger and Billy a small wave as they departed.

Ginger and Billy watched them go. 'You know, I don't think he really was pleased to have met you,' Ginger said.

Billy looked at her, feigning shock. 'You doubt him? I hope Natalie doesn't hear of this.'

'I won't tell if you won't,' she said, laughing.

'Mum's the word, then,' Billy said. 'Unless compelled by conscience, as I so often am.'

'Yes, I'll bet,' she said, shaking her head.

MONDAY

It wasn't yet seven o'clock and Natalie sat on the small porch of her cottage, taking in the cool of the early morning hour. The beach had been combed smooth by a high tide in the early morning hours and as it dropped out, a series of bright sandbars alternated with deeper channels creating a series of white and turquoise stripes stretching the breadth of the bay. The sun had risen early, but at this hour its best efforts only managed to bathe Porgy in a crystalline light: The punishing heat it delighted in imposing this time of year was still a few hours away.

The scent of the dewy blossoms surrounding the cottage mixed with the salty freshness of the ocean air and she inhaled deeply, pondering the dilemma of needing coffee to provide the impetus to go for coffee, deciding that that qualified as a crisis only in the near-perfect world of a Porgy morning. It was indeed ideal, and she made a move to get her phone and call room service but then realised that she would likely disturb her roommate's slumber as well as interrupt this rare moment. She settled back in her chair and gazed contently at the ocean.

The patter of light, quick footsteps came from behind the hibiscus hedge that hid the cottage from the central walk, and moments later Myron, second assistant to the concierge, rounded the squat bottle palm that marked the corner of the porch and walked smartly up the steps holding a tray with coffee, sugar and cream. He stood ramrod straight as he laid it unsteadily on the small table next to her. It was only after the tray was safe that he allowed himself a smile.

'Coffee compliments of the Mutt'n'Fish chili team, please, ma'am,' he said, stopping to catch his breath. 'Mr. Maximillian asks would you come to the Cur'n'Cuda if you please, ma'am.'

'The Curren what?'

'Pardon, ma'am,' he said, and after a quick gulp of air, continued. 'I meant to say the Mutt'n'Fish Pub and Restaurant. Mr. Maximillian and Mr. Scoonie would like to see you there.'

The aroma from the tray was waking Natalie's sleepy synapses.

'Cur'n'Cuda. Dog and barracuda?' she murmured. 'Ah, that's the Mutt'n'Fish?'

'Yessum.'

'Very clever.'

'Yessum.'

'Your own?'

'Pardon?'

'Did you make it up?'

'Oh, no ma'am, 's old, I think.'

'I see. And when am I expected there?'

'Directly you finish your coffee, ma'am, but don't rush,' he said, adding a final 'ma'am.'

Half an hour later Natalie was approaching the front porch of the Mutt'n'Fish when she saw Scoonie sitting on a bench facing the ocean with the morning breeze feathering his grey hair and moustache. His likeness to a lantern-jawed sea captain was compromised, however, by a string tie and western shirt. As she topped the steps he stood quickly, smiling.

'Ah, Miss Jones!'

'Good morning, Mr. Moxey. You wanted to see me?'

'Please, call me Scoonie,' he said. 'Yes, I do. As do Max and Billy as well. I hope you haven't eaten.' Without waiting for an answer he half-bowed and motioned toward the door. 'Shall we go in?'

'You look very nice this morning. I'm surprised to see a bolo tie in the Bahamas.'

Scoonie reddened slightly. 'I like to wear it on special occasions. Occasions having to do with my keen interest in chili.'

'It's not today, is--' Natalie said, puzzled.

'Oh, the Cook-off? No, no,' Scoonie interrupted. 'The Cook-off isn't until Awards Day, this coming Sunday. But come inside.' He offered his arm.

The breakfast rush was at its peak and they made their way slowly through the crowded dining room toward the captain's table. Scoonie took the opportunity to explain his attire.

'You know this tie and shirt were given to me by the Chili Society of Kerrville.' He looked at her significantly as they stopped to let a fully laden busboy pass.

'Is that right. I don't know Kerrville.'

'No?! Kerrville, Texas? Oh, it's a beautiful burg in the Hill Country northwest of San Antonio and it is absolutely bursting with chili aficionados. Experts...' Scoonie's spiel trailed off as they approached the table. Billy stood holding a chair for her and no sooner was she seated than a steaming bowl of chili was put on the table in front of her. Gladys appeared at her other shoulder with more coffee. While this choreography unfolded, Scoonie sat down, his moustache dancing impatiently above his smile.

Billy took the seat opposite his father and Maximillian came out of the kitchen and took his customary chair. Since she'd been seated, none of the cheerful men surrounding her had spoken a word. Maximillian nodded at her bowl, and Natalie took a tentative bite.

It was good. She smiled and took another. No, she'd been wrong. It wasn't just good, it was wonderful. Spectacularly wonderful. She closed her eyes and leaned back, trying to divine its secrets. It took all of five seconds.

Her eyes opened wide and she looked at each of them in turn.

'Coffee.'

Maximillian nodded.

'Cinnamon too?'

He nodded again.

'What else?' she asked.

'That's it.'

'No!'

'True, true,' Billy said. 'Inspired call, young Natalie.'

'It was just a guess.'

'And a good one.' Maximillian said, 'A single strong cup of Bahamas Coffee Roasters Junkanoo blend per four pounds of beef and we were halfway there. We had a variety of cinnamons flown in from Miami and we worked in the kitchen all yesterday afternoon, Billy and I did, and it all came together by nine o'clock last night. Very exciting. I admit, I hardly slept. The Ceylon did the trick. Just a touch made the difference.'

'Not too much,' she said.

'As you say, it's a delicate balance.'

'Well,' Natalie said, beaming. 'You did a wonderful job!'

'As talented as Maximillian and Billy are, my dear,' Scoonie said, 'they couldn't have done it without that inspired bit of direction. We owe you an immeasurable debt.'

Maximillian cleared his throat portentously. 'In light of that, we'd like to invite you to be a member of our little band, the Mutt'n'Fish chili team. No obligation, it is a purely honorary title if you wish, but we would be pleased if you chose to participate,' he said.

'If you are so inclined,' Scoonie added.

Natalie could see in their faces that this was no lightly bestowed tribute. Despite the hustle and bustle of the morning breakfast rush, the men's gaiety of a few moments earlier had given way to earnest faces around the circular table. The conversation, laughter, and clatter of silverware continued around them, but the three men watched her gravely.

'I'd be honoured…' she said just loud enough to be heard by those at the table.

'Excellent,' Billy said as the demeanour of the three brightened once more.

'Splendid!' Maximillian agreed and he and Scoonie banged their silverware on the table like schoolboys, oblivious to the stares of the other diners.

'...Although,' Natalie added quickly to stop them, 'who knows if I'll ever get back for another Cook-off.'

'You might surprise yourself, my dear,' Maximillian said. 'As I say, it's purely honorary if you wish.'

'Well, I am honoured, and I'll help in any way I can.'

It was late morning and Leonard was out on the porch under a squeaking ceiling fan, whistling happily. He had just finished polishing his size-fourteen pebble-grain wingtips in readiness for the awards party. It was six days away, but Leonard was a smart dresser and to him the preliminary preparations were an enjoyable prelude to the night itself. His belt lay beside him waiting for the saddle soap and as he reached for it Stewart exited his doorway onto the porch, eyeing his cousin warily through bloodshot eyes. Leonard gave him a censorious glance and began work on the leather without a word of greeting.

'What's wrong with you?' Stewart said, calling out Leonard's shocking breach of manners. 'Don't I even get a good morning?'

'Pardon me,' he said coldly. 'Good morning, Stewart.'

'Good morning. Why the nasty look?'

Leonard turned to him. 'Again, my apologies.'

'Accepted. But you didn't answer my question.'

Leonard reflected for a half minute before replying.

'You can tell me to mind my own business if you want to, and maybe I should, but...' He stopped. Lecturing Stewart was not something he could ever remember doing nor anything he welcomed at the moment, but duty called.

'But what?' Stewart said.

He took a deep breath and dove in. 'I don't like to see you drinking so much.'

Stewart stared at his cousin uncomprehending.

'I know,' Leonard said, 'I'm one to talk. But I've never seen you do this before and…'

Stewart held up his hand.

'I haven't been drinking.'

Leonard eyed his cousin critically.

'Have you seen me drinking?' Stewart said. 'Aside from that first night, I mean.'

Leonard didn't answer.

'The least bit kerpunckled up?' Stewart pressed.

He shook his head.

'Do you know why?'

'Because you haven't been?'

'That's right.'

'C'mon, Stew. Not yesterday morning, but the two before that and then this morning makes the third time I've seen you hungover.'

'Hungover?'

'That's what I said,' he said stoutly, determined to carry it through. Leonard grimaced. This was worse than he'd expected.

'Apparent hangover, I'll grant you that,' Stewart said. 'It might've looked like it, but it was fatigue. One hundred percent. I can't sleep. I haven't had a solid night's rest since I got here. It adds up.'

Leonard nodded. 'So you're saying the mornings when you've been bleary, dragging around, moaning…'

'Moaning!?'

'Well, everything but. You're saying none of it's from alcohol?'

'None of that was from alcohol.'

'I see.'

'You don't believe me,' Stewart said.

'If you say so, Stewart.'

'It doesn't sound like you believe me. I'm not Billy trying to put one over on you.'

'Of course I believe you. You're not Billy.'

Stewart nodded in agreement.

'Well, I'm glad it isn't drink; some people have trouble controlling that,' Leonard said. 'So why can't you sleep?'

'Just things on my mind.'

'It's not a girl, is it?'

'What gives you that idea?' Stewart snapped, horrified at his own transparency.

'Geeze, sorry,' Leonard said. 'Look Stewmeat, you need to tell me straight. Is this about Ginger?'

'No. It is not.'

'You wouldn't lie to me,' Leonard said. 'You're not Billy,' he reminded him.

'No,' Stewart said flatly, in no mood to elaborate further.

'Okay. Because I'm going to ask her out on the boat tomorrow.' Leonard watched his reaction carefully and he was relieved to see Stewart take it calmly.

'Good,' Stewart said. 'I'll bet she accepts, and you have a fine time.'

'You mean that, don't you?'

'Of course.'

They sat, each lost in his own thoughts until Stewart broke the silence.

'Have you met the owner of that ship in the harbour?'

'Ship is right,' Leonard said. 'I've never seen anything like it before, not even in Nassau. Those Russian yachts at the Atlantis aren't a patch on it.'

'You know the owner of it is here to marry Natalie Jones, the roommate of your friend Ginger.'

'Yeah, she told me that when I took her to Waltanique's. When we walked back to the cottage, he and Natalie were sitting on the porch. Antoine.'

'That's his name?'

Leonard nodded.

'They call him The Red Baron,' Stewart said.

'Yeah, that's what Ginger said, because of his red hair and I guess he's some sort of French bigshot, royalty or something,' Leonard said.

'What's he like?'

Leonard shrugged. 'Hard to say, I guess I was mostly paying attention to Ginger.'

'Of course.'

'He's all right, I guess. He seemed a little biggety, but he is French so maybe not really.'

'French, but not really what?' a lilting feminine voice called up from below. 'Speak up, we didn't quite catch that.'

Leonard looked at Stewart, horrified, and walked over, peering over the rail.

'Hi, Leonard. What's not really French?'

Oh, good morning, Natalie. Hi, Antoine,' Leonard said. He paused, and Stewart said a little prayer to the god of repartee to aid his cousin in his hour of need. Leonard's mind was rarely at its best when taken by surprise. After an awkward few moments, he spoke. 'That big yacht of yours, was it made in France?'

Leonard glanced back, and Stewart nodded admiringly at this deft reply.

'Actually, it was made in Belgium,' a French voice said.

'Oh, I see,' Leonard said, speaking a little too brightly.

'Who's with you up there?' Natalie asked.

Leonard turned to Stewart and motioned him to the rail. 'Stewart and I were talking about your yacht, you know how he likes boats.'

As Stewart moved to the railing, peering over, he heard Natalie say to The Baron, 'It's Stewart Moxey, the sailboat racer.' Stewart leaned out and waved down to them. Natalie was her normally radiant self and she waved back. Next to her the redheaded baron stood stiffly erect.

'Stewart, this is--'

'How do you do,' The Baron said, cutting her off. 'I am Antoine, pleased to meet you.' Stewart returned the greeting and smiled despite the large gears grinding in his chest.

'I watched you take the cup in the Corfu Challenge last year,' The Baron said. 'I must congratulate you on your extraordinary luck on the final leg.'

'Yes, well,' Stewart said, 'a little luck predicting wind shifts is always welcome. There was an indication in the eucalyptus trees on the bluff and we were fortunate the skipper of the Guépard missed it.'

'Yes, it so happens we were at school together.' The Baron shook his head, unable to hide his bitterness. 'I told Alain he must have been sleeping, to permit that. He had you easily.'

Despite the man's condescending tone, Stewart found it easier to keep his attention on The Baron than his companion. 'That's a beautiful part of the world,' he said, in an effort to redirect the conversation.

'Yes, I have an uncle that lives in Capri, so I rarely miss the race season there. Will we see you this year?'

'No, I'm taking some time off.'

'So you won't be racing? They've moved it to a later date, you know.'

'So I hear, but I'll be on Porgy for the foreseeable future.'

'You're cheating us of our revenge, you know.'

Stewart smiled grimly without answering.

'Natalie and I are making the race our belated honeymoon.'

Despite his interior continuing to lurch, Stewart was able to give an intelligible answer, though he later couldn't recall what it was. Presumably a parting remark because The Baron gestured goodbye with a finger salute and Natalie flashed a smile as the couple continued on their way down the walk. Leonard turned to Stewart as they resumed their seats. 'What did you ever do to him?'

2ND TUESDAY

At precisely an hour before noon the sun was doing yeoman's duty lighting the seawater to a state of such crystalline clarity that a Nassau grouper in the eight-pound range would have been hard-pressed to go unnoticed from forty yards away. Stewart was less than half that distance from a large sponge when just such a fish darted from behind it to a sea-fan garden and, pausing there only a moment, to the far side of a familiar coral-head. Unhurried, Stewart made his way to the massive mound of greenish-yellow coral and dove down on top of it. Taking care to keep his knees from scraping, he pulled himself across and stopped at the far edge, peering over the side. He knew the difference between a grouper that suspected it was being pursued and one confident that it had escaped notice, and this fish was clearly a member of the latter group.

Stewart was spearfishing off the northwest point of the Arm's bay, and due to long acquaintance with this particular coral-head dating to childhood, he knew there was no hole or cave of consequence on the far side into which a fish of that size could retreat. There was, however, a slight depression in which he'd known groupers to hide, contorting themselves with that species' amazing suppleness in order to blend with the coral.

He pulled back the spear of his Hawaiian sling, aiming down and back as he pushed out over the edge. As he'd hoped, this grouper was a strict follower of his species orthodox method and it was bent into the side of the coral with a bulging eye and a who-shot-John expression on its face. An instant later Stewart released his spear and freed the fish from all the cares of this world. Gathering his lunch in hand, Stewart finned to the beach.

As he walked up to the Mutt'n'Fish carrying his catch, the fish caught the attention of the brunch customers on the porch pushing the limits of the restaurant's bottomless coffee policy. Stewart held it up obligingly to oohs and aahs. His attention, however, was caught by a supine figure on the far side of the porch, and skirting the perimeter, he was surprised to find his younger brother gazing up at the sky with a dead stare. Having determined that Billy was breathing, he laid his catch and gear in the shade and jumped up next to him. The indolent figure stirred and noted the grouper.

'Nice fish,' he said, his voice flat.

'Yes, I found him out by the big burr head, the northern one.'

'Very dependable, that old rock,' Billy said in the same toneless voice.

'He was squished in the depression on the west side.'

Billy was silent.

'Is there a reason that you're lying out here?'

'Of course.'

'What would that be?'

'It's too depressing in there.'

'In the Mutt'n'Fish?'

'So you haven't heard? I guess not.'

'So speak up, boy. Fill me in.'

Billy rolled onto his side and sat up next to Stewart. 'Yesterday afternoon Maximillian got a letter from the museum's attorney. It turns out that that visit from Threepea was no bluff.'

'Go on.'

He took a deep breath and spoke with effort.

'Remember that business about shutting down music nights? That was nothing. Finger mullet. It looks like they can shut down the Mutt'n'Fish completely.'

'What rot! That can't be.'

Billy held up a world-weary hand. 'The museum had a survey done when they bought the old Thompson place, and it seems that the back thirty feet of the Mutt'n'Fish sits on their property. Some old boundary mix-up. And there's a twenty-five-foot setback, as well. So about a third of the restaurant belongs to the museum and another third is illegal encroachment.'

'So what did Abraham say?' Stewart said, referring to Abraham Rolle, their lawyer and an old family friend in Nassau.

'Max talked to him first thing this morning,' Billy said. 'Abe went straight over to Land and Survey. He called back about half an hour ago and confirmed it. That's when I exited.'

'Confirmed what?'

'Confirmed that the new survey is in fact correct.'

'If that's true, there must be a reasonable legal remedy for this sort of thing.'

'Abraham said there is.'

'Well sure. There you go…'

'Provided both parties are reasonable. And in this instance, that is far from the case. Threepea and her attorney have made it clear that they're out for Max's scalp. They're threatening to enforce their claim and level their portion of the property. Their attorney said, and I quote, "The fate of the middle portion of the structure, the part on the setback, is a matter for negotiation". Threepea is said to be salivating.'

'I can't take this on an empty stomach. I haven't even had coffee yet. Join me?' Stewart said, picking up his fish.

'I wouldn't venture in there unless you're prepared to witness despair in a very raw state. I've never seen Max in such bad shape.'

'But I had my heart set on boiled fish,' he said petulantly, nodding at the grouper.

'Take my advice and save it for tomorrow. It'll be fine in the walk-in,' Billy said, and he waved a busboy over to take the fish.

'That leaves my stomach...where?'

'How about Waltanique's?'

'Yes, fritters,' Stewart said, smiling. 'I haven't been there since I reached. I don't have my wallet, you'll have to treat.'

'I'm not getting mine, it's in there,' Billy said, pointing at the restaurant. 'I don't mind swinging by your room on the way, though.'

'No, you wouldn't, would you.'

Unbeknownst to Billy and Stewart, at that moment The Hall was the scene of high drama of another sort. Its centrepiece was Leonard lying in a hospital bed in his room, being orbited by a nurse while a doctor stood on one side of him and Ginger Hobbs on the other.

The doctor was looking at Leonard while Leonard stared ardently at Ginger. She in turn watched the doctor, alert to any indication of alarm. It was a daisy chain of rapt attention.

Leonard's besotted gaze and fixed smile worried the medical man; he was young and had never had a patient in the throes of love; in his experience such a frozen expression couldn't be anything other than the product of an addled mind, perhaps one that had been starved of oxygen.

Ginger squeezed Leonard's hand as she studied the doctor. His look of concern had not escaped her.

As Stewart and Billy were approaching The Hall, the ubiquitous second assistant to the concierge came running down the walkway.

'Didja hear?!'

'Good morning, Myron,' Stewart said censoriously, reminding the young man of his manners.

'Good morning. Didja hear what happened, sir?'

'Yeah, Billy was just telling me.'

'Mudda sic, man,' he said and caught himself. 'I mean, sir. His room is bulging with doctors and such and a real hospital bed That's what the helicopter in town was all about!'

The two men stopped, puzzled.

'What are you talking about, boy?' Billy said. 'What room? What helicopter?'

'Leonard's! I thought you said you heard?'

'What happened to Leonard?'

'I dunno, they shooed me away. He has a mighty bandage on his head. Looks like he might've taken blows from someone.'

Ginger was standing in conference with the doctor when Stewart and Billy rushed in the door, and she fairly leapt in their path. Raising her hands, she brought the men up short.

'He's resting at the moment!' she said.

'What happened?' Billy said, offended less by Ginger's abrupt blocking manoeuvre than her proprietary claim to his cousin.

'Leonard suffered a head injury.'

'Was it a row?'

'What?!'

'How'd it happen? Is it serious?'

Stewart peered around Billy and Ginger. Leonard smiled weakly and waved with his fingers.

'Serious enough,' she said.

'What does that mean? Billy demanded.

'It means he doesn't need any excitement right now.'

'When did this happen?'

'Earlier this morning,' she said in a clipped manner. 'Very early.'

'Why weren't we told?!'

When Ginger didn't answer, Billy started to push by her. The Valkyrie spread both arms wide, glaring at him, and Stewart stopped his brother with a hand on his shoulder.

'Leonard insisted, and we made a deal,' she said darkly. 'He allowed me to fly a doctor and nurse in from Nassau if I wouldn't alarm anyone here. And he said particularly you two.'

'He said you weren't to tell me?' Billy started to push past her again when the sharp young doctor appeared at her side.

'We're family, can we see the patient?' Billy said.

'She's right, no excitement,' the doctor said with an arch look. 'You can have ten minutes but keep your voices down.'

Ginger moved hesitantly aside, letting them pass.

'What's going on here, are you all right?' Stewart said as they reached the bed. Billy walked around to the opposite side.

'I'm fine. Absolutely fine,' Leonard said, and apart from the bandage on his head, he looked it.

'Is that why you're lying here wearing a turban? On account of everything's fine?' Billy said. 'And what's this doing here?' he added, shaking the hospital bed.

'Don't do that!' Stewart said. 'The man's injured.'

'How'd this happen?' Billy said, ignoring his brother.

'It's all right, Stewart, I'm fine,' Leonard said and turned to Billy. 'I just slipped and hit my head on the console...'

'This happened in Patticake?' he said, referring to Leonard's boat.

'Yeah, I was giving Ginger a little tour--turns out she's a great girl, I mean I already knew that, but she's way past great, she's the best. Really the best.'

'Slow down and less of Ginger. How did you slip?' In conducting the investigation, Billy was keeping his voice down as instructed but the interrogative tone had Leonard on edge and he resented the fact that Billy was focusing on a minor, negative aspect of what was, to date, the best day of his life. Nevertheless, he continued dutifully.

'I must've slipped in some fish slime, just being a little careless...only a bump and a few stitches on the noggin but what scared her was I blacked out for a moment.'

'A moment?'

'Well, not more than a minute or two.'

'A minute or two! You must've whacked it good.'

'Well actually, the passing out might be why I fell,' Leonard said evasively. 'Don't say anything to Ginger but I think the excitement of taking her out in the boat might've gotten to me.

Last night I hardly slept, and I was keyed up all morning like you wouldn't believe. I mean look at her! Can you blame me?' he said, nodding in Ginger's direction.

'Wait, wait a minute,' Billy said, eyeing his cousin suspiciously. 'Exactly where did all this happen?'

'Can you believe she had the doctor and nurse flown in by helicopter from Nassau? This bed, too. I kept telling her how silly it was, but she was worried about me.'

'That must've cost a small fortune,' Stewart said.

'Well yeah, exactly what I said but she didn't blink. Said she wasn't going to take a chance with me, and money was absolutely no issue. Those were her words.' He was beaming.

'And all this over nothing?' Billy said sceptically.

'Honestly, Billy, it was nothing.'

'Nothing?!' Ginger interrupted, walking up officiously. 'You should have heard the doctor when I told him what you were doing. Hello, Stewart, hello, Billy,' she said in belated greeting. 'What he calls nothing is swimming to impossible depths chasing a huge, what was it?'

'A hogfish,' Leonard said quietly.

'And all to impress me. And then, climbing in the boat and immediately passing out and gashing his head open. The doctor said it could have been very serious.'

'Excuse me, miss, one more thing,' the doctor called, motioning Ginger over.

'Excuse me,' she said, and gave Leonard a peck on the cheek before disappearing.

'That girl,' Leonard said solemnly, 'is the best, really the best. She….'

'So you were freediving. Spearing.' Billy said, nodding. 'But you still haven't said where you were.'

'We went to a few places,' he said vaguely. 'Rhino Rock. Seventh Heaven. Just showing her around, you know.'

Billy held up his hand. 'How big was this hogfish? Two pounds? Ten pounds? Fifteen?'

'Yeah.'

'Yeah, what? Fifteen?'

'Around there,' he said, obviously hedging.

'It was bigger?!'

Leonard stared straight ahead, avoiding Billy's eyes.

'There hasn't been a twenty pound hog at Rhino or Seventh Heaven since day one of creation,' Billy said, speaking evenly to his cousin.

He turned to look at Stewart. 'You know where he was.'

Stewart gave a slight, resigned nod.

'And probably how deep,' Billy added. 'For a twenty pound hogfish.'

'Don't exaggerate,' Leonard said. 'I didn't say twenty pounds.'

Billy ignored him and continued to stare meaningfully at his brother across the bed.

Stewart shook his head at Billy. 'Now's not the time.' He moved toward the door and motioned for Billy to follow. Billy turned as if to go but stopped at the foot of the bed. He was at a quiet boil now and Stewart knew from long experience that there would be no quick end to this. Billy whipped the sheet aside and, wrapping his fingers around the big toe of his cousin's size-fourteen foot, began to twist. Stewart rushed back and grabbed his hand, pulling him toward the door, but this only caused Leonard more pain and Stewart stopped. When Billy was in a determined frame of mind, nothing short of force was effective and the last thing Stewart wanted was a scene.

Billy scrutinized Leonard's face as he increased the pressure. Beads of sweat had broken out on Leonard's forehead and he suddenly opened his eyes wide and glared at his cousin.

'Yeow!' he shouted as it became too much and Billy jumped back a half-step, relaxing the pressure but still holding on to the toe.

The three men turned to see the doctor and Ginger look up from their conference. Leonard smiled, waving to assure her that all was fine. She and the doctor smiled back, but Ginger watched them suspiciously as she resumed the conversation.

'What is it, Billy?' Leonard said irritably, in a forced whisper.

'Sorry,' Billy said innocently, 'but I thought you'd dozed off. That's dangerous after a concussion, you know.'

'Do I have to call the doctor for you to leave?'

'This might be a lousy time, Leonard, but Billy's not wrong to be upset,' Stewart said as he moved back to his cousin's side.

Leonard sighed. 'Stew, this was special. It wasn't just that this morning was one of those magic mornings out there, but I had Ginger with me. No wind. Just dead glassy. Only a puffy cloud or two. It was one of those days when the water looks sorta sluggish...'

'This isn't a novel,' Billy said, interrupting.

'Remember that word you used to call it...' Leonard said to Stewart, ignoring his younger cousin. 'Jell-O something.'

'Gelatinous,' Stewart said.

'Yeah, that's it. It was like that, like clear Jell-O flowing around in slow motion.'

'I was just in the water out front,' Stewart said, indicating his swimsuit. 'I can see how it must've been perfect out there.'

'It was, and this is the first time I've done that, just this one time--'

'It only takes once,' Billy said.

Leonard ignored the interruption. 'There were three big black-headed males on top of the west pinnacle and I got out the hand-line and jigged for fifteen minutes, but they weren't having it. Not even looking at it after the first few jerks. You should have seen Ginger, she was so excited, it was like we could reach out and touch them...' His eyes glistened as he recalled it.

'Anyhow,' he said, returning to the present, 'I made one dive, got one fish and climbed back in the boat. Honest.'

'Didn't someone just point out that once is all it takes?' Billy said.

'Look, Billy, it was me taking the risk and to tell the truth I'd do it again and more if that's what it took to get Ginger's attention. She's the best thing that's ever happened to me and if you think I'd give her up to please you or anyone else, you're welcome to stick your head in a crab bucket.'

Billy gave his cousin's toe a good twist and the response was a stifled exclamation just as Ginger was approaching. She'd been keeping an eye on them after the first outburst and she took in the whole situation in an instant. She gave a yelp—what Billy forever after referred to as a 'rebel yell'—and raised her hand to swat Billy. He ducked and eyed her warily. Only the strict training of the finest Swiss finishing school held her arm back.

'Just what do you think you're doing!' She hissed, 'he's an injured man.'

'It's nothing,' Leonard bleated, still wincing a little from the pain. 'He's just goofing around.'

Ginger ignored Leonard's plea for clemency and directed a mortifying glare at Billy that Missy would have envied.

'I wasn't goofing around,' Billy said evenly. 'I was reminding Leonard of a sacred trust that he broke today, one that could have easily ended in tragedy.'

'And you thought that attacking him would be helpful? Adding pain to his injury?'

'Are you aware of the dangers of diving alone?'

'What?' she said.

'The danger of diving alone. I'm sure you've heard that.'

'Yes, I have heard that.'

'Have you heard that that is doubly true for spearfishing?'

'No, but it stands to reason,' she said, her tone icy.

'Most importantly: The Pinnacles. That place Leonard took you. Did you know that you were out in the Tongue of the Ocean?'

'Leonard mentioned something like that, but I don't know what that is and the engine was so loud, I didn't ask.'

'The Tongue of the Ocean is an underwater trench that extends down between Andros and the Exumas and it stops about eleven miles west-northwest of Porgy. Not far from where you were, it's three and a half thousand feet deep.'

'Somehow this natural history lesson is going to excuse how you were treating Leonard?' she said, an edge to her southern drawl.

'Bear with me. The point is, that is some roomy ocean and there are proportionately large sea creatures out there. That's what accounts for the good deep-sea fishing around here. Are you following this?'

Billy was on his soapbox now.

Ginger nodded. The fire in her eyes seemed to have banked a bit.

'We, the three of us,' Billy went on, 'agreed long ago we wouldn't spearfish out at the Pinnacles alone. It is the single location out of hundreds that we agreed was absolutely off limits at all times to solo hunting. Under any circumstances. No exceptions. Other places, we allow a little rule-bending, but there? Absolutely not. Leonard broke a blood oath this morning that has stood until even date.'

'Is that true?' she said, turning darkly to Leonard.

'Billy's exaggerating a little...' Leonard said, looking askance to avoid her penetrating stare.

'Not a bit,' Billy broke in. 'And Stewart will back me up on this.'

'Billy's right,' Stewart said as Ginger turned the chilling glare on him. 'I don't mean he was right to twist his toe,' he added quickly, 'but about the Pinnacles. It's foolhardy to dive, never mind spearfish, out there by yourself. It's sketchy enough with a partner.'

Ginger turned and directed all the withering wattage of her fury at Leonard. A look of delighted satisfaction crept onto Billy's face as he saw his cousin's eyes widen in alarm. But then just as quickly, a beatific smile spread across Leonard's face. Ginger's frightful stare had transformed into an expression of tender affection.

'So you thought it would take dangerous heroics to win my heart, you foolish man?'

'What!' Billy said, his voice pitched high at the injustice. 'That was a seriously stupid stunt he—'

'And your corrective was to attack him in his injured state?!' she said, turning on Billy. She took a quick half step toward him and he jumped back, bumping into Stewart.

'I'll have a word with him, Ginger,' Stewart said, taking his brother by the arm and starting for the door. 'We can't thank you enough for taking care of Leonard like this.'

'Certainly, it's my pleasure,' she said sweetly and turned back to her patient, cooing words of comfort as the two went out the door.

Billy turned on his brother.

'Thanks so much for the moral support back there!'

'Sure,' Stewart said, returning Billy's sarcasm undiluted.

'That was a textbook case of delayed shallow water blackout!'

'Yes.'

'At the Pinnacles!'

Stewart nodded.

'Far from help,' Billy said.

'Yes.'

'What if it hadn't been delayed?'

Stewart nodded again. 'I don't want to think about it.'

'Exactly! And you drag me out, telling her "I'll have a talk with him". Like I'm the one that needs to be lectured!'

'You weren't accomplishing a thing back there; his head is in the clouds. Both their heads are, can't you see that?'

'Is it really you, you, lecturing me on love? That is rich. They met, what, three days ago? Four?'

'Who knows, maybe that's enough,' Stewart said.

'What? I've been hearing for twenty years that I don't know the difference between love and infatuation.'

'You don't.'

'And now you're saying go easy on Leonard for the most boneheaded stunt ever because he's deeply, passionately in love after a couple days?' Billy said, shaking his head. 'Romantic advice from the expert that hasn't had a serious girlfriend in a decade.'

'I've been a little busy.'

Billy rolled his eyes.

2ND WEDNESDAY

Stewart sat up in bed and looked at the clock: five-forty a.m. He'd have liked nothing better than to lie back and enjoy three more hours of sleep, not that he could remember two in a row lately, but he knew a repeat of disturbing dreams featuring Natalie Jones was all he'd get. Why his psyche had seized upon this girl was a mystery, unless it was looking for the perfect foil to a good night's sleep. As an agent of insomnia, he thought bitterly, she was unsurpassed.

Hadn't he firmly and categorically dismissed anything beyond a casual acquaintance with her? That should have put an end to the whole thing. It seemed patently unfair that a simple misunderstanding stemming from their first meeting should continue to dog him.

There was a long list of mundane errands in Willstown that he'd been putting off, but stacked against tossing and turning in his bed, it would be a lark. He showered, dressed, and gulped a cup of reheated coffee. It was a few minutes after six, but like all Bahamian towns, Willstown awakened early and he'd be there with bells on.

On his way out he saw a dim light flicker under Leonard's door.

He put his ear to the door and tapped lightly. 'Is anyone up?' he said quietly, straightening quickly as it opened.

'Morning,' Ginger whispered as she slipped out. 'What's up?'

'I saw the light and wondered if someone was up. How is he?'

'He's still sleeping.'

'But he's doing okay?'

'He slept straight through the night. I stayed up to monitor his eupnea. Absolutely fine.' She smiled timidly.

'Yoop what?'

'Eupnea, standard respiratory rate. Even breathing.'

'I see,' Stewart said. 'And you say you were up all night?'

'Most of it. The doctor said he was out of danger, but I didn't want to take a chance.'

Natalie hadn't exaggerated when she'd called her friend the nurturing type.

She put her hand on Stewart's arm as he turned to go. 'Was that—the diving, I mean—as dangerous as Billy said?'

Stewart nodded. 'I'm afraid it was.'

He saw her lips quiver and she shut her eyes. Tiny droplets appeared in the corners.

'But he's fine, thank God,' Stewart said to comfort her, and changed the subject. 'I'm going to town, is there anything you need?'

She wiped her eyes. 'Sorry. No, nothing that I can think of.'

'I'll have my phone if you do.'

She nodded sweetly to him. The girl is a wonder, he thought as he climbed the hill in the fresh morning air.

Stewart's errands kept him in town until well after lunch, and on his return he dropped off his purchases and hurried to the Mutt'n'Fish, hoping against hope they hadn't run through the lunch special of conch chowder. All he'd had to eat was a quick tuna-and-grits at a takeaway in the early morning hours and he was hungry. Entering, he could see a full convocation in the back of the restaurant with every seat around the captain's table occupied. Looking for an open seat nearer the door, he caught sight of Maximillian's enormous hand motioning him to the back. He could see his father in his customary seat as well as Billy and Gladys, but as he neared the table he realized the two figures with their backs to him were Natalie and Ginger. He hadn't spoken to the former since their heated conversation four days earlier when she'd revealed herself to be a noxious shrew, and he veered to the other side of the table. Billy stood, jostling chairs to make room for Stewart between Ginger and himself.

'How's the patient?' Stewart asked her as he squeezed in between them.

'Still doing fine. I left him sitting on the porch in a rocker. I'm just waiting on a takeout for us,' Ginger said, sloshing red wine in a glass.

'How are you holding up? The past twenty-four hours haven't done you in?'

'No,' she said, adding under her breath, 'if things had gone differently, they might've.'

'All's well that ends well,' Stewart said and she raised her glass in agreement.

'I hate to ask,' Stewart said, directing his question to Maximillian, 'but any good news about the Mutt'n'Fish?'

He shook his head slowly and the gold tassel hanging behind his ear swung gravely.

'I'm sorry,' Stewart said, realizing he'd possibly left Ginger and Natalie out of the conversation, 'but do you know about this?'

They both nodded.

'In all the recent excitement you might not have heard,' Maximillian said, 'but due to service above and beyond the call of duty, young Gnat has been conscripted to the cause. She's now a certified member of the Mutt'n'Fish chili team.'

'What on earth did you do?' Stewart said, turning to her. 'Billy himself was only admitted on the back of naked nepotism.'

'Is that right?' she replied. 'Well, I am honoured. But I think the entry standard must be very low. All I did was make a lucky guess.'

Maximillian snorted, investing it with as much disagreement as he could manage, and turned to Stewart. 'When we win the pot this year, it will be largely thanks to this young lady.'

Despite Stewart's light treatment of the matter, the fact that Natalie Jones was worming her way into the affections of those nearest and dearest to him was no cause for celebration in his estimation. The sooner the pint-sized incubus was gone and forgotten, the better.

'Concerning the ongoing tragedy,' Maximillian said, clearing his throat emotionally, 'the fate of the Mutt'n'Fish continues to hang in the balance. Yesterday Scoonie had a promising idea, but it didn't pan out. I'm ready for the worst at this point.'

'What's that?'

'The worst?'

'No, what was dad's idea?' Stewart asked.

'I remember hearing something,' Scoonie said, 'about your great-grandfather Silas turning over the Moxey collection of family geegaws to the museum on a contingent basis.'

'A loan then?'

'Possibly.'

'Meaning, maybe we still have some claim to it?' Stewart said.

'Maybe.'

'And if we reclaimed our stuff, that would hurt them?'

'Hurt?' his father snorted. 'They'd be ruined.' His tone rose as he warmed to his theme. 'What would they be left with, Max? A whale backbone and half a dozen pottery shards?'

'Not much more,' Maximillian agreed, nodding at the floor. 'It would mean devastation for them. The value of the remaining assets might amount to enough for a final dinner if it didn't run to drinks.'

Stewart nodded. 'So that would be leverage against their land grab?'

Maximillian nodded.

'Is there a contract, some record of it?'

'Silas was such an old stickler for detail, there must've been,' Scoonie said. 'He's the one that put together the family archive.

But if it ever existed, it doesn't seem to now. This morning we searched through all the files stored in the old cistern and there was nothing. We could've used your help, by the way. Natalie here pitched in. Worked like a trouper.'

'The '68 hurricane destroyed some of your family's records,' Maximillian said, turning to Stewart. 'That's what worries us.'

'What about Abraham?' Stewart said. 'Wouldn't he have a copy in Nassau?'

'He had the whole office on it for hours this morning. Abraham himself called back an hour ago,' Scoonie said and his sagging moustache told the tale.

Stewart grimaced. 'Wouldn't the museum have a copy?'

'Abraham mentioned that,' Maximillian said, 'but if they do, it's not likely to come to light, is it?'

A fog of despondency settled on the group.

'We could,' Stewart said, breaking the mournful silence, 'go have a look for ourselves.'

'Yes, go ask Threepea to let you thumb through their files.' Maximillian snorted. 'Just don't slide your foot in the door when you ask, you're liable to lose a toe.'

'I was thinking of going in over a windowsill. After closing, avoid the rush.'

'She lives there now.'

'Of course,' Stewart said. 'What am I thinking.'

'Threepea went to Nassau yesterday,' Gladys said. 'Ida said she won't be back till tomorrow morning. She and Nellie have been working in the evenings putting the displays back together. She said they don't start till the painters leave.'

'And when's that?'

'Four-ish.'

'Then how long do they work?' Stewart asked.

'Four hours or so, Ida said.'

'So we'd have to wait until nine or ten to be safe.'

'Wait for what?' Ginger said.

'A burglary?!' Natalie said, looking excitedly from face to face.

'Do we even know if the records are all there, in one place?' Billy said. 'Aren't they still in the process of moving everything?'

'It's all been moved already,' Gladys said.

'It's all at the Thompson house now?' Billy said sceptically. Gladys nodded.

'Maybe we should have a look,' Stewart said, turning to his brother.

'We?' Billy said quietly.

'You and me, boy,' Stewart said.

Billy gave his brother a meaningful look and his expression turned dark. It took a few seconds for Stewart to decipher the message.

'Oh, no. Not that,' Stewart said, closing his eyes as he shook his head.

Billy stared blankly ahead without answering.

'What?' Maximillian and Natalie said simultaneously, both directing the question to Stewart.

Stewart held up his hands in surrender and gestured toward his brother.

'Thank you, Brother,' Billy said sarcastically. 'Very nice. A very deft pass.'

'What do you want me to do?'

'Oh, I don't know,' Billy said. 'Perhaps honour your promise, Mr. *Honourable*.'

'That was--'

Billy raised his eyebrows, interrupting Stewart. 'They have an expiration date now, promises do? First Leonard with the Pinnacles, now this?'

'What are you two talking about?' Scoonie asked. He was still looking at his eldest son.

'I can't say. It's about some old oath,' Stewart said.

'The very ground we're on right now is on the verge of being deeded to a criminal group of women,' Maximillian said, indicating the back of the restaurant with a sweep of his big mitt. 'And you two are wasting our time with riddles.'

'Yes, let's have no more of this,' Scoonie said to his youngest. 'Billy, what's this about?'

Billy was silent until the weight of the group's attention became too much.

'It's haunted,' he blurted out.

'What?!' Maximillian and Natalie again spoke in tandem.

'What?' Scoonie added, a half-step behind.

'The Thompson house. It's haunted. I mean, just look at it.'

All eyes but Stewart's were turned on Billy, who tilted his head back as if addressing the ceiling.

'I know because I've seen them. Jumbies. Three genuine jumbies. Stewart was there, we snuck in on a dare. He saw them too, all three of them. Clear—As—Day. Except that it was dead midnight.'

'When was this?' Scoonie asked. 'Since Stewart's come back?'

Billy shook his head and waved his hand in a gesture of long ago.

'When?' his father demanded, but Billy closed his mouth and eyes.

'It was the summer between my second and third year at Loughborough, I think,' Stewart said. 'So Billy was in grade five.'

'This is about some jumbies you imagined back in grammar school!' Maximillian said to Billy, incredulous. He shook his head and turned to Stewart. 'You too?'

Stewart sat back in silence, his lips stretched taut.

'He won't admit it,' Billy burst out. 'He never has. He says it was a trick of the light. Yes, right. Three tricks of the light coincidentally at the stroke of midnight, the recognised hour of spectral hijinks. Absolute tripe.'

Natalie raised her hand. 'Jumbies?'

'Ghosts,' Maximillian said.

'Well, that's a relief,' she said. 'I thought they might be bats. I don't like bats.'

He looked at her, his brow wrinkled. Her comment seemed beside the point.

Natalie noted Maximillian's confusion. 'Oh, I was worried because I've decided to go with Stewart,' she explained.

Billy looked at her. 'You can't do that!' he said brightly, unable to hide his delight.

'You can't do that,' Stewart repeated flatly. 'Anyway, didn't I hear you tell Ginger that you're going to dinner on the Papillon this evening? Because that's when I'll be going.'

Saying this was an admission that he'd been eavesdropping on the girls' quiet conversation when his attention was ostensibly elsewhere, but nipping this notion in the bud took precedent.

'Aren't burglaries generally scheduled after dark, in which case dinner will be over? I wouldn't miss it for anything in the world,' she said. 'Criminal mischief in the service of a good cause is a cherished dream of mine.'

'Out of the question. You're getting married next week,' Stewart said, 'and that would be some trick from a gaol cell.'

'He has a point,' Ginger said.

Natalie shook her head reproachfully at her friend and turned to Stewart. 'You sound like you're resigned to getting caught. I see now how badly I'm needed.'

'If you won't listen to reason, then listen to this: I'm not taking you.'

Stewart said this with such feeling that no one spoke for a moment.

'But will that stop her?' Billy murmured as he stood and sidled away from the table.

'Billy, you slinking—'

'An excellent point, Billy,' Natalie interrupted, standing and moving quickly between the two to cut off the fierce glare Stewart directed at his brother. 'At nine o'clock tonight I have every intention of creeping into the museum in a black t-shirt, black leggings and an adorable pair of black sneakers, which sadly, I've had no occasion to wear yet. I look forward to being a very stylish burglar.'

'Housebreaker,' Gladys said. 'That's what we call them.'

'Oh, I like that. A stylish housebreaker. This sounds like the event of the season.' She looked at Stewart. 'If you'd care to act as my accomplice, I'd be delighted with the company. I suggest we set aside all past personal disagreements and pull together for the sake of the Mutt'n'Fish.'

'Hear, hear!' Maximillian said emotionally, pushing the fez back on his head and smiling broadly at the two girls as they prepared to leave.

'Of course he'll take you, my dear,' Scoonie said. 'Or rather,' he added, turning to Stewart, 'Natalie will take you.'

Stewart rolled his eyes.

A busboy picked up a stack of takeaway containers sitting on the bar and brought them over to the girls.

'I'll see that he's ready on time,' Billy said, avoiding Stewart's glare.

'Wonderful, I hope to see you then,' she said to Stewart. With a bright ta-ta, the two girls departed. It was quiet for some time until Gladys turned to Stewart.

'What did she mean by "past personal disagreements"?'

Stewart waved his hand dismissively.

'Well I think you need to find you a girl like that one,' she said to him. 'Do you a world of good.'

'Oh yes, she hangs on my every word.'

'That's the last thing you need.'

At 9:02 that evening Stewart and Maximillian were sitting on boxes in the Mutt'n'Fish stock room, waiting. Stewart jiggled his leg nervously.

'You need a nip of something,' Maximillian said, getting heavily to his feet.

'I'm telling you, I'm fine,' he answered peevishly.

'Well, I'm getting one for me then. You're making me jumpy, vibrating like that.'

Stewart put his hand on his knee to stop it. 'I think she must have come to her senses and changed her mind.'

'Not that girl.' Maximillian looked at his watch. 'It's just a few minutes after.'

As if on cue, they heard voices and Scoonie came through the back door and, holding it open, stepped aside, ushering Natalie in with his hand held high. Dressed in black from her sneakers up to a black silk scarf framing her face, Natalie was stunning, more like a film star stopping by to pick up an award than a novice burglar.

'I'm positively buzzing,' she said, looking at Stewart. 'Aren't you excited?'

Though Stewart merely smiled mildly in reply, this was a gross understatement regarding his interior. As usual in this girl's presence, his emotions were in an uproar.

The support team chattered away, with Scoonie particularly animated, but Stewart was taking very little of it in. His striking partner in crime was dominating all available circuits.

Their confederates were not short of advice about how to go about breaking in, what to do if they were discovered, how to conduct the search, etc., and it was a full twenty minutes before they were able to leave. They exited the back door of the kitchen and made the short walk up the dune to a towering ficus hedge that separated the grounds of the Mutt'n'Fish from the backyard of the old Thompson place. As they pushed their way through the dense growth, Natalie put her hand on his shoulder for balance. It was as if a high voltage wire had been applied to his spine and he jerked upright, hitting his head squarely on an overhanging limb. It made a hollow thud, and hearing a muffled giggle, he turned to see her biting her lip.

'I'm sorry, was my hand cold?' she said, stifling her smile with an attempt at concern. He shook his head and pushed on through. Not that it had hurt much, but what was wounding was his buffoonish missteps in this girl's presence. It was humiliating, the way his dignity invariably suffered in her presence.

The moon slipped out from behind scattered clouds as they entered the yard, bathing the landscape in an ivory glow.

'Can we stop for a second,' Natalie whispered, dropping to one knee. She shook her hair out and turned her head up, retying her scarf. The moonlight coming over his shoulder shone full in her face and she smiled absently at him as she arranged her hair. Though Stewart had never denied that on their first encounter Natalie's beauty had affected him deeply, he'd definitively determined that the effect had been aided by his weak emotional state and abetted by the hangover. Perhaps even the dramatic lighting of the storm had been a factor.

But now, with the strength of her appeal staring him full in the face, he had to admit that, judging her on a strictly objective basis, she was about as attractive as human beings come. Well, good for her, for all that was worth. He didn't begrudge anyone their natural-born advantages; it simply made her shortcomings, so starkly evident the day she'd interrupted his gardening, that much more disappointing. Disappointing and yet curiously fortunate, for without that insight his reason might be overwhelmed by these emotions, which were still, embarrassingly, in thrall to her.

They crossed the grounds and, as planned, stopped behind the trunk of a stout gum elemi tree to study the house. All was dark and silent. Creeping onto the back porch with growing anticipation, they froze at the creak of the ancient floorboards and then again as Stewart tried to force a window open, but there were no signs of life. The second window he tried was unlocked, and pushing the stubborn sash up, he motioned for Natalie to climb through. Biting her lip, she took his hand to steady herself and slipped in.

As Stewart followed her over the sill, he was assaulted with the odour of fresh paint and the undeniable exhilaration of wrongdoing. Filing cabinets were pushed together in the middle of the two offices, surrounded by drop cloths and walls primed or newly painted.

They opened the curtains to the back porch and, by the light of the moon filtering in the windows, moved the file cabinets around until all the drawers were accessible. Natalie found a chair, and turning on her flashlight, bent over and started on the bottom drawer. Stewart had been briefed by Abraham, their lawyer, on what the assignation would likely look like and Stewart described it to Natalie; the newish, white papers that made up the bulk of the files could be safely dismissed: the document, if it still existed, would almost certainly be wrinkled and yellowed with time.

Stewart stood watching Natalie's delicate fingers dance over the files and couldn't help noting the graceful curve of her back and her auburn hair bound thickly by the scarf. She turned her flashlight on him.

'Did I take your spot?'

Coming out of his trance, Stewart shook his head. 'No, no, I was just lost in thought...thinking about...something.' Red-faced, he pointed through the doorway. 'I'll be over here so we don't cover the same ground twice.' He found a chair in the next room and pulled it up to a file cabinet, concentrating on the task at hand.

At first a mild air of collegiality reigned, and they exchanged hopeful remarks through the open doorway, but after an hour of diligent searching failed to produce anything remotely like the purported document, optimism began to wane and there was a noticeable falling off in the joie de vivre department. What a lot of bureaucratic nonsense a little museum generated, was the shared sentiment.

Natalie finished the files in her room and started on a cabinet in the hallway. He couldn't see her, but he could hear her working away and her proximity was distracting. He willed his attention back to his job and started on a new drawer. His gaze struck a promising folder in the back, fat with ageing, stained papers, and he opened it carefully, not wanting to damage the crumbling documents.

Suddenly, magically, there it was. It looked so much like what he'd imagined that he mistrusted his tired eyes for a moment. Holding his breath lest the grail evaporate, he pinched it gingerly between the fingers of both hands and pulled it out. Putting it in his lap, he examined it line by line with the failing flashlight beam until there was no doubt.

'Eureka!' he shouted. 'I've got it!'

Hearing a bustle behind him, he sat back, exhilarated, and held the old, foxed document above his head. Pointing the beam of his light upward to illuminate it, he turned, smiling broadly.

He then sprang four inches off the seat of the chair, for coming up behind him was not his partner in crime, the diminutive fashionista, but a spectre just as Billy had described; a dark, sinister, billowing figure of indeterminate shape. Stewart's heart froze as he reflexively turned his light on it, revealing it to be none other than Threepea herself, advancing into battle. She'd purchased a caped outfit in Nassau that accounted for her ghostly aspect and for Stewart's heart missing a beat. Perhaps it was best that Billy hadn't come.

He gulped as he felt the paper snatched from his grasp and realised his arm was still extended above his head. Threepea turned and bellowed behind her, "I've got him, Constable!"

Stewart heard the clomping gait of heavy boots, and the leering face of Constable Cartwright entered the beam of his light. Though the constable was a large man himself, at the moment he was dwarfed by Threepea, inflated in triumph.

'I'm right here, Mrs. Pinder,' he said, peering around her. At the realization that the apprehended party was none other than Stewart Moxey, the constable's reaction was astonishment; his eyes couldn't have protruded further if they'd been mounted on stalks. He resembled a large spiny lobster squeezed into the stylish uniform of a Bahamian policeman.

'Mudda sic!' he said. 'Stewart, what are you doing here?'

'I think we can safely assume, Constable,' Threepea said with a peevish air, 'that Mr. Moxey is in the process of performing a robbery, a housebreaking, a burglary. That is obvious to the meanest intelligence. Here, apparently, was the object he hoped to purloin. And there,' she said, indicating the open window visible in the next room, 'is how he gained unauthorized access to the premises.'

Stewart's heart lodged high in his throat as Threepea walked over to the wall and turned on the lights. He anticipated the discovery of Natalie at any moment but somehow his stylish partner had melted into the shadows.

'Stay with this man, Constable, while I have a look around,' Threepea said, as if reading his mind.

'Perhaps I--' the portly constable began, but she stopped him with a raised hand and he leaned back against the file cabinet and looked at Stewart with resignation.

Though Threepea took less than a minute to scan the adjoining rooms, the search seemed interminable to Stewart. When she finally returned, he breathed a silent sigh of relief and the three of them trooped outside.

The constable was struggling with Threepea's accusation of Stewart and worked to get a satisfactory explanation from the accused, but Stewart remained mute. Talk, he reasoned, would only delay the constable leaving the scene. With Natalie on the premises, he preferred that the area become police-free at the soonest possible moment. With any luck, she'd already left through the window and was already back at the Mutt'n'Fish, sharing their tragic tale.

Seating Stewart in his jeep, Constable Cartwright returned to the porch.

'I'll take it from here on out, Mrs. Pinder. You can rest your mind on this matter, I will get to the bottom of it.'

'How do you plan on handling it, Constable?'

'Since the suspect is offering no explanation tonight,' he said officiously, 'I'm afraid we might have to wait until tomorrow to clear this up. I'll present myself at the Arms first thing tomorrow morning to untangle this business. I find that these things often resolve themselves in the light of day.' With every word he regained a measure of the dignity that Threepea had offended earlier with her bossiness.

'How do you propose to do that, Constable?' she said in a sceptical tone.

'Having, as I do, a long and straightforward relationship with the suspect and his family, I don't foresee a problem. However, I plan to be, as I said, at the Moxey Arms the first thing tomorrow morning and if Stewart, that is, young Mr. Moxey, can give no satisfactory explanation of his presence on your premises, steps will be taken. The necessary steps. Trust me, he won't step foot off this island until the matter is settled to your satisfaction. Your interests, and those of your organization, are foremost in this investigation, ma'am.'

'No, Caleb Cartwright, Mr. Moxey will spend the night in gaol.'

He was silent for a moment, biting his lower lip.

'You want me to lock Stewart up? Stewart Moxey?'

'Isn't that the usual procedure when housebreakers are caught red-handed? Do you customarily scold them and send them on their merry way to the comfort of their own bed?' She turned away. 'I'm appalled at this breach of police procedure, Constable.'

'But this is Stewart. Think how it will look to…' He grimaced.

'I imagine it will look like precisely what it is,' she said evenly. 'The son of a venerable island family chooses a wicked path and turns to a life of crime. It is tragic but certainly not unique.'

The Constable switched to chewing his upper lip. He played his last card.

'There's a problem with the gaol, ma'am. It's broken. The lock on the cell door, I mean. We're waiting on a part from Tampa.'

Once again, the pitiful note of pleading.

'I suggest a length of chain around the bars and a padlock. That should be sufficient to hold him. I don't think that Mr. Moxey is a hardened criminal, not as yet.' She paused. 'I happen to know that Police Commissioner Yockey is particularly vexed with the lax nature of law enforcement on the out-islands. He regards it as remarkably slipshod. He remarked on it when I was last dining at his house. He's married to a cousin of mine in Nassau, you know.'

The constable swallowed and began to reply but before he could utter a word she froze him with a glittering eye and turned, sweeping majestically into the house. The stricken expression on his face gratified her; it was an assurance that her dramatic powers were still compelling. I've still got it, she said to herself as she passed through the door and up the stairs.

The faces in the neighbouring windows faded from behind their respective curtains as the jeep drove away and a wave of telephone calls rippled outward across the island. Within the half hour, only those Porgians choosing to ignore a ringing telephone at one in the morning remained ignorant of the news that Stewart Moxey, the pride of Porgy Island, had been jailed on charges of housebreaking.

Natalie, too, had been watching the proceedings from a window, one overlooking the front porch of the museum; and watching, she had chafed at the fact that Threepea had carelessly rolled up the document and carried it outside with her. Natalie watched as she waved and gestured to the policeman with it. If only she had dropped it on the side-table by the door as she followed Stewart and the constable outside.

It wasn't until their conversation came to a close and Natalie saw Threepea turn toward the house that she realized she hadn't given any consideration to her next move. The sensible course was to backtrack to safety, but that would mean accepting a bitter defeat when they'd been on the cusp of victory. It was the proverbial fork of fortune and she came within a hair of playing it safe and slipping out the way they'd come in; Apalachicola's daughters, however, are made of sterner stuff, and swallowing gamely, she turned and ran quickly up the stairs.

She'd just reached the top step when the door hinges squeaked, followed an instant later by the stairway light coming on. Turning to enter the upstairs hallway, she heard the heavy tread of Threepea ascending and prayed she hadn't been seen. As intrepid as Natalie had proven herself in choosing the stairs over a safe retreat, panic now gripped her, and she turned in to the first doorway that presented itself. The footsteps grew louder and she struck out blindly across the room. In the dim light she glanced off an overstuffed chair, skirted a bed and dresser, and headed for the dark outline of a door to an adjoining room. One, she prayed, with an exit. She passed through the doorway with that sinking feeling familiar to any outlaw that has ridden into a box canyon with the hanging posse close behind. She'd entered a bathroom.

Threepea entered her bedroom and turned on the overhead light, spilling illumination into the bathroom doorway. The light revealed a bathtub dead ahead and Natalie crossed to it on tiptoe before stepping gingerly in. She pulled the shower curtain closed and held her breath, praying against hope that she hadn't been heard. The squeak of the springs as Threepea sat down on the bed had cloaked the noise of the shower curtain and Natalie exhaled slowly. At least momentarily safe, she leaned back against the cool tile and caught her breath.

Threepea sat on the bed examining the document, humming away merrily. The next few minutes were punctuated with delighted giggles as she read and then reread the document and the extent of her good fortune sank in. She hadn't wanted to return to Porgy this evening. She didn't like taking the late flight out of Nassau and then there was the expense of a private ferry to bring her over in the dark and night crossings always gave her the heebie-jeebies and on and on, so many reasons. But now, now! All of that was justified ten times over. A hundred times.

She reviewed her good fortune: Her great, good luck catching a glimpse of the flashlight beam dancing around the office as she approached the house; Cartwright responding to her call in a timely manner—the first was the merest chance and the second, unprecedented. And finally: Catching Stewart Moxey in precisely his moment of triumph! The whole delicate train of events would have been thwarted by the slightest variance at any point. She closed her eyes and held the paper to her breast. Exhaling deeply, she sent a quick thank you heavenward.

Natalie was doing some praying herself and, if anything, in an even more heartfelt manner. Presently the bed complained again, and Natalie heard footsteps approaching the bathroom. Her mind raced to formulate a plan of action, but the multitude of unknown factors stymied her: Did Threepea have the document in hand? Would she become violent when surprised? How did Bahamian courts treat foreign lawbreakers? Natalie set her delicate jaw and resolved to trust her instincts. It was precisely this iron mettle that made her such a formidable sailing competitor, yet despite extensive experience in race committee disputes, she'd never had to wrestle an amazon twice her size.

Her heart pounded so loudly in her ears that she couldn't imagine how it was that Threepea didn't hear it. The milky shower curtain festooned with sand dollars and starfish wouldn't hide her for an instant once the light was on. Threepea's shadow, followed by her looming figure, suddenly filled the doorway and Natalie's knees weakened as she watched a large bejewelled hand reach for the light switch. The light flashed on and at the same moment a loud knocking issued from somewhere. Someone was at the front door. Threepea's hand switched the light off and disappeared. An instant later Natalie's legs gave way, a blunt refusal to continue providing support under such trying conditions. It was too much to ask, her underpinnings signalled to headquarters. She sank to a crouch with her arms wrapped around her knees and resumed breathing.

'Threepea, it's me, Ida!' a distant voice called.

'Coming,' Threepea shouted as she clattered down the stairs.

The kettledrum pounding in Natalie's ears subsided and she strained to hear the conversation.

'I just heard what happened! Stewart Moxey housebreaking!' Ida said as Threepea opened the door.

'You heard right, girlfriend. I caught him with this!' she said, waving the document.

'What is it?'

'Come up, I'll show you.'

They hurried up the stairs like a couple of excited schoolgirls and entered the bedroom in a fit of giggles. Threepea steered Ida into a chair and sat down on the bed across from her. Whether someone as large and formidable as

Pamela Pims Pinder can ever be described as giddy is an open question, but she was as close as Ida had seen since their days at grammar school.

'I caught Stewart Moxey himself thieving an old document right out of one of our file cabinets.'

'But what is it?'

'Just what I said, some crusty old document. An Assignation, it says. It's something about the Moxeys turning their collection over to the museum. Look at the date, the second of March 1938. You can be sure he was stealing it for the wicked purpose of hobbling the museum's mission. This can be traced right back to my cousin and your brother, you may count on that.'

'Can I see it?'

Threepea handed it over hesitantly as Ida put on her reading glasses. She read slowly and carefully, and halfway down the page she started visibly.

'Could they take all of this back?' Ida said, tracing her finger down the long list of items on loan from the Moxey family. 'It's practically everything!' she said. 'Does anyone else on the board know about this?'

Threepea shook her head. 'I'm sure they don't. I myself had no idea.'

'You'll have to call an emergency meeting!' Ida said.

'Well,' Threepea said, speaking carefully, 'there is no doubt that is what you and I would want, as the most senior members of the board...that is...if circumstances were different...' she said, laying considerable stress on the last phrase before regrouping. 'Consider, however, that there are powerful forces willing to go to any length, to criminal lengths, to take possession of it. That was demonstrated not one hour ago!'

Ida nodded, her eyes wide, and waited for Threepea to continue.

'What I mean is,' she said, again choosing her words with care, 'perhaps it's time to put aside our own wishes...'

She faltered for a moment.

'In service to the greater...' Ida offered helpfully.

'Exactly, thank you. In service to the greater good. I would never forgive myself if this document fell into the wrong hands just because of some selfish desire on our part to save it for the other board members' idle perusal.'

As always, she spoke nobly and well, and Ida wasn't sure that strains of "March on, Bahamaland" weren't faintly audible.

'Yes, yes, I see what you mean. But what can we do?'

'Why, destroy it. Burn it!'

Ida couldn't hide her shock.

'You'd do that!'

'I would, and I will. It must be put beyond the grasp of these philistines. Those that would retard the advancement of this community for their own gain. Certainly. When I became president I pledged to protect and promote the interests of the museum, and by extension our whole community.' She straightened regally. 'And that I am bound by honour to do.'

'Couldn't we just hide it somewhere it couldn't be found. Somewhere safe?'

'And then what if we were subpoenaed and ordered to produce it? This gets to the heart of the problem; you and I, being honest, law-abiding citizens, would be helpless. Our upright character would force us to turn it over. We would be compelled by the integrity of our own consciences. You see that, don't you?'

Ida nodded mechanically.

'Do we want to risk that? It would be the end of the historical society and all we've worked for. Like that!' She clapped her hands and Ida jumped, as did the secret occupant of the bathtub.

'Did you hear something?' Threepea said and Ida shook her head. Threepea looked suspiciously at the bathroom doorway, but she turned back and continued.

'Yes, the end of all our dreams for the museum, just as it promises to blossom and bless this community with truth, beauty, and, I have no doubt whatsoever, international cultural repute. Imagine the damage this old yellow sheet of paper could visit on this island and, by extension, the Commonwealth of the Bahamas, I dare say.'

'Yes, yes, yes, yes, yes.' Ida clucked. 'I'm sure you're right.'

'Of course,' Threepea said, her customary confidence returning on the strength of her own rhetoric. 'It's the only way, the proper way.'

'The proper way,' Ida echoed shakily.

She handed the paper back gingerly and Threepea pulled it from her grasp, producing a lighter from her purse.

'Now?' Ida cried. 'You're going to do it right now? It's late, I should go...' She stood and edged toward the door.

'Idamae Angelina Thompson, sit down! Are we in accord here? Didn't we just agree that this is the proper course? The selfless course. Is this document not from the museum's own files? Doesn't that make it the property of the Foundation? Can we not, as the Foundation's highest elected representatives, do with it as we judge best?'

'But what good will burning it do?' Ida said, suddenly brightening. 'Surely they have a copy.'

'Ida. Think. Would they go to the trouble to thief ours if they did?'

'No, no, of course you're right,' Ida fluttered. She took a deep breath. 'Yes, yes, I agree. For the Foundation.' She sighed and sat down heavily, fanning herself.

Natalie had been listening so intently to the conversation that for the past few minutes she'd forgotten her own perilous position, and she flinched as the floorboards creaked and Threepea's heavy tread approached the bathroom. As the ominous shadow again filled the door, Natalie rose to her tiptoes. Her spine felt like a backstay stretched to the limit by a spinnaker. The imposing shadow stopped just inside the doorway next to the sink and Threepea turned to Ida, who could feel her formidable friend's gaze drawing her into the act.

'Isn't it a fact that this is the Foundation's property and I am the Foundation's highest-ranking member?'

'Yes,' Ida said, nodding slowly, adding, 'Aye.'

'Do you, as the second-highest-ranking member, concur with me in this matter?'

Ida chewed her lip.

'For the good of the Foundation? For Porgy? For the future of your own grandchildren?' Threepea said, her voice rising.

'Yes,' Ida croaked. 'Yes.'

Through the shower curtain Natalie could make out Threepea holding the lighter and the old stained paper over the sink. She braced herself to leap out at the first sign of a flame, but beyond that her plan was unformed.

'By the authority vested in me by the Porgy Island Museum and Historical Foundation,' Threepea said solemnly, and she clicked the lighter. Nothing. She clicked it again.

'This isn't working. Do you have one?'

Ida stood nervously. 'I might have some matches in the car.'

'There's a box in the bedside table, the drawer,' Threepea said irritably. 'No, the one on this side of the bed.'

She put the document down on the edge of the sink and walked impatiently over to the table. Natalie could hear her rummaging in the drawer. It was the break she'd been waiting for and stepping quickly out of the tub, she scooped up the paper and hurried to the window. It was open, and pushing the screen aside, she slipped through the gap. Then as nimble and swift as a chickcharnie, the supernatural three-toed creature once so common in the Bahamas, she scampered across the back-porch roof and, wrapping her arms and legs around a stout cistern pipe, slid down. As her feet touched ground a bellowing cry of anger and loss issued from the window above.

Constable Cartwright had had to stop by his house to get fresh sheets for the gaol bunk, as well as a padlock, and by the time he and Stewart reached the station it was nearly eleven o'clock. Stewart's thoughts had been so intensely concentrated on Natalie that he hadn't spoken since they'd left the scene of the crime. The constable assumed this was due to anger directed at him and, being a soft-hearted man and fond of his

charge, he apologized as he made up the bed. Having to play
the stern authority with someone he considered a man of
integrity as well as a friend was clearly painful to the sensitive
soul.

'Stewart, I know you're vexed with me, but you don't leave
me a choice. You're making it hard, not explaining what this is
all about.'

This shook Stewart from his worried musing.

'I'm sorry, Caleb, uh, Constable Cartwright, but I've got
nothing for you tonight. You'll just have to lock me up.' He
pointed at the phone on the desk. 'Can I make a call?'

'Of course.'

Cartwright pulled a cell phone out of his pocket.

'I'll leave my phone with you; the landline hasn't worked
right since they confuddled up the lines last year.'

He motioned Stewart into the cell and fished the chain
through the bars, locking it. Shrugging, he wished Stewart
pleasant dreams and left.

Stewart rang up the Mutt'n'Fish and Maximillian answered.

'Max, have you seen Natalie?'

'Stewart! She's not with you? Wait.' There was a pause. 'You
won't believe this, but she just this moment walked in. Where
are you?'

Stewart closed his eyes and a wave of relief rolled outward
from his centre until his toes, fingertips, and the crown of his
head tingled.

'Stewart, you still there?'

'I am!'

'Are you in gaol? We heard...'

'What did she say?'

'Not a word yet. She is smiling though. She's holding
something—now she's in your father's arms and he's swinging
her around. We got a call saying you were in...' Maximillian's
voice trailed off.

'Yes, I'm in the gaol. I'm staying the night, don't worry--'

'She got it,' Maximillian said, his voice a hoarse whisper.

'Pardon, could you repeat that?'

'That girl has it. She has it, the paper, the assignation,' he said, his voice still chalky. The large man's natural dignity normally subdued demonstrations of emotion but he was overcome at the moment and all Stewart heard was a low, happy bleat. Maximillian was choked up and finding it difficult to speak, but this was just as well because the constable's phone battery had died.

Throughout history those unfairly imprisoned have made the point that a man may be bound in chains in the dankest dungeon, but you can't shackle a free spirit. Stewart's spirit was currently qualified to serve as the OED illustration of 'unshackled'. He leaned back against the cool tabby wall of the ancient cell, beaming a smile out to the empty police station, to the Commonwealth of the Bahamas, and beyond. If he'd suddenly found himself in the penthouse suite of the Atlantis Resort on Paradise Island with its fresh sea breezes and expansive view of Nassau's glittering lights, it wouldn't have elevated his mood an inch. There wasn't any room.

He was astonished at his earlier attempts to convince himself that Natalie was anything other than the finest female to have delicately trod the earth. Even the initial estimate on the day they met, when he'd reckoned she bumped up against the ceiling of perfect womanhood, now seemed sadly lacking. This demonstration of spunk and selfless enterprise revealed previously unimagined regions of wonderfulness. Now the wisdom of his own nervous system—repeatedly interrupting his sleep, playing havoc with his emotional state during waking hours, and generally making him miserable—was obvious; it had been trying to wake him to the undeniable truth. He reckoned it was fortunate that such comprehensive dissonance hadn't short-circuited his system altogether. Despite an examination of her from every angle, he could detect only one failing in Natalie's whole glorious and singular make-up, and that was her current choice of a life-mate.

He had a few days to correct that. He leaned back with his hands behind his head; he'd need every bit of energy he could muster for the coming campaign. While waiting for much-needed sleep to overtake him, he recalled the tableau imprinted on his mind's eye of Natalie gazing up at him on the museum lawn, arranging her hair in the moonlight.

This acceptance of fate was followed by a flow of serenity and soon every corner of his parched psyche was flooded. Half a minute later he was sound asleep.

2ND THURSDAY

Two hours later at a few minutes before two a.m., a dark figure leaned against a palm trunk on the far west side of Willstown Harbour watching the moon dodge in and out of passing clouds. The figure was contemplating the rich seagoing lore of the Bahamian archipelago, particularly the native seamen reputed to be as adept as any in the world at seat-of-the-pants navigation in treacherous shallows. With spring-steel legs, cast-iron stomachs, and elastic ethics, they are the heirs of a pirate tradition dating back over a hundred years before the American Revolution. It's said that some among this elite group of men have the ability to navigate from the Turks to West End by moonlight with no more than a flask of rum in their hip pocket and a prayer for a fathom of water on the banks.

The skills of Bahamian mariners have been called upon in such varied service as that of smuggling arms to the Confederacy, leading flotillas across the Gulfstream in both World Wars and, most heroically in their own estimation, ensuring a steady flow of alcoholic spirits to their dry brethren across the Stream during the dark years of Prohibition. Any need of their colossal neighbour to the north—when expressed in sufficient monetary terms—was met by these intrepid seamen.

It was on these super-mariners that the hopes of the impatient figure rested, although rest implies ease and comfort, neither of which he was experiencing to any degree at the moment. The deal had been that they would arrive no later than one o'clock and he'd been slapping the occasional sand fly for over an hour. The Chili Cook-off was only three days away and a delivery Kingston considered to be necessary insurance in that contest was imminent

Yes, it was the great man himself out on the rocks in the wee morning hours. He hadn't stayed at the helm of the largest department store chain in the tri-state area due solely to nepotism. He knew a few things and one of them was that when it was necessary that something be done right, you do it yourself, and the job at hand required the utmost secrecy and sensitive handling. In fact, it was the step he was taking tonight that had emboldened him to send a sample of his chili to the Mutt'n'Fish team days before the competition—an unheard-of level of brazen confidence. Imagining their alarm at his reckless courage gave him a tremendous thrill. Even if their new recipe approached the level of his own, which he very much doubted, it wouldn't matter after tonight; provided, of course, that the blackguards he'd hired made good on their delivery.

At long last, a sinister stiletto of a boat eased into the crowded anchorage of the Willstown Harbour roadstead. Both the long hull and row of motors across the stern were painted a mottled primer grey, dulling its outline in the bright moonlight. It moved silently through the tightly packed boats on a single trolling motor, its four massive outboards tilted out of the water. The engines trailed long wisps of steam, a testament to the boat's mad sprint across the Gulf Stream. The craft swung to starboard and nudged its bow up to the western point of the harbour, where Kingston stood teetering on the rocks waving a lumpy duffel bag in the glare of the boat's spotlight. Before he knew what was happening, a boat hook from the bow slipped out and caught the bag, pulling it from his grasp and reeling it in. He grunted in complaint as the boat eased backward with the tidal wash and the bag was passed below.

'Where's my nephew? Where's Julius!' he called in a loud whisper.

'You relax yourself, boy, we going count it,' a voice from the boat called out.

'Hey!' Kingston hissed, 'keep your voice down.' His nerves were vibrating like a plucked bowstring and, unable to contain his agitation, he began pacing the shore. Three long minutes later two figures emerged from the cabin of the craft and moved to the bow.

'Lay down under the rail,' a coarse Bahamian voice ordered loudly and the stout figure, moving stiffly, did as it was told.

'Stop shouting!' Kingston said as loudly as he dared.

Suddenly the unmistakable whine of electric servos lowering outboard motors into the water came to his ears.

'Don't start those things!' Kingston cried as the massive motors rumbled to life.

The engines shifted into gear and as the moon slid out from behind a cloud, he could clearly make out his sister's youngest child—at twenty-two years old one of earth's more useless creatures—lying on his side across the bow with his chubby hand gripping the railing above him. Drained of its native pinkish hue, his nephew's face fairly glowed in the moonlight as the boat approached shore again. The young man's eyes rounded to saucers as the boat surged forward in the grip of a seemingly suicidal impulse, but an instant before the bow crashed into the rocks, the motors shifted into reverse and, with the assistance of a helpful kick, he rolled off the bow and into the water not five feet from shore. The boat continued backing away with the engines throbbing loudly.

'Quiet!' Kingston shouted at the boat, thoroughly incensed. Now that these pirates had their money, his instructions that the operation be conducted in silence were being ignored. In a fit of frustration he picked up a rock, and taking aim at the departing boat, launched his missile. It ricocheted off the near engine and in retaliation the helmsman opened the throttle wide, sending an ear-splitting roar across the still water. This was followed with loud blasts from an air horn.

A rollicking wake spread out as the craft ploughed seaward, setting every boat in the harbour rocking. Lights appeared on all sides and voices rose in protest. Kingston rushed into the shallows and pulled the miserable human cargo onto shore, pulling and pushing until the two of them stumbled into the bushes. Wet, disoriented, and seasick, the lad began to complain loudly at the inhumanity of it all, but before Kingston could get a hand over his mouth, continued blasts from the air horn and the angry shouts of awakened mariners drowned him out.

Kingston found himself perversely pleased with this young man's discomfort. Up until now his nephew had led far too coddled an existence due to his sister's too-tender heart and too-soft head. Though he hadn't given it much thought previously, this raw treatment was likely to prove therapeutic for the boy, who, his mother had said, spent most daylight hours watching movies and his evenings attending the local playhouse. This encounter with the wide world was an opportunity for Julius to face life's grim and earnest side. Kingston blushed inwardly at this evidence of his own benevolence. He didn't normally give himself a lot of credit for helping others, it not being anything that interested him, but then, he reflected, hadn't he heard high-minded generosity described as disinterested charity? No one he knew, he said to himself, was less interested in it than him.

Admittedly, he was saving himself a bit of money by not hiring a real actor, but the inconvenience of having to mollycoddle this inexperienced amateur would more than offset any savings. He doubted his nephew appreciated the sacrifice he was making on his behalf. Certainly not at the moment.

The chorus of angry voices hadn't abated, and a crowd was forming on the wharf. Kingston watched as yet more lights appeared, among them the harbourmaster's apartment above his office. A growing knot of incensed sportsmen, sailors and concerned citizens had formed at the foot of the stairway demanding satisfaction, and judging from the tone, there was very little to go around. Kingston was beginning to feel a marked lack of it himself as he realized that he and Julius were stuck in the bushes until the uproar died down and the crowd dispersed. It was essential that they make their way to the Butterchurn VIII unseen.

The way things stood, the only ones in the Willstown Harbour area experiencing any degree of satisfaction were a swarm of sand flies convened in the bushes hiding the two men. For this little band of tropical no-see-ums, it was a case of one minute not knowing where their next meal was coming from and the next having an embarrassing surfeit of flesh magically appear front and centre. It was enough to make a bug believe that even it had a part in Providence's larger plan.

At eight o'clock sharp, less than six hours after Kingston's nephew arrived and nine hours since the already infamous museum burglary, Scoonie and Maximillian met Constable Cartwright in front of the Porgy Island Museum and the three men climbed the steps to the porch. Mrs. Pamela Pims Pinder opened the door before they had a chance to knock, stepping out with magisterial dignity. She was in immaculate form from the soles of her high-heels to her starched and pressed collar. North of that, however, it was a different story. Underneath the proud features it was evident that strong emotion had been at work and that the person behind the mask hadn't spent the night in rejuvenating slumber. In addition to fatigue, her grim expression suggested repressed emotion of a potentially volatile nature. The general idea, if not the precise term, of *a loose cannon* occurred to the three men simultaneously and they stepped back in unscripted unison. After a moment of uncomfortable silence, she spoke.

'Good morning, gentlemen.'

'Good morning, ma'am,' Maximillian said, with the constable and Scoonie mumbling agreement.

'I was just on my way to your office, Constable,' she said.

'Yes, ma'am. I hope I've saved you the trouble.'

'You will have, provided you brought with you the forms necessary to press charges of housebreaking and attempted burglary, as well as the form to file a report of a successful theft that occurred on the premises after your departure last night.'

'A successful theft?!' Constable Cartwright said. 'After I left?!'

'I believe that's what I just said. After the young Mr. Moxey was apprehended, apparently an accomplice remained behind in hiding and later effected the theft of museum property.'

'Surely not, ma'am. Why wasn't I alerted?'

'I judged there was no imminent danger to my person and the lateness of the hour dissuaded me. More to the point, however, the so-called "hotness"—to use the argot—of the trail is somewhat immaterial in this case. I am confident that I can direct you as to where to begin, and end, your investigation.'

Here she swivelled an accusing eye on Scoonie and Maximillian. Constable Cartwright, busy scribbling on his clipboard, missed this dramatic visual accusation.

'What time did the incident take place?' he said, continuing to write.

'Approximately eleven twenty.'

'That wasn't long after I left!' he said, looking up.

'That is correct.'

'And you yourself witnessed it?'

'Both Idamae Thompson and I were present.'

'Ida was there?' the constable said, raising an eyebrow. 'Can either of you identify the thief?'

'I'm afraid not as to appearance.'

'Yet you did witness the theft?'

'I was in the next room when it occurred, as was Mrs. Thompson.'

'Can you give me any sort of description of the perpetrator?'

'I'm afraid that beyond bold and devious, no. Neither Mrs. Thompson nor I can be of help in that respect. The thief was very skilful.'

'You saw nothing?'

'No.'

'But you heard something?'

'Very little. As I say, the thief was cunning.'

A derisory snort issued from Maximillian, and Scoonie bowed his head, biting his lower lip. He turned away in an effort to muffle his laughter.

For Threepea and the two men, it was a shared moment of déjà vu, taking all three back to Threepea's first year of teaching at the Porgy Island All-Age School. Two of the little savages in her class now stood before her in adult form, neither apparently having benefited from forty-two subsequent years of life's stern lessons.

'You seem to be enjoying yourselves, gentlemen,' she said. 'Perhaps you have something to share?'

Maximillian, fighting a timeless reflex to elbow Scoonie in the lower ribs, collected himself and straightened.

'Yes, ma'am, I do. This might change the direction of things this morning,' he said, pulling the assignation from his pocket.

Had the fire in Pamela Pims Pinder's eyes been a shade more literal it would have consumed Maximillian and Scoonie, along with the vexing document, in a demonstration of Old Testament fury. Experience dating from their tutelage under Threepea, nee Miss Sawyer, had steeled the two aging lads for this; it was an inoculation against a fearsome glare that had survived four decades. The constable, however, wasn't so lucky: Caught flat-footed in a metaphorical tribute to his profession, he stumbled back and fell into a porch chair. The ageing chair groaned but held.

'Constable Cartwright, arrest these two men! That is the very stolen property in his hand,' Threepea boomed to the seated public servant. His instinctive response was to continue right where he was, and he obeyed it.

'Threepea,' Maximillian said calmly. 'We're prepared to settle this on a mutually beneficial basis.'

Here he did elbow his compatriot.

'Yes, yes,' Scoonie croaked, clearing his throat as he fumbled with his reading glasses. He held a prepared statement in front of him:

'As the ranking member of the Moxey family, I am prepared to sign over the entire collection of historical items to the museum. In return, all we would ask is that a niggling strip of property, a very insignificant piece belonging to the Foundation, be deeded to Maximillian, that is, Mr. Sawyer, your cousin, here...' He quickly pointed to Maximillian in case there was any confusion in the matter, and when he tried to resume, found he'd lost his place.

Maximillian took over for his addled friend. '...And additionally, that all charges be dropped in connection to the events of last night and an assurance that there will be no future legal actions taken against the Mutt'n'Fish Pub & Restaurant Ltd. regarding property encroachment or curtailment of entertainment nights.'

Like doused embers, Threepea's eyes faded to small, smouldering coals.

'Is that all?' She sniffed sarcastically. An intelligent woman, she'd known from the poignant moment when she'd discovered the document missing from the edge of her sink that she was beaten, and her actions of the morning had been the Hail Mary effort of an indefatigable warrior. She turned to the agent of the law still seated in the pink Adirondack chair.

'Constable, I wish to withdraw the charges against Mr. Stewart Moxey. You may release him.'

'No housebreaking charges?!' he said with protruding eyes, reviving the previous night's impersonation of a baffled lobster. He hadn't the slightest idea what was going on.

'None,' Threepea said.

'And no burglary report? I'm referring to the successful...'

'No report at all, no charges of any kind,' she stated with finality.

She turned back to Scoonie and Maximillian.

'Gentlemen, speaking as president and board chairman of the Porgy Island Museum and Historical Foundation, your offer of a full and permanent assignation under the conditions you have outlined is accepted.'

'We'll have it drawn up,' Maximillian said.

'Fine,' she said. 'Good day, gentlemen,' and with no discernible emotion she pivoted stiffly to re-enter the museum.

Maximillian cleared his throat just as she reached the door and she froze with her hand on the doorknob.

'I'd like to thank you, Mrs. Pamela Pims Pinder.'

'You're welcome, Mr. Sawyer,' she said without turning and disappeared inside.

The two men declined a ride, preferring a pleasant walk to the station, and they met Stewart just as the constable released him. Despite his line of work, Caleb Cartwright was no fan of legal drama, and the deflated resolution of the case suited him to his toes; his cordial relations with Stewart were restored and the comfortable cell bunk was now free for a late morning nap.

On the walk back Stewart gave his account of the previous night's events, and he listened in turn as Maximillian related Natalie's version. By the time they reached the Moxey Arms, each of them had fallen silent, lost in his own thoughts. Stewart headed for The Hall to see how his cousin was doing and the two older men turned off on the walkway to the Mutt'n'Fish. As they mounted the steps, Scoonie turned to Maximillian.

'You know, I have to admit, I had sympathetic pangs for Threepea back there. She's really not such a bad sort.'

Maximillian laughed softly. 'You're suffering from the "Hemingway Syndrome." '

'What?'

'Remember Santiago?'

Scoonie thought for a moment. '*The Old Man and the Sea*?'

Maximillian nodded. 'Santiago said he loved the marlin as he fought it and he loved it afterwards. Because it fought so tirelessly and so nobly.'

'Threepea is no marlin,' Scoonie pointed out.

'No,' Maximillian agreed. 'She's considerably more cold-blooded. You should never forget that.'

It was nearly lunchtime and Natalie heard the door to the cottage open and close.

'Is that you, Ginger?' she called from the bathroom.

'It's me, darling,' Ginger said in a drawling French accent.

Natalie came out in a sundress, looking bright and fresh. 'I hope that isn't your impression of Antoine.'

'You look fabulous, where are you going?'

'I'm having lunch on the Papillon. How about coming with me?'

Ginger shook her head. 'I'd love to but I'm meeting Leonard at Waltaniques. I'll take a rain check.'

'Are you sure? Lobster.'

Ginger shook her head.

'Look how excited you are!' Natalie said, and her friend blushed. 'I guess five-star French cuisine with The Baron and I can't stand up to conch fritters with Leonard. We're having mimosas,' she added to tempt her friend. 'You could invite him.'

'No, he's been talking about this for two days. And, really, I've been looking forward to having fritters with him. He enjoys them so much, it's infectious.'

'You're practically giddy!'

'I can't deny it.'

'So, what's his full name?'

When the two were roommates in boarding school, they'd determined that the point at which one learns a boy's middle name was a sure sign of love.

'What!' Ginger laughed. 'I haven't thought of that in years.'

Natalie nodded, still demanding an answer. Ginger stood as if readying herself for a recitation and took a deep breath.

'Leonard Willoughby Sawyer,' she announced sonorously. They both collapsed in laughter.

'So you don't know yet.'

'No. That's what it is.'

'Really?' Natalie said, her eyes wide. 'Willoughby with an o-u-g-h?'

Ginger smiled and nodded.

'That's more like a royal proclamation than a name.'

'And in his case, absolutely appropriate. He's a king among men. His manners, his generosity, his divinely deep voice. And that accent.'

Natalie listened happily as her friend waxed eloquent on Leonard's many sterling qualities, but when Ginger circled around to expound on his unparalleled sweetness for the third time, she saw that Natalie's attention had wandered.

'I'm sorry, I'm repeating myself now. I can see I'm boring you with my blathering on about him,' Ginger said, laughing. 'Now you'll know better than to ask me.'

Natalie smiled at her. 'I'm sorry. I really do like hearing about him and I particularly like seeing you so happy. It was just that something occurred to me. But I'm keeping you...'

'No, first tell me what's bothering you. I could see you were upset about something earlier. You've been distracted lately.'

'It's just something I overheard Antoine say last Sunday. I'm sure I'll find out it was nothing. Go on, you'll miss your lunch date.'

'I'm not going until you tell me. What was it?'

'No, go on! Like I said, I'm sure I'm inventing problems.'

Ginger set her jaw and stared at her friend. 'Spill it.'

'Okay, but remember I said there's probably some simple explanation. I heard Antoine saying that he'd ordered a boat just like the Papillon.'

Ginger's eyes widened.

'You mean ship, don't you? That's pretty great. I didn't know he was that well off.'

Natalie chewed her lip, avoiding her friend's eyes.

'Aren't you pleased?' Ginger said. 'I'd love to have a giant yacht like that. It's like your own private cruise ship!'

'That boat cost two hundred and fifty million dollars.'

'Whew! Really!' she said, her eyes wide. 'Well if he has the money, why not? Even if it cost every penny he's got, it's not like you're ever going to go hungry.'

'The thing is, I don't think he does.'

'Does what?'

'Have the money.'

'Of course he does. He must. He wouldn't order it if he didn't...would he?' Ginger said.

Natalie did look at Ginger now but didn't answer.

'What makes you think he doesn't?' Ginger said, pressing her.

'His cousin told me he and his mom were struggling to keep the estate together. And my dad had him investigated and he says the same thing.'

'Your dad had him investigated!'

Natalie nodded.

'Whoa. That's pretty serious.'

'You know how he is with me; Daddy's little girl.'

'Yeah, I always thought that was cute.'

'Yeah, well he claims the detective said that Antoine is close to broke.'

'Claims? Your dad wouldn't lie. He's about the last person I can imagine lying. Next to Leonard, of course.'

'Of course,' Natalie said with a fleeting smile. 'Dad's not a liar, but to keep me from "ruining my life"?' She traced quotes in the air. 'But I've committed myself to Antoine and I owe him my trust. He said everything is okay.'

'You asked him if he was broke and he said no? That must have been awkward.'

'Not quite that direct, but we've discussed finances and yes, he as much as said that everything on his side is fine.'

'There's a lot of room between financially fine and ordering a yacht that cost a quarter of a billion dollars,' Ginger said, always no-nonsense.

Natalie nodded. 'I know he was irritated by Kingston Butterwort that day. He's mentioned it twice. I wonder if he said that just to...'

'To shut Butterwort up or maybe one-up him?' Ginger finished for her.

Natalie winced. Ginger could tell neither possibility sat well with her friend.

It was early afternoon before Julius, Kingston's newly arrived nephew, woke in a nasty, disoriented state. After dressing grumpily, he stumbled out onto the deck of the Butterchurn VIII where a crew member spotted him and, as instructed, quickly shuffled the complaining young man back to his cabin with the assurance that breakfast would be brought to him in a matter of minutes. True to his word, the steward was back shortly with a lavish spread and word that his Uncle Kingston would be there soon.

Julius had just taken the edge off of his considerable appetite with the eggs, bacon, sausage, hash browns, toast, jelly, and pineapple yogurt. He was excited by the discovery of a delicious but mysterious jelly when his uncle walked in. His deep bitterness toward Kingston had been considerably lessened in the course of filling his stomach and the first thing out of his mouth was, 'What is this, it's beyond description!'

He held up a piece of toast heaped with quivering amber jelly.

'Toast and jelly,' Kingston said, puzzled. Though he'd never credited any of his sister's children with the slightest intelligence, this was jarring.

'Yes, of course, but what's the jelly? It's exquisite.'

'Ahh,' Kingston nodded, understanding dawning. A deep appreciation of food was part of the Butterwort genetic imprint and though it might be painful, he had to face the fact that Julius was family.

'Good stuff, isn't it? That's guava jelly, locally made. I have it myself every morning, buy it by the case. You should have it in a roly poly,' he added with a significant look.

'Isn't that a bug?' Julius said, wrinkling his nose.

'It's an excellent local pastry. Well worth searching out. If you're cooperative, I might have some brought to you.'

Smiling back at his uncle in this moment of shared culinary appreciation, Julius realized that this wasn't at all the tone he'd planned to open with. His mother had impressed on him the importance of taking a stiff line with her brother at the outset. If he didn't, she'd warned, he'd be crushed beneath the heel of Kingston's cruel manipulations. Steeling himself for confrontation, he took a gulp of coffee and put the toast down for later. He'd want a soothing bite or two after dealing firmly with his uncle.

'Criminy, Uncle, why did you drag me down here? I was busy when you called Mother, you know. In fact I was on the verge of landing a part in a commercial.'

'I need a hand and you're just the one that can help me. I'd think you'd be happy for the chance to get out in the real world, toughen up a bit, prove yourself. You can be useful here.'

'I don't need to toughen up. I'm plenty tough,' he said defiantly.

His uncle leaned over and poked him in the stomach, and when Julius jumped back with a squawk, he laughed loudly.

'What's that prove? And why do I need to be tough anyway?'

'The world's a rough place for you creative types. This is a chance to show you're up to the challenge.'

'But why me? You could've had Meg or Katie come here. Even Mary,' Julius said, running down his roster of sisters. 'They've got nothing better to do, nothing...' he searched for the bon juste '...artistic. All they do is talk on the phone and shop.'

'Had to be a man. Or at least somewhat male-ish.'

Other than a harsh glance at his uncle, Julius let this pass.

'Why?!' he said peevishly. 'How about Rod, then? Or Michael?'

'Too tall. Too thin,' Kingston said, citing two of Julius's cousins' respective disqualifications. 'And you're an actor, aren't you? I need an actor.'

This brought Julius up short, and he suppressed a smile. In spite of his pique, it was gratifying to be recognised as such by this celebrated philistine.

'You're still calling yourself an actor, aren't you?' Kingston pressed.

'Of course. I just said I had to give up a promising role in a television commercial to come here, didn't I?'

'Those people in commercials are called actors, are they? Anyway, this is bigger than that.'

'What is it?'

'Ever played a Mexican?'

'Well, a Hispanic. I played Sancho Panza last year…'

'Yes, that sounds about right. How'd it go?'

' "Played with verve and rare spirit". That was the *Cloverdale Observer*. "Breathing new life into the role of the Don's side…"'

'Actually, this fellow's American,' Kingston interrupted. 'An American Mexican.'

'Oh, a Mexican-American. A Chicano,' He pronounced 'American' with an extravagantly rolled 'r'.

'Hey, that's pretty good. Maybe you can do this.'

'For whom is this performance intended?' Julius sniffed.

'Look, if you can convince the bunch around here that you're this Mexican fellow, I'll feather your little artiste nest with crisp new dollars, now and possibly into the future.'

'What "bunch" do you refer to? Is this for some local playhouse?' Julius said, showing signs of a pout.

'No! Do you think I'd go to all this trouble for something as silly as that?'

'Oh!' Julius said, suddenly animated, 'It's not a film is it?' He could hardly contain himself.

'No, it's not some silly movie show,' Kingston replied, happy to quash any budding hope. 'This is something more important.'

The young man looked at him sceptically.

'I'd like to hear what's more important than a film role, Uncle.'

'For starters, stop calling me Uncle. One slip like that could send this whole thing off the rails. And this is no goofy Hollywood picture. This will take real acting.'

'So what is it, exactly?'

'I need you to impersonate this fellow.'

'That sounds illegal!'

'There's no legal or illegal about it.'

Julius's suspicions were fully alert now. He hadn't spent much time with his uncle in recent years, but he'd heard from his mother and aunts of the depths to which the family oligarch was capable of sinking. The three women had no shortage of mocking invective when the subject was their autocratic brother, and their long-time favourite was, 'the moral bathysphere'. It came back to Julius now: TMB. The term had always seemed like a mean-spirited insult, but it was starting to sound merely descriptive.

'Think of it as a test,' Kingston continued, 'which if completed to my satisfaction, will encourage me to continue funding your "career".' His thick fingers traced quotation marks in the air.

Julius chewed his lip. He appreciated the extent of his uncle's resources; it was another popular topic with Kingston's sisters. He was the nozzle that controlled the flow of the family fortune, directing it where he would.

'Give it serious thought,' Kingston said. 'If you plan to stick with this acting business, you'll still be wanting to eat, I imagine?' He poked his young nephew's ample mid-section again, guffawing loudly, and it sounded to Julius's ears as jolly as a fork dropped into a garbage disposal. He sat quietly considering his plight.

'How is it I'm to "play" this part?' he said finally, resigned to his fate.

'That's more like it. You'll be "playing" Fernando Lopez, an American Mexican fellow from—'

'The term is Chicano. Or at least Mexican-American.'

'All right, all right,' Kingston said testily, making a concerted effort to restrain himself. It was a measure of this scheme's importance to him that he was able to check the impulse to clout his nephew in the ear. 'This fellow's from Texas. He backed out of judging the Chili Cook-off at the last minute—'

'I'm judging a food contest!'

'Yes, you are. Do you have a problem with that?' He looked at Julius meaningfully.

The futility of resisting once again washed over the young man. He smiled weakly. 'I guess not. Why did he quit?'

'Who? Oh, the judge. It doesn't matter. But he's gone now.'

'Gone? What does that mean?!' He'd caught a sinister note in his uncle's reply and it reminded him of his mother's admonition that he should put nothing past this man.

'I said gone and I mean gone. He and his whole family. Trust me, they won't be showing up from where I sent 'em.'

Julius swallowed. 'And his whole family! They're gone too?'

'Yeah, I just said that, didn't I? I took care of the whole bunch. Wasn't cheap, either, I'll tell you.'

Julius recoiled in horror. What particularly frightened him was the casual tone his uncle used admitting to such a heinous act. That he discussed it so casually indicated such things were routine for him. This man was every bit the monster his mother and aunts had maintained. Julius's breathing quickened to a staccato wheezing and if Kingston hadn't been so preoccupied lamenting the cost, he'd have seen the young man's complexion go from its typically fruity pink to something like a blanched cauliflower. Julius felt faint, and just as consciousness was fading, he heard Kingston speak.

'I sent the whole bunch to Disneyland—in California, mind you. I didn't want them coming this way, to the Florida one, you know—and I had to pay for a full week. Grandkids too. It was a small fortune, but it will be worth every penny if you don't botch this.'

Julius struggled to pull himself upright as the blood returned to his head.

'You paid for them to go on vacation?' he said, his head wobbling.

'What do you think I've been telling you?' Kingston shook his head at the obtuseness of the younger generation. 'So, can you do it?'

Julius nodded weakly.

'Yes?!' Kingston demanded.

'I'll do my best,' he said.

'You've got one job while you're here and that's to convince everyone that you're this Lopez fellow. Manage that, and while I'm sure you'll still be an unemployed actor, at least you won't be a starving one. Comprende, Senor Lopez?'

'Si,' Julius said, swallowing hard. He was far from home and at the mercy of a madman who held the purse strings to his future. He'd have to make the best of it.

The evening of the prep party found the porch of the Mutt'n'Fish crowded with early arrivals watching the sun sink into the sea as it simultaneously painted the underside of the clouds with a garish display of reds and oranges. Feeling it had done enough, the sun unceremoniously dropped below the horizon, prompting a third of the viewers—about the average—to claim they'd seen a green flash. In the face of jeering from the rest, they insisted you just needed their practised eye.

As the crowd filtered into the restaurant arguing the point, a large, merry group came up the walkway. It was Kingston Butterwort and The Baron, their combined entourages surrounding them and mingling loudly. Kingston's voice boomed out from the centre of the group, arguing a point with The Baron. The prep party was invitation only, but it had been open to the Butterworts from its inception and tradition deemed that they be welcome. Though this was a source of long-standing aggravation to Billy and Scoonie, Maximillian was hesitant to tamper with precedent. He stood at the door, greeting arrivals.

Kingston entered the restaurant in his customary blustering manner, shaking hands with everyone. He was followed by The Baron, who walked with the air of a matador favouring the peasantry with a visit. His towering first-mate trailed him with a wooden crate of wine on his shoulder.

'I hope that's not alcoholic?' Maximillian said.

'It is not permitted?' The Baron said with exaggerated surprise.

'You've brought salt to Inagua,' someone said, laughing.

'No, it's fine,' Maximillian said to him. 'But if we have an excess of anything, it would be alcohol. Still, I applaud your generosity.'

'Yes, I'm sure you are well supplied, Monsieur Maximillian,' The Baron replied, 'but I bring something unique. This is wine from The Château Rouge, my family's vineyards, and it is the finest Cabernet Blanc in the world.'

'The finest?' Billy said, walking up with a raised eyebrow. He, like any chef worth his pink Himalayan salt, was a self-anointed wine expert and though he hadn't cared much for The Baron at their first meeting in the churchyard, he was willing to let bygones be bygones if a first-class wine was involved.

'Unquestionably. As I say, it is from my family's vineyard.'

'Let's try it then,' Billy said, producing a corkscrew with a magician's finesse.

'You are prepared,' The Baron said, raising his own eyebrow.

Billy nodded, motioning the first-mate to put the crate down, and they began prying it open.

Stewart stepped up and shook The Baron's hand.

'Welcome. I hope you enjoy yourself tonight,' Stewart said as warmly as he could manage.

'Certainly, I'm looking forward to it,' The Baron replied, in an equally cool manner.

The band was setting up and musicians and technicians bustled around them with microphones, video cameras, and other electronica.

'This looks very, what is the word...elaborate?' The Baron said.

'It's a last run-through for the band before tournament night,' Stewart said. 'They video themselves and use it to iron out any kinks in their performance.'

'Ah, and very nice for us. They practice, we enjoy.'

Billy called to The Baron, holding two glasses of wine aloft, and Stewart, having fulfilled his duty as a host, withdrew. Billy would have to represent the family's hospitality to the Frenchman, for try as he might, Stewart couldn't feel anything but the deepest distaste for the man intent on marrying the girl destiny had marked for him.

A minute later Billy sat down, staring blankly, an expression of quiet rapture on his face.

'You approve, Monsieur William?'

'That might be one of the finest wines I've ever tasted,' he said reverently. 'Without question the best Cabernet Blanc.'

'Of course you are correct. I think you didn't believe me. I find you Bahamians very sceptical, but I must say it is a quality for which I have respect. It is very French, especially in regards to food and drink. Your corkscrew if you please, Monsieur Billy. I will open a few bottles so they may be breathing while we finish this one. You would help me enjoy them?'

'By all means, boy,' Billy said.

The band launched into 'Ufo', an Eddie Minnis classic, and the party was off.

An hour later, Billy and The Baron were sitting off to the side, into their third bottle of wine, and when Billy got up to speak to a friend, the Frenchman waved Stewart over.

'The name of the band,' The Baron said, '"Potcake and Porgy"; the porgy I know of. It is a fish, a succulent fish. But potcake, what is potcake?'

'Potcake is the Bahamian term for mutt. A dog of mixed breed,' Stewart said. 'The crusty rice at the bottom of the pot is called potcake and it's generally thrown to the dogs. So that's how it got started, they say.'

The Baron nodded. 'I see. Very colourful. So Potcake and Porgy, the Mutt and the Fish. I am correct?'

'Yes, exactly right.'

The Baron picked up an open bottle of the Cabernet Blanc.

'Please have a glass with me. So far, there is only Billy and me to enjoy this wonderful wine.'

'Bahamians like their rum,' Stewart said, motioning around him. 'Rum and gin. But yes, I'll have a glass.'

Maximillian walked up.

'Enjoying the music, gentlemen?'

'Spirited,' The Baron said, but that was as far as he was willing to go.

Maximillian nodded and turned to Stewart. 'Hercules has entered the zone well ahead of schedule, I'm afraid. I think he was already pretty well oiled when he rolled in.'

'Is Constable Cartwright here?'

'I'm going to call him now. I just thought I'd put you on notice.'

Stewart nodded, and Maximillian hurried off.

'There is a problem?' the Frenchman asked.

'Let's hope not. The man there, his name is Hercules.' Stewart nodded toward a large black Bahamian in shorts and high boots, laughing wildly with a group of men. 'He's apt to let himself go at times like this.'

'Let himself go?'

'Cut loose. Carouse. He's just returned from three weeks at sea,' Stewart said. 'He tends to bottle it up when out fishing and then get a little expansive ashore. His idea of a good time is a good row.' Stewart raised his fists to illustrate. The wine was making The Baron's company more tolerable.

'A hard worker and prince among men when sober,' Stewart continued. 'But at times like this it takes a troop of men to contain him. Once he blows, I mean.'

'Blows?'

'Explodes!' Stewart motioned with his hands.

The Baron nodded. 'He is large,' he observed. 'Strong?'

Stewart nodded. 'And since fighting is his favoured form of recreation, he's a handful. It would be no picnic to go up against him one-on-one.'

'No picnic?' The Baron said.

'No fun. Dangerous.'

'I see.'

The Baron smiled mildly and looked Stewart up and down. 'You are frightened of him?'

Stewart nodded again. 'But don't worry, the constable should be along soon.'

'The policeman can handle him?'

'Hercules will take on five, ten men, when he's rolling, but put one man in uniform and he's a lamb. He was in the Royal Bahamian Defence Force, and he has outsized respect for a uniform, even when drunk. I should say particularly when he's drunk, because that's the only time he gets out of hand.'

Maximillian reappeared with a worried look. 'I can't raise Cartwright.'

'Well, you're right, he's getting wound up,' Stewart said.

'I haven't seen Leonard either, but without the constable we're going to need him and a few more,' Maximillian said, scanning the crowd.

'Leonard said he wasn't coming tonight, but I saw Clyde and Lucius on the porch.'

'Leonard missing the prep party!'

'So he said.'

'Well, keep an eye on Hercules and I'll go round up who I can,' Maximillian said. 'But this isn't going to be easy without Leonard.'

As he turned to go, the Frenchman put a slender hand on his shoulder.

'Monsieur Maximillian. I can assist,' he said.

Maximillian looked at The Baron and at Stewart. The Frenchman was drunk, he decided, but it was more humanity than he'd expected from him.

Maximillian nodded. 'What about that first-mate of yours, could we enlist him?'

'Leave it to me, Monsieur.'

Maximillian raised an eyebrow at this, but there was no time to argue. He thanked him and went to find the other men.

Five minutes later Maximillian was back with reinforcements. The recruits eyed Hercules uneasily.

'The last time this happened,' Billy said, 'I was sore for a week.'

'Billy,' a wiry black man said, 'cast your mind back. Whining the way you do, I think you forget who it was had his collarbone broke.'

'Why, that must've been you, Clyde,' Billy said, his voice heavy with sarcasm. 'I forget, probably due to the concussion I got prying you from Hercules's grip.'

Clyde shook his head at Billy's account.

Maximillian broke in. 'Darlings, we've all suffered our share of cut-ass from Hercules, but enough sniping. Unless Leonard shows up in the next minute or two you're going to need each other and more.'

'Leonard's not coming,' Stewart said impatiently. 'No sense putting it off any longer.' He'd been away for most of Hercules's fighting career, but the one time he'd seen the giant on a rampage had left a deep impression. In his view, the sooner the row was over, the better.

'Okay, we'll have to do without him,' Maximillian said, holding up his hand. 'Gentlemen, surround him and try not to be too obvious. Wait for my whistle.'

The men moved through the crowd, taking up their positions. Stewart stayed close to The Baron, unsure of his intentions. He couldn't help wondering what a blow from Hercules would do to the slender Frenchman. At the very moment this occurred to him, The Baron stepped toward Hercules with his trademarked insolence as if determined to answer Stewart's curiosity. Stewart reached out to stop him, but The Baron proved surprisingly quick and Stewart's hand closed on air. He stood face-to-face with the impressive Bahamian. The Frenchman was a rooster, complete with flaming red comb, demanding a bull's attention. It was well known that Hercules's state of mind prior to wreaking havoc was a good-natured hilarity that only someone prepared to take his lumps would dare to interrupt. The six men stood tensed, awaiting Maximillian's signal to act.

The tension spread outward through the crowd and the music came to a ragged halt. A circle formed, filling in the gaps between Maximillian's task force, but these were strictly spectators wanting a good view of the coming carnage while leaving ample room for Hercules to exhibit his art. Most of the crowd keenly anticipated the coming fight.

Maximillian's concern was getting The Baron out of the way before they jumped Hercules, but the trick was pulling him back without triggering the human powder keg prematurely. As if reading Maximillian's thoughts, The Baron reached out and put a hand on Hercules's shoulder, interrupting the giant's laugh. Hercules spun to face him squarely, and seeing The Baron's smug and patronizing smile, his expression turned dark. He reared up into a fighting stance, seeming to suddenly swell to half again his size. A wave of awe passed through the crowd. No matter how many times one was witness to the unleashing of this man's exuberant rage, it never failed to impress.

Though contrary to his every inclination, Stewart was going to have to risk taking The Baron out of the line of fire before the men subdued Hercules. The room was still, a hush so complete that when a bottle was knocked over it rang like a bell announcing the start of round one.

The Baron stood calmly erect, a lamb before the slaughter. When Hercules cocked his right arm, Maximillian's fingers went to his lips, but before the sound of the whistle reached any ears, Stewart had lunged for The Baron. This was followed a fraction of a second later by the release of Hercules's punch.

Though both Hercules's renowned haymaker and Stewart were aimed at The Baron, neither found their mark. The absence of any Frenchman where there had unquestionably been a Frenchman an instant earlier left Hercules's fist free to trace an unimpeded, whistling arc, narrowly missing Stewart's jaw as he himself continued on across the circle and into the crowd on the far side.

Though not witness to it, Stewart was assured later that The Baron was not idle in the interim. According to witnesses, he performed a series of lightning-fast oriental gymnastics rarely seen outside of Hong Kong movie houses. When Stewart untangled himself from the crowd and turned to survey the damage, Hercules was on his knees and The Baron was on top of him with a knee pressed in his back. The giant's right arm was twisted behind him and he was bent forward, his face pressed against the floor. As Billy later lamented, the onlookers had, to a man, perfectly slack jaws, and anyone with prior knowledge of The Baron's form could have, with even the most conservative odds, cleaned up on an unprecedented scale.

The Baron appeared at his ease, breathing heavily but calmly, while Hercules's lungs wheezed like a blacksmith's bellows. Maximillian and his hastily assembled task force took a step back. They'd all been a split second too late to lay a hand on either man.

'Monsieur Hercules,' The Baron said, bending down to the big man's ear. 'You were preparing to do me mischief, were you not?'

There was a muffled reply.

The Baron relaxed the pressure, giving Hercules some breathing room.

'I'm sorry, please repeat.'

'Yeth, Yeth,' Hercules said, and he nodded as enthusiastically as a face spread liberally on a hardwood floor would allow.

'You are prepared to be nice? Civilized?'

'Yeth.'

'Promeez?'

He relieved the pressure a bit more.

'Aye, I promise.'

The Baron released him and stood with his hands on his hips as Hercules came to his feet, rubbing his arm. The massive man appeared to be completely defused.

'You are sore?'

Hercules nodded.

'No bad feelingz, I trust. You forced me, you see.'

'Yessir. Yeah, I see that,' Hercules said, hanging his head. He couldn't have been more compliant if The Baron had been the Commodore of the Defence Force himself.

The deep ring of spectators began to migrate toward the bar to discuss what exactly they'd witnessed. With history in the making, no facet was too small to be examined and the rising tone indicated that enthusiastic evaluations were underway.

The Baron had his hand on Hercules's shoulder and they were chatting happily. As the two approached the bar, the sea of celebrants parted and swallowed them. Kingston Butterwort called loudly that a round was on him, having forgotten in all the excitement that drinks were on the house. A cheer went up from the contented crowd anyway.

Billy turned to Stewart, his eyes wide and excited.

'The most amazing part is that that skinny frog and I just massacred the better part of four bottles of wine and I count myself lucky to be standing.'

Stewart nodded without smiling. He had to admit that it had been an impressive performance, but he didn't have to like it. Stewart moved away as Billy turned to Maximillian and Clyde and the three began comparing notes and marvelling at what they'd just witnessed.

Stewart was disappointed that in the wake of the incident even Billy seemed to have forgotten the fact that The Baron was a sinister incubus utterly inimical to his brother's future happiness. The bandstand was empty, and Stewart retreated to it, taking a seat on the drummer's stool. He toyed idly with the drumsticks as he watched the crowd. Watching them cheer The Baron with undisguised adulation, the ridiculous nature of his quest to win over Natalie Jones from this popular favourite was brought into stark relief. How he'd ever thought he could steal the affections of the girl from this charismatic aristocrat crammed to bursting with sophistication and extraordinary skills, he couldn't imagine.

What did he have to offer? His sole distinction was the ability to make one sailboat go a little faster than the next one, while his rival was plush with wealth, fame, and royal blood, not to mention celebrated vineyards and this recently revealed expertise in the oriental arts. The man was catnip to women and why not? His previous night's resolve to win her away from The Baron now appeared absurdly quixotic. Seeing himself for the first time as he must appear to Natalie, he realized he ought to be grateful she hadn't reacted to his clumsy attempt with outright derision. After facing the fact that this girl was essential to his happiness, now, not twenty-four hours later, he had to swallow the bitter truth that a better man had the prior claim.

He stared listlessly at the crowd lining the bar, three rows deep. They sang and swayed en masse, well lubricated and pleased with the evening's entertainment. He suddenly felt very tired. As he stood to go, he watched a gap open in the crowd surrounding the bar and The Baron emerged, pressed on all sides by backslapping admirers. He managed to slip away from the group and approached the bandstand carrying two large mugs.

'I see you have found a refuge from the mob,' The Baron said, hooking a stool with his foot and pulling it close to Stewart. He spilled a little of one of the drinks on Stewart as he sat down.

'Pardon, I am a little unsteady.'

Stewart dismissed it with a shake of his head. 'The lads seem to approve of you,' he said, unsmiling.

'A friendly mob,' The Baron said carefully, 'is still a mob.' He dismissed them with a wave of the mug, spilling more. 'Would you finish one of these for me?'

'I would,' Stewart said, 'if I weren't leaving.'

'Indulge me a few minutes' conversation, Monsieur. I have wanted to speak with you.'

Watching him sway unsteadily, Stewart decided he could spare a few more minutes. The Baron didn't look like he'd be upright much longer, anyway. Apparently the Frenchman wasn't as impervious to rum as he was to his native wine. Stewart settled back onto the stool and accepted the mug.

The Baron smiled crookedly and leaned forward, pressing his drink up against Stewart's arm.

'Yes, join me in celebrating.'

'Your upcoming marriage?'

He nodded. 'My upcoming marriage.'

'That was an impressive bit of fighting with Hercules,' Stewart said, changing the subject.

'That was nothing. Nothing.' The Baron snorted. 'You Bahamians are very easily impressed, I think.'

Stewart took a sip from the mug. He coughed and gave a quick, involuntary shake, looking at the drink with a harsh, accusing glare. 'That's a Roundhouse made with too much 151, if I'm not mistaken,' he said. He got up and put the mug on a nearby table.

'Yes, a Rum Roundhouse, I was told. It is strong, but good. This is my second,' The Baron said, taking a drink. He swallowed and wiped his mouth before continuing. 'I'll be getting married soon now to my little Natalie.'

'Yes, so I hear,' Stewart said, not pleased to return to the subject.

'You like my little Natalie.' The Baron turned his head coyly and leered at Stewart. 'I know this.'

'Yes,' Stewart said. 'She's very nice.'

'No. No, I mean you like her very much. Very, very much. A crunch, perhaps?'

The Baron's head wobbled as he spoke.

'You mean crush,' Stewart said.

'Oui, yes. Merci. A crush. Thank you.'

'But no, I don't have a crush on her.'

'Natalie says no also when I say this,' he said, laughing. He pointed to his eye. 'But I see. Yes, I see. She knows too, I think.'

He noted Stewart's stricken expression and smiled.

'Don't worry, your secret is safe with me,' he said. 'With us!' He laughed loudly. 'Between us three.'

Stewart got up and took a quick swallow from the mug.

'Yes, celebrate with me. No bitterness between us, between men. For you, she is a passing fancy. There are many fish in the sea,' The Baron said. 'For her, for me, it is perfect. She will be titled, a baroness. I will become rich...'

'Rich? You are rich,' Stewart said. 'By any reasonable standard, anyway,'

'No, by no standard.' He turned and made the sad, exaggerated face of a mime. Stewart smiled indulgently at this man crying poor.

'Truly,' he said, seeing Stewart's scepticism. 'I am impoverished. A common tale, I am an aristocrat with many obligations but very little money.'

'That boat of yours, the Papillon isn't it, is worth about the gross national product of this country.'

'It belongs to a cousin,' he said. 'The fuel was a wedding present from my uncle.'

'What money does Natalie have?' Stewart asked. 'Not that it's any of my business.'

'No, Monsieur Stewart, it is, as you rightly say, not your business. But I will tell you because I feel for you tonight. I sense that your feelings for my Natalie are greater even than I suspected.'

Wincing inwardly, Stewart struggled to maintain an expression of indifference.

'Brixton Steel,' The Baron said.

Stewart nodded. It wouldn't be long now; the man was babbling.

'You know this company?' The Baron asked. 'Of course you do.'

'What about it?'

'It is her family.'

'Natalie's?'

The Baron nodded, smiling sweetly.

'Brixton Steel?'

'She is one of three heiresses, her older sister and a cousin. Oh yes, and her brother. She could buy many yachts the size of my cousin's. A fleet,' he mused, tilting his head and leering drunkenly. 'And I am underwater, as the saying is.'

He laughed at his own joke and punched Stewart in the arm.

Stewart nodded. 'Does she know this?'

'That she is so rich! You joke, my friend.'

'No, does she know that you aren't?'

'Not in great detail.' He shrugged. 'But it does not matter. I have a plan. A plan to increase the money. I have developed this plan for many years, in preparation for the right time. But until Nat…until now, I could not implem—imp—I could not do it.'

'And that's why you're marrying her?'

The Baron shrugged, and his head fell to the side. He straightened it and over-corrected to the other. 'She is beautiful.'

Stewart nodded.

'She is loyal,' he continued. 'Very loyal. That, to me, is of the utmost importance. She is socially adeeept. Well educated. She will make a good moth--'

'But you don't love her, particularly?' Stewart said, mystified.

The Baron held up his hands defensively, but the look in his eyes gave the game away. Stewart was astonished in the deepest sense of the word and repeated the question to himself, this time as an extraordinary statement of fact.

'You don't love her!'

'Of course I do, she is perfect for me,' The Baron said quickly. The horror of revealing his true feelings seemed to have momentarily sobered him and he spoke clearly. 'We are perfectly matched. She is adorable. She worships me. How could I not love her?'

'He doesn't even love her,' Stewart repeated to himself. He stood and walked around the drums, astonished at this new knowledge. Not loving Natalie Jones! He wouldn't have thought it possible.

He turned back and examined The Baron. The man was now a curiosity, an unusual, hardly human creature. He shook his head in disbelief. 'For money?'

'I'm marrying her for all the reasons I've said. Many reasons!'

'But not love.'

'You Anglos and your "love". What do you know of it? Passion? Infatuation? And what do you imagine a mistress is for?'

Stewart stared at him.

'The wife is for the household. The family. For children," The Baron said, his anger building. 'Prackical—practical reasons.'

'Such as expanding the bank account? Pardon my French, but you're quite a scheming ass.'

The Baron sat staring at him with hate building. Finally he found his tongue. 'And you are a stupid, bourgeois, Bahamian blockhead, but I repeat myself!' He laughed and jumped to his feet, his hands running through a flurry of Gallic gestures. Stewart, still in disbelief that any man could fail to fall irretrievably in love with Natalie Jones, turned away and so missed the exhibition of rude sign language. Lost in dismay at this revelation of the Frenchman's feelings, he stared upward in shocked contemplation.

'A big, dull blockhead,' The Baron said loudly, in an effort to get his attention. In his drunken fury he stumbled back and caught his heel on a microphone stand and, with arms wind-milling, fell back into the guitars and drum kit with a terrific din. It was fortunate that the mug was nearly empty, keeping the spillage on the electronics to a minimum; but looking at it fairly, if he hadn't downed its contents perhaps he wouldn't have fallen at all.

Stewart turned at the sound of the crash and watched as The Baron was swallowed by a forest of instruments, microphones, and wiring. It was an arresting sight keenly attended to by the men at the bar, but Stewart couldn't work up any interest; his attention was completely occupied by the recent revelation. He did note movement in the tangle of instruments, so The Baron was presumably alive. He turned to go.

The first-mate and the others in The Baron's entourage ran to his aid and began the delicate work of disentangling him from the equipment. The musicians also rallied around to help, although their careful handling of the instruments betrayed their sympathies.

Those not busy with the rescue effort watched as Stewart made his way to the door. No one was sure what had happened, and the speculation centred on whether The Baron had fallen on his own or had been roughly handled by Stewart. The consensus was the latter, providing, as it did, a pleasing symmetry to the evening that the audience appreciated

2ND FRIDAY

When the pattern of the southeast trade winds lapse and the wind skews to the west with any intensity, as happens occasionally in the southern Bahamas, waves and whitecaps make their way into the normally placid Ambergris Bay. Those that like to play rough in the surf enjoy the waves kicked up during these times, but anyone looking for calm water in which to relax is advised to go elsewhere.

Natalie's plan to go shelling was upset when the wind did this very thing, swinging to a compass heading of two hundred and seventeen degrees and pushing in waves from one end of the bay to the other. Ginger wanted to do a little birdwatching and the two girls appealed to Wallace, the Arm's active and diligent concierge, seeking somewhere on Porgy that might accommodate both. He had just the place; hidden around the northern arm of the bay lay a delightful series of tide pools that would meet both of their demands. When imparting this privileged information, his manner took on the air of one revealing state secrets. They were on the porch of the front desk office and Wallace looked around before pointing out the winding path that led around the point.

'Keep following that little ironshore trail,' he said, keeping his voice down. Two children exited the door and he stopped abruptly, resuming when they were out of earshot.

'You'll want flip-flops for that first part, and once you're around the corner, the shallows are sand with tide pools tucked in along the rocky shore.'

'Will there be many people there?' Ginger asked.

Wallace shook his head. 'I don't share the location with families. The pools are a respite not just from the wind and waves, but also from shouting, crying, beach balls, and particularly,' he added with a shiver, 'boogie boards.'

He followed this with a knowing look. He rarely shared his conviction that children were the scourge of a refined resort, but these girls had an air of sophistication that assured him of their good sense.

'The trade winds will be back directly, and tomorrow the bay should be its placid self again,' he added, smiling.

A half hour later the girls were on their way with snacks, drinks, a shell bag and binoculars. The path went from sand to the rough and rocky limestone called ironshore, but once around the point they removed their flip-flops and waded out onto a white expanse of sand flats. In the lee of the limestone point, the wind died and the water's surface was unmarred by a ripple. The tide pools lining the point were as limpid as an aquarium. The two made their way through the pools, delighted with the darting, jewel-like fish and flamboyant sea anemones waving in the wash.

'Did you see your new beau this morning?' Natalie asked.

'Yes, we had an early breakfast before he went out fishing,' she said happily.

'I wondered where you disappeared to so early! I'm surprised he was up.'

'He likes to be out on the ocean at first light. In fact he delayed it to have breakfast with me at six-thirty. Why?'

'Antoine woke at the break of noon with a hangover like you wouldn't believe. I told him that will have to be his bachelor party bash.'

'Leonard didn't go to the party.'

'I thought all the men went.'

'No, he spent the evening with me. He said it was the first time he's missed it since he was sixteen.'

'That's sweet.'

'I thought so too. I insisted, but he wouldn't go. He even had his clothes all picked out and everything. And he does seem to like a good time with his buddies.'

'Apparently Antoine enjoyed himself a little too much. I've never even seen him tipsy but judging from his hangover...'

Ginger cut her off with a laugh. She handed the binoculars to Natalie and pointed ahead. Focusing on the two seated figures in the distance, Natalie began laughing herself. It was Maximillian and Scoonie sitting on the shore with their pants rolled up, enjoying a smoke. The two were half reclining against a smooth limestone rock, dangling their feet in the water. They were deep in conversation.

'I forgot to tell you about Lopez,' Scoonie was saying, 'I suppose because so much has been going on with the new recipe and then last night's party...that was amazing, that Frenchman.'

'First, what did you forget to tell me? Before you forget to tell me what you forgot.'

'Yes, sorry, well, I finally heard back from Lopez.'

'The new judge! That's a relief!' Maximillian said. The newest addition to the three-man chili judging panel had been a cause of concern for the past two weeks.

'Yes, I got an email from him last night. He's due to reach tomorrow.'

'That's cutting it close,' Maximillian said. 'Did he say why he hadn't answered your emails?'

'No, but he wrote from a new address, so maybe there was some disconnection or other,' Scoonie said. The tech world was a vast mystery to him. 'I was so glad to hear from him, I didn't think to ask.'

'I'm just glad we don't have to use Foster. Having a judge from Exuma always leads to the worst whining.'

'Yes,' Scoonie said, 'I hope this new fellow's as sharp as they say, especially when things look so good for us this year. I have every confidence in this new recipe.'

Maximillian nodded. 'Thanks to that girl. Although it's disturbing how fortune sometimes hangs by the thinnest of threads.'

'Yes,' Scoonie said. 'Imagine if Billy hadn't hailed her when she stuck her head in the door that day.'

Maximillian shivered. 'Just the thought gives me an attack of nerves! Mudda sic, boy.'

'Mudda sic,' Scoonie agreed. Neither of them could fathom how a chili neophyte like Natalie could zero in so unerringly on the recipe's weakness, such an apparently niggling fault yet so significant. They sat shaking their heads.

'I'm fine with Ollie, and of course couldn't be happier to get Ornery Jake back, but this new fellow,' Maximillian said, returning to the subject of judges. 'What do we know about him?'

'Not much,' Scoonie admitted. 'But Jake said he judged at New Braunfels last year.'

'Where'd you say he's from?'

Geographical pedigree was important. The judges for the Cook-off were traditionally recruited from one of the big three chili states: Texas, New Mexico, or Arizona. As the birthplace of chili, Texas was the favoured talent pool, but the other two states were no slouches. Ollie Aulin was the foremost example of that, a former trail cook from Phoenix and the acknowledged dean of chili judges. Ornery Jake was his half-brother.

'West Texas,' Scoonie said, answering the question. 'He's a Chicano fellow. Jake assured me he has a most discerning palate. He claims the man can pick out Italian oregano trying to pass as Mexican with a sniff or two...' Scoonie illustrated with a delicate fanning of his fingers, followed by a sudden double-take as he looked in the distance. Maximillian followed his friend's line of sight to the two girls wading towards them.

'Look what's coming,' Scoonie said.

'Ah! The naughty boys,' Ginger called out when they were close enough to be heard. 'So this is where you hide to do your smoking.'

The two men started to stand.

"Sit back down, both of you,' Ginger commanded.

They eased back into their seats and Scoonie upended his pipe to tap the tobacco out as Maximillian moved to douse his cigar.

'Don't do that! At least not on our account,' Ginger said. 'My daddy, God rest his soul, smoked cigars till the day he died, and I do miss the smell.'

'A woman that likes cigars,' Maximillian said with amazement. 'I didn't know God made them.'

'We aren't staying anyway, we're out getting some exercise,' Natalie said.

'And looking for birds. I'm particularly on the look-out for a rynchops.'

'A what?' Scoonie said.

'A skimmer,' Ginger said. 'A black skimmer.' She illustrated the bird's open-mouth feeding technique with her hand.

'Ah,' Maximillian said. 'A scissorbill.'

Scoonie nodded. 'We call them scissorbills. You'll have to come back in the winter, that's the only time we see them.'

'I was afraid of that.' She cocked her head at Maximillian. 'Did you shave? Didn't you have a moustache?'

Maximillian shook his head, mystified by the line of questioning.

'She's wondering why you look different,' Natalie said to Maximillian, laughing. She turned to her friend. 'It's the hat.'

Ginger cocked her head, puzzled.

'Where's your fez?' Natalie asked him.

'Ah!' Ginger drawled, understanding dawning. Maximillian had on a large-brimmed straw hat, these excursions into the midday summer sun being the only time he abandoned his trademark top.

'I'm protecting my delicate skin.'

'And those precious freckles, I hope,' Ginger said.

'Well,' Natalie said, turning to her companion. 'Shall we leave these gentlemen in peace to enjoy their illicit pleasure?'

'Not just yet,' Ginger said, sitting down next to Maximillian. 'You know me, I never willingly abandon anything illicit. Besides, I have questions these two are uniquely qualified to answer.'

'Chili,' Scoonie said knowingly to Maximillian. He turned back to Ginger. 'Ask away.'

'No, not chili,' she corrected him.

'No matter, we'd enjoy the company and a change of subject,' Maximillian said.

'Yes,' Scoonie agreed. 'Yes, some fresh conversation. Maximillian and I have known each other so long...'

'...that we find ourselves finishing the other's sentences,' Maximillian said.

'You two remind me of an old married couple,' Gnat said, bringing a stricken look to both men's faces.

Ginger inhaled deeply as a trail of cigar smoke crossed under her nose.

'Sometimes I think of taking up cigars myself, I miss the aroma so,' she said, holding her breath as she spoke. She exhaled. 'But it's just a bit too un-lady-like.'

The men puffed away contentedly, and no one spoke for a few minutes. Natalie was settled comfortably in the pool watching the small tropical fish against the backdrop of bright corals.

'So,' Ginger said, breaking the silence. 'How about you gentlemen dishing the dirt on Leonard Sawyer, my wonder-man.'

Scoonie was baffled. 'Dishing what?'

'Dishing the dirt,' Maximillian explained. 'Nasty sip-sip.'

'Ah,' Scoonie said.

It was the girls' turn to be nonplussed.

'Sip-sip?' they said together.

'Gossip,' Maximillian translated.

'That's exactly what she wants,' Natalie said. 'But I warned her to be careful what she wishes for.'

'I'm prepared to hear the worst,' she said, comically jutting her chin. 'I say that in the full knowledge that nothing about that honest soul could prejudice me against him.'

'Well, all you'll get from us is a biased view,' Scoonie said. 'We both think the world of Leonard.'

'As I expected. You both seem intelligent.'

'He's our nephew, you know.'

'Whose nephew?'

'Both of ours. His father is my brother,' Maximillian said. 'His mother was Scoonie's wife's sister.'

'He's the only family link between us, I guess,' Scoonie said.

Maximillian nodded. 'As far as we know.'

Ginger looked at Maximillian. 'Your brother was Leonard's father?'

Maximillian nodded.

'Stepbrother?'

'No.'

'Half-brother?'

'No, full brother,' Maximillian said. He smiled. 'He's too white, you're thinking. Leonard is, I mean.'

Ginger looked at him sceptically. Maximillian put his hands on each side of his face and pulled the skin back, streamlining his features, and she gave a gasp of recognition.

'Yes,' he said, 'in my somewhat slimmer youth, there was a marked resemblance between Leonard and myself. But my brother pulled bright from head to toe, you see. A Brit friend of mine says he looks like a Yorkshireman in early spring, which is some exaggeration, but Bahamian genes do go their own way, the saying is.'

'Pulled bright?'

'Bright. You know, light-skinned. And then Leonard is even brighter than his dad.'

'Well, that explains those sumptuous lips you go on about,' Natalie said to Ginger.

Ginger giggled nervously.

'Is it a problem for you?' Maximillian said.

'You're asking because I'm a Southerner.' It was more a statement than a question.

'I guess I am,' he said.

'Not a bit,' Ginger said matter-of-factly. 'Now, what else have you got?'

The two men looked at each other a little warily, Ginger noted.

'He's about the best fisherman on this island,' Maximillian offered. 'Rod, cast net, handline, Hawaiian sling. Only a couple of other fellows are in his league. That's saying something on Porgy.'

'And he's as honest as they come,' Scoonie said. 'The fellow is without guile.'

'Yes,' Maximillian agreed. 'And he can cook. Fills in for Billy sometimes and you can hardly tell. I don't even know how he picked that up.'

'So he's perfect,' Ginger said with mocking sarcasm.

'Well, he can be a rough tease sometimes. He fairly tortures that bunch at the Conch & Coronet—the bar down by the docks—for what poor fishermen they are. They aren't, but that's his teasing. He likes getting under their skin and some fellows down there resent it, but he's too big for them to stop it.'

'I hope you can do better than that. I want some inside stuff.'

'He never was much good at air hockey,' Scoonie said, 'not that we play any more with the table broken.'

Ginger rolled her eyes.

'And plaiting, he can plait like a Red Bay granny,' Maximillian said.

'What like a what? Gnat said.

'Plaiting. Weaving palm leaves. He's very good at it. Hats, baskets, mats. Good with his hands.'

'Yes, yes,' Ginger said, 'enough of this. Yes, he's a sweetheart, yes he's likeable--'

'Oh, very likeable. Everyone likes Leonard. Aside from those C & C boys, you'd have a tough time finding anyone on

Porgy that didn't speak highly of him, other than his, ah...'
Here Scoonie stalled and conversation died for a few
moments.

'His drinking,' Ginger finished for him, looking steadily at
the two men. 'You two have been dancing around it like Fred
and Ginger.'

There was a longer pause as the two men looked at each
other, both weighing the appropriate degree of candour.
Neither wanted to hurt Leonard's chances with this girl, but
just as there's no point denying that the sun will rise tomorrow,
so too there was no percentage in denying that Leonard
mopped it up on an industrial scale.

'He does drink a bit at times,' Scoonie said.

'Yes, at times,' Maximillian agreed.

'Fairly regular times,' Scoonie added, avoiding the girl's
eyes.

'How regular?' Ginger said firmly.

'Well,' Maximillian said, 'five o'clock sharp, generally.'

'Every day?!'

The two nodded.

'But however immoderate his intake...' Maximillian said.

'And it's always immoderate,' Scoonie added.

'...he's ready to go the next morning. It doesn't interfere
with his work, his attitude, anything.'

'He's what is known as a fully functioning alcoholic. His
biggest problem is,' Scoonie said, 'he doesn't know what a
hangover is.'

'No,' Maximillian agreed. 'He's never had the experience
that makes it such a rich and cautionary lesson for the rest of
us. He's up and spinning like a top after the worst debauchery.'

'Maybe so, but all that alcohol can't be good for him,'
Ginger said.

'No, you wouldn't think so, would you,' Scoonie mused,
'but he's as healthy as a horse. I mean, look at him.'

'The last time anyone can remember him having so much as
a cold or the flu was his last year of high school,' Maximillian
said. 'He just doesn't get sick. It's remarkable.'

Staring down at his feet, Scoonie nodded agreement. 'Everyone remarks on it.'

Ginger looked from one to the other sceptically.

'No, it's quite a mystery,' Maximillian went on. 'The theory I hold is that the disinfectant properties of the alcohol kill the germs.'

'Does anyone ever say anything to him?' Natalie asked. 'An intervention?'

'Oh, he knows we all worry about him. He's sensitive to any mention of it,' Scoonie said. 'But the fact that even when utterly submerged he's still a gentleman--'

'Unfailingly gracious,' Maximillian agreed.

'And Bahamians are forgiving as can be with a fellow as long as he isn't rude. That's the line you don't cross.'

Ginger smiled crookedly with a distant look in her eye, and it was impossible to tell how she was taking these revelations.

'Yes,' she said quietly. 'Evening cocktails have been interesting. At first I thought maybe it was because it's tournament season.'

'Tell her the Cuba Libre story,' Scoonie said in an attempt to lighten the mood. Ginger watched a pained expression cross Maximillian's face.

'I think we've said enough for the time being.'

'Maximillian, tell me the story,' Ginger pressed.

The big man shifted his bulk, pausing so long it seemed he would ignore her request. The two girls continued to look at him expectantly and finally he sighed and spoke.

'One day Billy and I were sitting at the bar with a couple of other fellows and as always, at five o'clock in comes Leonard and he give Gladys that little two-finger salute of his, meaning he'd start with his usual, a Cuba Libre made with 151.'

'That's just a rum and Coke?' Gnat said.

'With a squeeze of lime,' Maximillian said. 'So Gladys filled a glass, added some ice, sat it down on the bar in front of him and went back into the kitchen. Leonard picked it up, took a long drink and started choking, spewing the stuff all over the bar, the floor, the stools. He coughed and sputtered and wheezed, it was awful. Naturally we jumped up and slapped him on the back and shook him around a bit. No one had any idea what was wrong. I thought it had to be a piece of ice down the wrong pipe.'

Scoonie laughed and Maximillian paused to giggle. Ginger and Natalie exchanged looks. The humour escaped them.

'So Gladys comes out of the kitchen with a bottle just as Leonard is getting his voice back. He pointed to the glass and, practically shouting at her, says, "You almost poisoned me, Gladys. That stuff's gone off!" She squinted at him a second or two and then burst out laughing. It turned out it was only Coca-Cola and ice; she'd run out of rum and had gone to get another bottle. It had been so long since Leonard had tasted straight Coke, he didn't recognise it. He thought the stuff had gone bad.'

Natalie laughed with the two men and then caught herself when she saw that her friend was staring with a quiet smile on her lips.

'Well,' Ginger said. 'My feeling is that all the liquor has just been filling a gap in his life that I mean to fill. I'm no teetotaller and I won't try to make him one, but there isn't room for quite that much alcohol and me in his life.'

Since the discussion with his uncle the day before in which Julius had learned what was expected of him, he'd been in a funk. He'd expected to spend at least some time in the Bahamas relaxing by the seaside in the sun, and yet it appeared even that was to be denied him.

'You mean I can't even go to the beach!'

'No, too risky. The less you show your face in public, the better. And anyway, you can't go in the water with that wig.'

'This "operation" of yours requires me to pose as a Chicano, Uncle. Don't you think I need a little colour for the role?' He pulled his shirt up, exposing a field of white tinged with small pink freckles.

Kingston winced and nodded. 'Yes, I've seen more attractive fish bellies.'

'And how old is this man that I'm playing?'

'Don't worry,' Kingston said. 'I've got a girl coming in on the boat today to take care of all that. It's what I came to tell you.'

'What do you mean?' Julius said.

'What it means is, you can be sure that I've taken every detail into consideration. I'm bringing in a make-up person who, I have been assured, will transform you into a convincingly swarthy and middle-aged Mexican.'

'A genuine dramatic arts make-up artist?' Julius said sceptically.

'Direct from Hollywood, California. She'd better be the real thing, she's charging me a fortune.'

Julius couldn't hide his excitement.

'An actual make-up artist. This is so cool.'

'You just work on your end of it. I don't care if you're the spitting image of the Frito Bandito, you're not poking your nose outside until you have a Mexican accent down cold.'

'Who's the Frito Bandito?'

'Before your time. Just get to work on that accent,' he said on his way out. 'If she arrives as scheduled, and she'd better, tomorrow evening is a trial run in the full get-up.'

It was almost noon and Julius had watched his uncle board the sportfishing boat and leave the harbour. He sat with his hands cradling his chin, staring out of the window of his cabin at the boats bobbing in the harbour roadstead. Though he was under strict orders to stay inside and practice his accent, the young thespian was a natural mimic and had matched the telephone recording Kingston had given him within minutes. He pulled off the tight-fitting, itchy wig he'd been instructed to wear at all times. It was very uncomfortable.

'All the more reason to get used to wearing it,' Kingston had said. He'd even stipulated that Julius sleep in it, but not even the threat of poverty could induce him to do that. Maybe the make-up artist would know how to fix the itching.

His immediate concern was his growling stomach. The boat's kitchen had been instructed to deliver whatever he wanted, but Julius was interested in the local fare. When his mother had informed him that he'd be helping his Uncle Kingston with a project in the Bahamas, Julius had done his due diligence on the internet and the reviews of local conch and fish dishes had excited his adventurous palate, always keen for new experiences. Glancing at his notes, he came to Waltanique's Conch Stand, and read the enthusiastic description printed directly from BahamaLouie.net:

"Though only a fraction of the size of The Willstownian Restaurant or the celebrated Mutt'n'Fish," it read, "this tiny Porgy eatery, little more than a kiosk with a lean-to porch and three ramshackle tables, is known throughout the Bahamas for serving the best conch fritters of the island chain. How proprietress Waltanique Sands turns what is too often a heavy, greasy creation into the light, airy and scrumptious 'Niquefritter' is a closely held secret and it's rumoured that she's turned down five-figure offers for the recipe."

It went on to list the notable celebrities that had eaten at the stand, and reading the names of several giants in his chosen field of acting, Julius decided that fearsome uncle or not, he would eat at that conch stand and today his lunch schedule was wide open. He wasn't going to sully the experience with the scratchy hairpiece, but with his sensitive skin and the sun at its peak, he would compromise and wear the sombrero Kingston had given him.

The online map of Willstown proved accurate and ten minutes later, having successfully escaped the yacht undetected, he found himself standing in front of little more than a shack with a faded sign that read 'Waltanique's Fritters & More' and from which emanated the most tantalizing aroma. He'd arrived at the peak of the lunch rush and though there was a long line ahead of him, it gave him the opportunity to study a stunning girl taking orders. This ample beauty was Missy's niece and she was working at the stand for the summer before returning to college in England. He noted her beautifully radiant skin, the colour of which, he mused, was Dark Sulawesi with two teaspoons of heavy whipping cream, his preferred breakfast beverage. Her large brown eyes had an oriental cast, her lips were full and sculpted and her voice had the most musical Caribbean lilt. She had a much more sumptuous figure than is currently fashionable, but for Julius this was no deterrent, for he liked a woman of substance. The skeletal sleekness celebrated by current fashion always put him in mind of a shrunken chicken wing, a thing that never stimulated his appetite.

Her attractiveness worked on him like a beaver and when he finally shuffled forward, face-to-face with this Rubenesque ideal, he found himself at a loss for words. They stood gazing at one another, Julius with a crossed look of budding love and embarrassment, she with the questioning look of a busy order-taker dealing with a long line of hungry lunch patrons.

'Yes sir, what will you have?' she asked the tongue-tied young man for the third time. Truth be told, on her side there was also some interest. She too appreciated an ample physique and thought the limp blond hair sticking out under the wide brim of his hat striking. His features, which heretofore the distaff half of humanity had deemed vapid and uninteresting, she viewed as amiable and attractive. He was just the sort of big, sensitive type she liked.

The fritters lived up to the advance billing, but Julius, a man normally attentive to every nuance of flavour, returned to the Butterchurn VIII after lunch with only the vaguest impression of the celebrated dish. His stay on Porgy, which thirty minutes earlier had loomed in his impressionable imagination as a dark and ominous cloud, had acquired a silver lining. Somehow, he'd have to get to know this girl. Could The Moral Bathysphere have inadvertently done his nephew a good turn?

Stewart was resolute as he approached the Upper Pink Cottage. The calm focus he'd felt in the gaol the night of the museum robbery had been shaken by the events at the Prep Party: First The Baron's display of fighting prowess and the celebration of it followed by his astonishing drunken admission of his mercenary motive for marrying Natalie. Stewart had never been adept at navigating difficult emotions and these events has set his psyche rocking. He meant to have an open and frank conversation with Natalie and let the chips fall where they may.

That's what he told himself. Actually, his confidence in the rightness of his cause had returned, and he was sure he could bring her to acknowledge destiny's intent.

He knocked on the door of the cottage and Ginger opened it, her phone sandwiched between her ear and shoulder. She raised her eyebrows in greeting.

'I'm talking to your precious cousin,' she said, smiling.

Stewart nodded. 'Is Natalie in?'

She shook her head. 'She went for a walk about ten minutes ago.'

'To town?'

She shook her head. 'Just around the grounds, I think.'

'Thanks,' Stewart said, and giving a little wave, set off. On a hunch, he began following his favourite walkway and a few minutes into the search he came across her sitting on a bench in a shaded bower that faced slightly south, catching a corner of the cooling trades.

'Ah,' he said. 'You've found a pleasant spot.'

'Yes, this is my secret hideaway.'

'It's a favourite of mine too. May I join you?'

'Certainly,' she said, sliding over to make room. Stewart sat awkwardly and followed her gaze out over the Mutt'n'Fish and the southern arm of the bay.

'Well,' he said, indicating the restaurant, 'you're a hero twice over now that you've saved the Mutt'n'Fish.'

'You mean we saved it,' she said. 'After all, you found the assignation. But what do you mean by twice?'

'Your help with the chili recipe. That ranks nearly as high with Max and Dad as your heroics at the museum.'

'You might be right,' she said, laughing, 'they seemed about equally happy with both results, although how a couple of chili ingredients rank as high as saving a restaurant is a mystery to me.'

'Oh I agree, but they'd just pity us for our misplaced priorities.'

The conversation lagged, and Stewart struggled with an artful way to introduce the subject of a girl marrying the wrong man. He'd hoped that somehow the segue into questioning someone's choice of a life mate would occur naturally in the course of their talking, but he was stymied.

Natalie stirred and started to stand, causing Stewart to speak.

'I hope this won't be your last time visiting us,' he said more abruptly than he'd intended.

Startled, she sat back down.

'Well, I don't know,' she said. 'Antoine generally goes to the Mediterranean or the Red Sea, but I know I'd like to come back. We chose Porgy for the wedding because it was between both families and the yacht happened to be in Miami, but I had no idea it would be so charming.'

'Yes, I guess you'll be married soon.'

'The wedding is next weekend.'

'That seems like short notice.'

Natalie wrinkled her brow. 'Short notice? It's why we came here, you know.'

'No, I know. I just meant that you and he only recently met. At least, that's what I've heard.'

'Who said that?'

'I can't remember, Leonard maybe. It isn't true?'

'No, it is. We met three months ago,' she said, eyeing him carefully. 'I just wondered how you would hear it.'

'Islands, you know. The coconut telegraph.'

'Yes, I've heard. Sip-sip.'

He nodded. 'You're learning fast.'

'It's a charming term. I guess you're one of those people that believe in long engagements.'

'No, not necessarily. But it's a big step, you do want to be careful.'

'Now you sound like my father.'

'Well, I won't question your father's judgement,' Stewart said, forcing a laugh.

'Why do you say that?'

'Well, I'm sure he knows more about your situation than I do.'

'That's just the problem. He doesn't know anything about Antoine but what he's read or heard, every bit of it second-hand.'

'They've never met?'

She shook her head. 'But that hasn't stopped him from having strong opinions about him. Or expressing them.'

'What does he say?'

'Just nonsense. All critical and none of it worth repeating.'

'Really, all negative? Nothing helpful, no advice?' Stewart prattled on, looking for an opening to make his case.

'Well, nothing you wouldn't find in a book of platitudes; good things come to those that wait, patience is a virtue, better safe than sorry, that sort of thing.'

Stewart nodded.

'Our family has some money,' she said, 'and he thinks every man that I date is after it. When we got engaged, he was sure of it. He went as far as having Antoine investigated.'

'Really!'

She nodded.

'And?'

She shrugged. 'We haven't spoken since.'

'And you were close?'

'We've always been close. Extremely close until this. That's why I'm furious that he won't trust me.'

'I'm sure he's just looking out for you. I wouldn't judge him too harshly for that.'

'Why would you say that? Why are you and I even discussing this?' she said in a suddenly combative tone. 'It's bad enough arguing with my father and my brother.'

'Your brother too?' Stewart said.

'They're just alike. And neither one has met Antoine. At least you have, not that you sound the least bit more sensible. Really, you remind me of both of them!'

'I'm not criticizing your fiancé,' he said. 'But to their point, what's the rush?'

'You just reflexively take their side,' she said, shaking her head in disbelief.

'I'm not taking a side, but it sounds like damn good advice to me. Of course your father has your best interests at heart. Your brother too. Why wouldn't you listen to them?'

'So you have "my best interests at heart" too?' she said, parroting Stewart's tone. 'You don't know Antoine at all. In fact, you hardly know me.'

'You'd be surprised,' Stewart said.

'That,' Natalie said bitterly, 'is an understatement.'

'Why do you say that?'

'Why wouldn't I be surprised? You and I met a week and a half ago. We've talked a total of what, three times--'

'Recovering the assignation,' Stewart said, interrupting her, 'was hardly a single conversation.' Her mitigation of the burglary was wounding.

'No, you're right. That was an adventure and thank you for it. But their objection is to Antoine and you apparently agree with them, after what, one drunken conversation with him?'

Stewart didn't answer, not trusting himself to speak about it.

'I'm just mystified why you side with the only two people that know less about my fiancé than you do.'

'Don't put words in my mouth,' Stewart said, more heatedly than he intended. 'All I'm saying is, don't be so resistant...' He stopped and took a deep breath.

'So now I'm resistant?' she said. 'The only thing I'm resisting is my father's bizarre objection. And my brother's. And, apparently, yours!'

Yet another conversation with this girl was becoming open combat. He looked at the ground and took a deep breath. 'I think you know what you're really resisting,' he said evenly, determined to make his case before the conversation completely deteriorated.

'Oh, I know it, do I?' she said severely, folding her arms. 'Tell me what I know I'm resisting, please.'

Like a sensitive stomach peering over a cliff, he swallowed and took the plunge.

'Me.'

'You?'

'Me.'

'I'm resisting you!'

'Yes.'

'I'm resisting you?!' she repeated, her tone rising.

'Yes.'

'Not your opinion? Not your incredible insight?'

'No.'

'Just you?'

'Just me.'

Her eyes went wide in disbelief.

'You deny it?' Stewart said, brazening through. There was no turning back now.

'Why am I surprised?' She grimaced. 'I was told to expect this. I was warned.'

'By who?' he said. 'Not Ginger.'

Natalie pulled herself up to every bit of her five feet three inches.

'Antoine told me about your disagreement at the party last night and how you were drunk on your ear and said the most outrageous things. The worst of it is, I defended you, not imagining that you were capable of such talk. I thought he must've misheard you because he drank too much.'

Nothing could have stirred Stewart like this. After refusing to use the truth against The Baron, it turned out the man had slandered him with a deliberate lie. The temptation to lay out the truth chapter and verse nearly overwhelmed him and he came within a whisker of spilling it all. Instead, he simply said, 'I wasn't the one saying outrageous things last night.'

'Oh, it was my fiancé, was it? And what did he say?'

Stewart bit his upper lip, a physical check to the temptation.

'I'm all ears,' she said, fluttering her eyes.

'Can we leave him out of this?'

'Oh yes, let's. We'll banish the man—whom incidentally, I happen to be marrying next week—from the discussion of who I'm in love with. Does that suit you? Perfectly reasonable. Now that he's out of the way, tell me how you know that I'm infatuated with you.'

'I never said infatuated. It's...' He stopped, brought up short by her wide-eyed astonishment.

'Love?!' she finished for him, her arms crossed. 'Is that it? I'm deeply, hopelessly in love with you? If only I'd known! I could've avoided a lot of pointless wedding planning and expense! And you know what? My father will be thrilled. Really. And my brother. Because neither of them has any idea the extent to which you are absolutely out of your mind. That, or carrying around an ego that would crush any normal man.'

She said this with such vehemence that Stewart pulled back. She noted his reaction and smiled grimly before continuing.

'Mr. Stewart Moxey, in the enchanted world of your romantic conquests I guess you don't run into this reaction often, but on the off chance that you ever pursue another affianced girl that isn't out of her blooming mind, that was disbelief. Simple and unadorned disbelief that even a hound of your calibre would stoop this low.'

'You deny having any feelings for me?'

Natalie took a deep breath and exhaled slowly before she spoke.

'Because I am a fair-minded person, Mr. Moxey, I will humour you this much. You are attractive. You have a certain charm. Another place, another time, in another life perhaps, some feelings could possibly have grown between us. At the moment I confess I'm at a loss as to what those circumstances would have to be. But it is madness to consider it now. Absolute lunacy. I love a man and I am absolutely thrilled to be marrying him. Can't you see...'

'Do you love him? I mean in the deepest sense. In my case, I confess I never grasped the scope of the word until I met you.'

'Would you stop,' she said, giving a low growl of frustration he wouldn't have thought such a diminutive person capable of. 'Of course I love him. And I respect him more than any man I know.' She turned away, glaring at the clouds.

'There you go, that's what I mean right there,' Stewart said, regaining his footing. 'You wouldn't tack on "respect" like that if it were love. Love is quite enough on its own when you're neck deep in it.'

She continued staring up, not deigning to look at him.

'Does he love you?'

The question took her by surprise and it was a few moments before she answered.

'Yes, of course he does. And it's despicable that you'd ask such a thing. First you try and make me doubt my own feeling and now his--'

'No! I just want you to face this thing honestly. You came to Porgy--'

'I came to Porgy in love with my fiancé,' she said, interrupting him. 'I am—as of even date—still in love with my fiancé, and believe it or not, I have every intention of continuing to love him. For a lifetime. Does that surprise you? He and I have a beautiful future ahead of us and you're on some egotistical quest to sabotage it. And for what? One of your tacky conquests?' She shook her head at him. 'I confess that after our first conversation I was surprised by your shallowness, but I never suspected you of this level of selfishness--'

'I'm selfish...' He trailed off, speechless.

'Yes. I can't tell if you're really obsessed with me or if you see me as just another notch in your gun belt, but on the off chance that you truly care for me as you say you do, how about giving my future some consideration--'

This was too much for Stewart. Clearly, talk wasn't bringing them any nearer the truth and at the moment they seemed to be making record time away from it. Taking her shoulders in his hands, he pulled her to him and kissed her. It wasn't a long kiss, but it was sufficient to rearrange his world. As their lips met, hers were stiff and wooden, but an instant later they yielded, and this acquiescence set off a chain of explosive realizations: It was verification; validation. This crack in the seamless wall of denial she'd built between them sent him soaring and that accounted for the delay in his realizing that she'd pulled back and was pounding on his chest.

The pounding stopped as he slowly released his hold on her and he opened his eyes just in time to see the flash of Natalie's open hand as it met the side of his face. It was jarring—there was no disputing that—and it left his ear ringing, but he felt no pain, or, for that matter, regret. In his judgement, the slap wasn't an unequivocal no that meant, unequivocally, no. It was the involuntary and virtuous reaction of a confused and wrongly affianced woman. Stewart expected nothing less from the reflexes of an upright and principled person, but he was braced and he couldn't imagine her not sharing the same exhilaration on a deep and profound level. Supporting this view was the affirmation of her body: Weighing her responsive lips and pliant body against a single angry slap, it was no contest: The slap was clearly the outlier when everything was taken into account.

Natalie lowered her hand to her side and the two looked at one another. She was expecting an apologetic expression of remorse and embarrassment. Instead, she was met by the gaze of a man apparently pleased with himself, a man that had the answer he sought. She pulled her hand back and slapped him again. The ferocity of the second slap was half again the strength of the first and this time the pain did penetrate Stewart's euphoria. Without waiting for a response, she turned and stalked away.

Stewart's attributing the first slap to a reflexive and even commendable reaction was correct, but the fury powering the second wasn't just a response to Stewart's satisfied expression.

The real force behind it was Natalie's exasperation at the betrayal of her own flesh. If a girl's resolve can't stop a tingle from racing up and down her limbs or keep her toes from curling in delight, what can it control? For a maddening few moments she'd lost command of her body and it had collapsed in his arms with a wilting compliance it had never accorded The Baron. Never in such a complete and witless way and that was unforgivable. The question was, who wasn't she forgiving?

The question kept Natalie's anger at a boil all the way back to the cottage, and opening the door to find Ginger chattering away happily to Leonard did nothing to cool it. Not wanting to interrupt or speak with her roommate, she backed out of the door with a raised hand and carefully closed it. Sitting down on the porch, she glared with unseeing eyes at the distant sea and sky.

Ginger had seen the banked fire in her roommate's eyes, and sensing trouble she told her beloved that she would call him back. After a rather long exchange of endearments she hung up and, grabbing two cold drinks from the fridge, went out to the porch.

'Coke?'

Natalie's roiling emotion seemed to have affected her hearing and there was a very long pause before she acknowledged being spoken to. Ginger waved the drink at her.

'Yes, I could use that. Was that Leonard you were talking to?'

This brought an involuntary smile to Ginger's lips.

'I thought so,' Natalie said and turned away, lapsing into silence. Ginger knew her friend well enough to keep quiet until she resumed talking. This required a superhuman effort on Ginger's part, speech being for her only a little less necessary than oxygen, but long and intimate association had taught her that any prying at this point would only delay Natalie's opening up. Her friend's sour moods were all the more intense for being rare. Five interminable minutes passed before Natalie finally turned to her.

'You're really crazy about Leonard, aren't you?'

Ginger nodded.

'More than Mark or the Nutson guy?' she said, listing two of Ginger's past boyfriends.

'Chip Knutson. Oh yeah.'

'More than Ryan?'

'Much more. Natalie, this is different.'

'Really? You're in capital-L love?'

'I guess I am. No, who am I kidding. I know I am,' Ginger said, looking pointedly at her. 'There's nothing like it, is there? You should have prepared me for this.'

'What do you mean?'

'The intensity. You could have warned me how overwhelming it is, you know.'

Natalie nodded, her brow furrowed. She turned to her friend and her expression softened. 'Ginger, I'm so happy for you.'

'And I'm happy for you too.'

Natalie's face darkened again, and she resumed her careful study of the horizon. Finally Ginger ventured to speak.

'How is The Baron? I haven't seen him the last couple of days.'

'Oh he's fine. Just fine.'

'He must be busy with his mother and all his friends here now.'

'Yes, but he makes time for me. He's thoughtful that way.' Her voice was flat, and her eyes remained fixed straight ahead. This was a very strange Natalie. After another long silence, Ginger stood and turned to go back inside. She didn't know what to do about Natalie's moodiness, and her friend's mopey despondency was no match for talking to Leonard on the phone. As she reached the door, Natalie spoke again.

'I just had a very unpleasant conversation with Stewart Moxey. Or should I say, I had a conversation with a very unpleasant Stewart Moxey.'

Ginger walked back and resumed her seat. 'Again?'

'What do you mean?'

'Remember last week when you were warning me off him? You said after talking to him you were convinced he was a louse. You don't remember calling him an arrogant womanizer?'

'I guess I did. Anyway, I was right.'

'You never did tell me what he said.'

'The details aren't important. But I stand by that. He is a louse.'

'Well, are you going to tell me what he said this time?'

'No, it doesn't matter.'

Ginger stood again.

Natalie tugged her arm to sit back down.

'I was thinking about something Antoine told me...' she stalled, deep in thought.

'Yes?'

'You know that party all the men went to last night?'

'Not Leonard, he spent the evening with me. He said it was the first time he's missed it since he was seventeen years old.'

'That's sweet,' Natalie said vaguely.

'Yes, I thought so too, but go on.'

'He said that Stewart Moxey got drunk and said some outrageous things right to his face. Things about me.'

'The Baron told you that? It sounds like the whole evening was outrageous, fighting and lots of drinking.'

'Yes, I asked him about that too but all he'd say was that Stewart wouldn't stop badgering him with questions.'

'What kind of questions?'

'About me. About the family money. He said Stewart seemed excited when he heard I was a Brixton heiress.'

'So what's new? It always gets around, it's just the sort of thing that people find fascinating.'

'He said Stewart was strangely excited. Those were his words, "strangely excited". It really seemed to have upset him. Antoine, I mean.'

'Well it would, wouldn't it? I have to say though, that doesn't sound much like Stewart to me.'

'But then how well do you really know him?'

'I haven't known him long, if that's what you mean, but that doesn't fit with what I've seen. Leonard speaks very highly of him,' Ginger said.

Natalie gave the slightest eye roll, but her friend caught it.

'Don't patronize me,' Ginger said, pushing her friend playfully.

'I'm not.'

'I saw that.'

'Well, you are in love.'

'Yes.'

'And Leonard is his cousin.'

'More like a brother, really.'

'There you go, more to my point. Neither of you are objective about this. I think Antoine is a better judge. After all, he's looking after me.'

'And I'm not?'

'No, I didn't mean that. You're a wonderful friend.' She took Ginger's hand and patted it.

There was silence for some time until Natalie spoke.

'When Leonard kisses you, what do you feel?'

Ginger smiled slyly, considering it. 'Electric. That's corny, I know, but I can't describe it any better.'

'That's wonderful,' Natalie said morosely. 'And it was like that from the beginning?'

'We've only been seeing each other a few days,' she said, laughing. 'But yes.'

'That's right, I wasn't thinking. I wonder if sometimes those feelings come later?'

'I suppose it could work that way.'

'I just wonder if maybe I haven't stifled that side of things...' She trailed off.

'You mean with The Baron?'

'Well...yes. He's so confident and mature. So practical. I try to be too, but maybe I shouldn't have tried to match his maturity and discipline. I hope I didn't squeeze the romance out of it.'

'I don't think Leonard and I could do that if we tried,' she said, instantly regretting it as Natalie's face fell further. 'I wouldn't worry about it,' she added quickly. 'I'm sure everything will work out for the best.'

Natalie nodded blankly, and Ginger hurried back inside.

2ND SATURDAY

Billy entered Stewart's apartment, slamming the door loudly.

'Stewie, boy, wake up. The sun is shinin', conch are crawlin' and the fishes is willin'. Something wonderful this way comes.'

It was eight a.m. and Stewart had been sleeping soundly. Billy circled the room, stepping heavily and opening curtains as he chided his brother. Stewart lifted his head, shielding his eyes from the glare.

'Would you get out of here. I didn't manage to fall asleep until a couple of hours ago and I don't appreciate it being interrupted.'

'Sleep?' Billy said. 'Sleep will be the last thing on your mind when you see what I've got.'

'I'm not getting up yet, Brother. Come back when you're welcome, maybe this afternoon.'

'When you see this…' Billy held up a gleaming disc and spoke softly, 'whatever complaints you have will fade to nothing. Your drowsiness will evaporate with the morning dew.'

He made a dramatic sweep of his arm and, tilting the DVD near a window, reflected sunlight in his brother's eyes. Stewart jumped at him, but Billy was across the room in an instant and sliding the disc into the machine.

Stewart lay back on the bed. 'Come back after lunch, we'll watch whatever it is then.'

'No, you want to see this,' Billy said meaningfully, hitting play on the remote.

Stewart waved goodbye to his brother and turned to the wall, pulling the sheet over his head. He could hear the Potcake & Porgy band playing.

'Where's fast-forward on this blasted thing?' Billy said, examining the remote. 'Oh, here we are.'

'Billy, no joke, I'm dead tired,' he said, speaking to the wall.

'Yeah, that's what you think,' Billy said.

Stewart looked over his shoulder. 'If it's so important to you, I'll watch it the minute I get up. Now vamoose.'

Billy held up a hand as he watched the TV screen.

'Yes…where is, ah…here we are.'

Stewart was at the end of his patience when something caught his attention. It was his own voice speaking.

'You don't love her.'

And then The Baron.

'Of course I do, she is perfect. Ideal for me. She worships me. How could I not love her.'

'The video camera was left on,' Stewart said.

'The camera was left on,' Billy agreed, grinning at his brother's back.

'While we talked.'

'As you say, while you talked. And more importantly, while that gold-digging Baron talked.'

Stewart turned and propped himself up on an elbow. 'Amazing,' he said in a tired voice.

'Amazing is not the word. Here, Brother, is Natalie Jones served to you with all the trimmings. And I'd like to go on record as a hearty Yea vote. As does the Pater, I happen to know. And Max. In fact it's generally agreed throughout the compound that we could use a girl like her around here. To be honest, though, it sets the bar pretty high for me. I never saw you attracting anyone of her calibre.'

'This doesn't change a thing.'

Billy's brow wrinkled as he studied his brother. 'Are you all right?' He walked over and waved his hand in front of Stewart's eyes. 'This changes everything.'

'I'm not showing her that.'

'Of course you will.'

'I would never show her that.'

'What?'

'You heard.'

Billy looked at his brother, his emotions seesawing from disbelief to exasperation and back. 'You'd let her marry this guy, knowing this?'

'He was drunk, Billy.'

'Exactly. In vino veritas.'

'What, the truth?'

'A cigar for the man in his underwear,' Billy said theatrically. 'Yes, in wine, truth. You have an objection to her learning the truth?'

'Billy, how many engagements would hold up if videos of bachelor parties and drunken conversations were in wide circulation? And, more importantly, she's made it clear to me who she cares about and in no uncertain terms. Believe me or believe me not, it isn't your elder brother.'

'The worst part is, you think you're being noble,' Billy said, walking to the window and shaking his head. Stewart got up and ejected the disc. He put it in his bedside drawer and got back into bed.

'Was that the disc?' Billy said, turning. 'I'll take that.'

Stewart shook his head. He took it out of the drawer and slipped it under his pillow.

'I'm going back to sleep. See yourself out.'

'I know what this is all about, Stew.'

'Good, it saves me explaining. Goodbye.'

'You'd let her marry this serpent rather than act "ungentlemanly".'

'Goodbye, Billy.'

'I'm going, I'm going. And don't bother to thank me.' He stopped at the door. 'Brother, your principles are among your more unsavoury qualities.'

Julius was enjoying a midmorning slice of pie to tide him over until lunch and to strengthen him for the ordeal of having a thick silicon layer applied to much of his exposed surface. His transformation into Fernando Lopez was pending, with the middle-aged, west Texas chili expert scheduled to check in to his cottage at the Moxey Arms in the afternoon.

The make-up artist that Kingston had imported for the job, Clairice Hoffman, had arrived the previous day and she and Julius had spent the evening together. He'd found her to be delightful company. She was a seasoned worker bee in the Hollywood hive and though she teased Julius, she clearly liked him and indulged him in his dream that he was also a working professional in the arts. He was delighted with her insider shop talk and Hollywood anecdotes and she'd poured it on for his sake.

There was a light knock on the door and Julius looked cautiously out the window. It was Clairice. As he opened the door she smiled conspiratorially and slipped in.

'Are you ready for your metamorphosis?' she said, putting down two worn leather bags containing the tools of her trade.

'I guess,' Julius said. 'Is it going to be horrible?'

'Not at all. The secret is a calm state of mind. Have you ever practiced yoga?'

He shook his head, alarmed.

'Don't worry, you'll be fine,' she said. 'Claustrophobic feelings are compounded by stress, but I have a couple of techniques to keep you relaxed.'

She noted the worry still on his face.

'They worked for DiCaprio.'

'Leonardo?!' Julius said.

'No, Beauregard. Of course Leonardo. At first he shook like a leaf, but my methods soon had him as relaxed as a frog in a bog. And that's exactly what I told him.'

Julius laughed. It was wonderful to be in her capable hands. He listened carefully as she outlined the breathing method guaranteed to quiet the nerves of acting professionals. Closing his eyes, he began to sink into a relaxing stupor when Clairice turned to the single subject certain to get his heart racing.

'I tried that little conch fritter stand you recommended, the one where the girl works,' Clairice said, pronouncing conch to rhyme with launch. Any calm he might have felt from the deep breathing exercises vanished with the mention of Patsy.

'Did you see her?!'

'Biggish girl that takes the orders?'

Julius bridled at the adjective.

'She isn't big. Not as in too big. Voluptuous would be more accurate.'

'All right, voluptuous she was. With skin like I've rarely seen, I will say that. And I know skin.'

'Yes, and her eyes. And voice, what an accent. Lilting, wouldn't you say? And did you happen to notice how she moved?'

'Settle down, lover boy, or I'll never get this done,' she said, pressing his head back down. 'So, have you been back to see her?'

'I haven't dared. My uncle found out I went there yesterday and he's got the crew watching me like a hawk.'

'I'm surprised that Midwestern passion of yours hasn't brought out the daring in you.'

'It's going to if I don't see her soon.'

'Okay, I need you to stop talking until I give the word. I'm on your mouth and cheeks.'

She worked away as Julius sat with his eyes closed, concentrating on his breath. Finally she straightened and bent backwards, stretching. 'You can talk now, the sensitive work is dry enough.'

The door swung open and Kingston entered, causing Julius to jump.

'Uncle, can't you knock?'

'It's me,' Kingston explained, stopping to examine his nephew. 'Looking good, Clairice. You charge too much, but this looks promising.'

Clairice sniffed at him.

'You're aren't paying either of us enough,' Julius said. 'If there was a theatre union here, you'd find out what a couple of professionals are worth.'

Clairice smiled at this and nodded.

'Will Senor Lopez be presentable in half an hour?' Kingston asked, ignoring Julius.

She nodded. 'If not sooner.'

'Well, don't poke your head out until I get back for a look at you,' he said pointedly to Julius. 'The sport-fisher should be back by then too. I sent them on a run to George Town and the idea is our esteemed chili judge caught a ride back on it. Your big debut is coming up. You remember everything, I hope.'

'Yes, of course!' the young man said hotly. 'I'm already a trained actor, Uncle, whether you recognise it or not and I have the skills to remember the lines to a two-hour production. This will be child's play.'

He spoke with such vehemence that Kingston stepped back and smiled. 'Well, there's a spark! I'm glad to see it. Remember, though, stop calling me uncle or we're sunk. Now give me a quick rundown of your itinerary this afternoon.'

Julius rolled his eyes and recited in a world-weary tone: 'I'm to take my bags and go to the front desk of the Moxey Arms and announce myself as Fernando Lopez, take my assigned room, etc., etc.'

'Don't be so glib, your future hangs on this,' Kingston said. 'You shouldn't have any trouble if you meet Scoonie, he's not the sharpest, but be on your guard with Maximillian and Billy. And Missy, the manager, she's a smart one too.'

'Don't worry, I can manage.'

'Make sure you do,' his uncle said, turning his attention to Clairice. 'When you go to fix him up tomorrow, how will you find his cottage?'

'Julius and I have it worked out, don't worry,' she said. 'He'll be ready by two-thirty, three at the latest.'

'The middle of the afternoon? I was thinking midmorning!'

'I'm not going to sit around sweating in this all day tomorrow,' Julius whined, tugging at his rubbery jowls.

'Stop that,' Clairice said, slapping his hand. She turned to Kingston. 'Didn't you say the Cook-off doesn't start until late afternoon?'

'That's right, but I want him ready and set to go.'

'The silicon is uncomfortable when someone's not used to it. It'll be a lot easier for him if he doesn't have to wear it all day.'

He looked at her sceptically.

'Trust me, I know what I'm talking about,' she added.

'God forbid he should have to suffer the least little bit,' Kingston said bitterly.

'You do want him at his best,' Clairice said.

'Yes, yes. Make it two-thirty then. But not a minute later. I don't want them going looking for him and discovering a pink and blond piggy hiding in the Mexican's cottage,' he snapped. 'He'll be done in half an hour?' Before she could answer, Kingston went out, slamming the door behind him.

Clairice saw that the jab at his nephew had found its mark and she knew just the thing to lessen the pain. 'I never finished telling you about my visit to the conch stand, did I?'

'So how were the fritters?' Julius asked without enthusiasm.

'Delicious. And... what's her name?'

'Patsy,' he said.

'Yes, that's it, Patsy. I understand why you fell for her, she is a beauty. A large one, but a beauty nonetheless.'

Julius glared at her. 'Another backhanded compliment?'

'No,' she said. 'I mean that. Of course you recognise that she is somewhat supersized, as you are yourself. But she certainly is gorgeous; exquisite features. And her personality; forthright yet charming. No, my admiration is real, and I applaud your mature taste. Most guys your age won't even look at anything short of a human Barbie doll.'

Julius smiled as she coloured the silicone wrinkles with long strokes. Hearing someone agree with his appraisal of Patsy's qualities warmed his heart. On her side, Clarice was happy to encourage the floundering young man suffering under the thumb of an autocratic uncle.

'Yes,' she continued. 'It's a credit to you that you can see past a healthy waistline to a girl's inner beauty and character. If you lived in Southern California, you'd appreciate what a rare quality that is.'

'Thank you, you're a wonderful friend.'

'And you're a middle-aged Chicano gentleman,' she said, giving his chin a final swipe with a brush. She handed a mirror to him and Julius studied himself. He made a series of facial contortions and burst out laughing.

'I had to do that to be sure it was me. You're a miracle worker, Reecy!'

'I'm a professional, that's what I am,' she said, smiling. 'As soon as I colour your hands and arms, you'll be ready to go check in to your room. Well, after your uncle checks my work and that boat arrives. Will you be swinging by the conch stand to get a glimpse of Patsy on your way to the Moxey Arms, Senor Lopez?'

'Si, senorita, sin duda.'

Clairice laughed. 'I guess that's a yes.'

Leonard's boat was anchored just off the beach and he was bailing her out when Stewart waded out to it.

'What are you pulled up here for?'

'I'm going to take Ginger out for a ride, but she and Gnat are going to The Baron's to have lunch first.'

'Why're you bailing, Patticake's pump go out?'

Leonard nodded. 'Battery's shot.'

Stewart motioned for the other bailer as he pulled himself over the gunwale. A couple of minutes later Leonard looked up to see Stewart staring into the water, mesmerized.

'What do you see?'

Stewart looked up, startled. 'Oh, sorry. Got side-tracked,' he said, resuming his task.

'What's on your mind?' Leonard asked.

'I look like I have something on my mind?'

'You sure do.'

'Well yeah, you're right,' Stewart said. 'What do you think of Natalie and that Baron getting married? Has Ginger mentioned it?'

'Talked about it last night, matter of fact. She's not as thrilled for her as she was, I know that.'

Stewart brightened. 'Why's that?'

'She didn't say, she just said she hoped Gnat knew what she was doing.'

'And what do you think?'

'I don't know. What's wrong with him?'

'What did Ginger say?'

'Like I said, not much. And now you're not either. What's going on. What's the problem with him?'

'He's marrying the wrong woman, for one thing.'

'What's wrong with Natalie' Leonard said. 'I happen to think a lot of her.'

'Yeah, well, me too. And she's the wrong woman for him. They're wrong for each other.'

'Why do you say that, who'd be better?' he said as he stowed the bucket forward. He turned to face his cousin.

'Why are you smiling like that?' he said, studying Stewart carefully. 'You? You think you'd be better?'

'I didn't say that!'

'You didn't have to. When did this happen?'

Stewart shrugged. 'I'm just saying she shouldn't jump into--'

'Stew, one thing Ginger did say was that Gnat said some things about you that weren't particularly nice. I told Ginger that she, Gnat I mean, must be crazy--'

'Thanks.'

'No, never mind that. What I mean is, I think you're getting your signals crossed.'

'Natalie just said that because of an argument we had yesterday. It was a misunderstanding. She has this idea that I'm some Don Juan--'

'Who's Don Won?'

'A ladies' man, a player type. It's from all the silly press I get, but there you go, she believes it. There was no convincing her otherwise and it turned into an argument.'

'So you told her you're not a fast guy,' Leonard said slowly, 'thinking that she'd call off the wedding and send The Baron packing? Because you're not a player?'

'I was just trying to have a rational, calm conversation with her, and it all went south. The same thing happened when I talked to her last week. I don't know how to get through to her.'

'Through to her how? Saying don't marry this rich, royal fellow next week, hold off, you might like me?'

'I know. As crazy as it sounds, that's pretty much it,' Stewart said sheepishly.

Leonard shook his head in disbelief. 'And people say I'm the dumb one.'

As Natalie approached the Mutt'n'Fish, she saw just the person she was looking for standing at a table on the front porch. Billy was wearing bright blue rubber gloves and chopping with lightning efficiency as he crooned quietly along with Sinatra. He was pleased to see Natalie coming up the steps for he was in a talkative mood and had been looking for an ear to bend.

'Ah, Gnat. How is the bride?' he said in greeting, turning the music down.

'Morning, morning, morning, young Billy,' she said, affecting the local patois.

'Falling in with the native tongue, I see. Always a good sign.'

'I'm making an effort. How's my accent?'

'I've heard worse,' he said thoughtfully. 'At some point, I'm sure I must have.'

'Why the gloves?' she said, ignoring his gibe and shifting the topic. 'What are those things you're chopping?'

Billy held up what appeared to be a shrivelled pumpkin reduced to the size of a walnut.

'The goat pepper, aka the Scotch bonnet, the game and popular pepper of the Bahamas. It's a close Caribbean cousin of the habanero pepper, which you may or may not know is among the world's warmest.'

'I have heard of them, but I've never tasted one. Are they as hot as they say?'

'Blowtorches, each and every one. They'd be an excellent paint stripper if only they stopped with the paint. The goat pepper's heat might even outdo the habanero and its oils penetrate sensitive skin such as my own with frightening ease. Hence the gloves.'

'"Frightening ease. Hence the gloves,"' Natalie parroted. 'You certainly have the gift of gab; I wonder you're not a politician.'

'Yes, politics' loss, no doubt--'

'But I'm not here to talk about you,' Natalie interrupted, 'I...'

'An engrossing subject,' he said wistfully.

She put her hands on her hips and got down to brass tacks. 'I came about your impossible brother and...how can I put this nicely? His curious relationship with the truth.'

'Ah, yes, say no more. It's been a point of contention between us since grammar school, if not before.'

'I'm generally a good judge of character, but I--'

'On the subject of character,' Billy said, interrupting her. 'Before we drag his through the mud—nothing I enjoy more, incidentally—I feel honour-bound to point out that it's purely and simply a matter of temperament. A wayward Moxey genetic root, I'm afraid, that sprang to life when we were mere boys, if not before. They say our great-grandfather suffered from the same way of thinking.'

'If you mean by that that he can't help it, I don't want to hear it. I won't listen to you make excuses for him.'

'Me excuse Stewart's behaviour?' Billy snorted. 'I think you know me better than that. It drives me batty too, and has for a lifetime, but the simple fact is, he really can't help himself. He's had this adhesion to unadorned reality as long as I've known him. You can't imagine the complications it caused in our free and easy childhood.'

Billy looked up for a moment and saw Natalie eyeing him strangely.

'No really, I couldn't agree more,' he said, returning his attention to his work as he expounded. 'He can no more bend the facts in the interest of, say, diplomacy, than a cat can turn up its nose at lobster bisque. And you can't imagine how crazy cats are for bisque--'

'You must be daft! I'm...' Natalie looked at him in disbelief as she came to a stop, at a loss for words. Billy looked up from his work again, noting that she was curiously reddening.

'Daft?' he said, puzzled. 'You don't know how mad they are for lobby bisque? They're attracted to it like you wouldn't believe, a positive mania...'

'You're as loony as he is...' she said before once again sputtering to a stop.

'It's established fact,' he said, enunciating carefully as if explaining to a backward child. 'Trust me. As a pretty fair lobster diver, a cat owner, and a seafood chef, you can look to me as a triple authority concerning this simple...'

Natalie started to interrupt again, nearly knocking Billy off stride, but he was not a man easily interrupted on his way to making an important point.

'Give me a very few seconds more here and I'll yield the floor,' he said, holding up the knife and speaking quickly. 'You seem to be missing my main point, which is simply that our feline friends' fascination with lobster in a thick cream sauce— a demonstrable fact—is very like the pathological hold that truth has on my brother. It's irrational, I freely grant you that. But pragmatism is an entirely empty...concept...to...himmm...'

He trailed off into silence as he watched Natalie's complexion go from reddish to a frightening crimson glow.

She appeared to be holding her breath. Her inflated cheeks reminded Billy of a wind god in the corner of an antique map, but in this case, a wind god savvy enough to leap into a gap in the conversation at the first opportunity.

'Would you be quiet for one second!' she blurted out. 'You talk enough for any two old biddies.'

'Pardon,' he said, chastened. 'Got carried away. The floor is yours.' Billy was sensitive to complaints of his talkativeness.

'Thank you.' She composed herself and fixed him with a penetrating stare. 'Now! Somewhere in all that nonsense about cats and lobsters and pathology, it sounded like you were making the point that your brother is honest. Forthright. Above-board.'

'To a fault. After all, that is the matter under discussion here, isn't it?' he said breezily despite his confusion at her restatement of the obvious.

'Quite—The—Opposite,' she said through taut lips. Each of the three words might have been cut from granite and dropped on Billy from a great height. He looked at her from under a creased brow, baffled.

'The topic under advisement,' she stated coldly, turning away to present him with a severe profile, 'is your brother's appalling duplicity.'

Billy turned this over carefully in his mind before speaking. 'You must have Stewart confused with someone else. Tall, strapping, bullet-headed fellow almost as handsome as me. Says what he thinks and damns the consequences. Thinks nuance and deceit are synonyms. Maddeningly high-minded.'

'On the complete and utter contrary,' Natalie said, drawing herself up, 'he is the most shameless and bald-faced liar that I've ever met. You should have heard what he said to me just yesterday. Antoine and I aren't suited. Was I even sure that I loved him. Was I sure that he loved me! And other things so outrageous I'm not going to repeat them. He all but said that my marrying Antoine is a mistake, as if he knows anything about it, about us, about me. And as if it were any of his business if he did.'

'Did he give a reason why? Something The Baron said, maybe?'

'No, of course not! He didn't have any proof,' she said, glowering. 'How could he?'

Billy considered this without replying.

'Well?' she demanded.

'Give me a minute.'

Natalie's eyes blazed, but she held her tongue.

'How well do you know The Baron…' Billy finally ventured.

'What!' she cried. 'Not you too!'

'I mean, is it possible…'

She glared at him, shaking her head. 'And to think I considered you a friend…'

She broke off in exasperation and began sucking her teeth. Billy gazed in open amazement.

'You picked that up pretty quickly!'

'What? Oh, the teeth-sucking. Yes, I find it strangely calming. Which, at the moment, you ought to be thankful for.'

Natalie stood suddenly and began pacing in a disconcerting manner. Billy laughed nervously. It was preposterous of course, but he found it reassuring that he was the one holding a knife. Calling on his supple synapses to diffuse the situation, Billy was rewarded with a flash of inspiration.

He cleared his throat. 'Well then, I guess there's no sense in my defending him any longer.'

She stopped pacing and turned to him. The expression on her face told Billy that he'd caught her off balance with an agile bit of psychological jujitsu. Momentarily stunned into silence, she turned and contemplated the far distance before turning back to him. "So now you admit it. He is a lying cad, isn't he?'

'The only advice I'm going to offer is, avoid him.'

'Have nothing to do with him at all, y-you mean?' she stammered.

'That's exactly what I mean.'

She nodded, gathering herself. 'I'm glad that you're finally being honest with me: He can't be trusted; he was toying with

Ginger's feelings; now he's toying with mine. He is a shameless womanizer, isn't he?'

Billy didn't respond. His conscience had the elasticity of a Bulgarian weightlifter's suit, but here it stopped him short of slandering his brother with a statement so precisely opposite the truth. There are limits even for you and me, his conscience seemed to say, and Billy had to agree.

Natalie, busy meditating on his advice, didn't press for an answer.

'Yes,' she said quietly as if to herself. 'That is sensible. Thank you, William.'

The corners of her mouth were turned down in a caricature of either sadness or resolve, but which of the two it was impossible to say. Deep in thought, she waved absently to him and wandered off.

'You'll be at the Chili Cook-off tomorrow, won't you?' Billy called after her.

She turned around, expressionless.

'I guess. The Baron wants to go.'

'I'll expect you there.'

'Why?'

'Well, you're on the chili team.'

'That's right,' she said flatly. 'I'd forgotten.'

'It's a lot of fun. It'll take your mind off of things.'

'Yes.' She nodded. 'Things.'

2ND SUNDAY

Awards Day dawned sunny and clear and the Mutt'n'Fish spent the morning hours undergoing final touch-ups in preparation for the day's festivities. It was set to kick off at three p.m., giving churchgoers plenty of time to seek preemptive forgiveness for the highly anticipated excesses to come. The one-two punch of the Porgy Island Billfish Tournament Award's ceremony followed by the Chili Cook-off and Dancing Party in the evening amounted to the blowout of the year for the island.

The Mutt'n'Fish bar was open for the duration of the celebration, but the kitchen was closed; instead, Porgians had set up food stands outside selling all manner of Bahamian fare:

Fish: fried snapper, broiled barracuda, grunts and grits, boiled grouper.

Lobster: boiled, sautéed, deep-fried, barbecued, and bisque.

Conch: salad, chowder, burgers, fritters, scorched, and cracked.

The usual suspects on the side: peas and rice, crab and rice, mac an' cheese, plantains, and coleslaw.

For the sweet tooth: guava duff, rum cake, roly poly, and benne wafers.

Stands serving Gully Wash, the popular Gin and Coconut drink, were also prominent. Both these and rum merchants were necessary to relieve the pressure on the Mutt'n'Fish bar, which laboured under a crush of custom from three in the afternoon until the wee hours of Monday morning.

The fishing awards kicked off the celebration with trophies and medals passed out from the platform on the front porch amid much cheering and jeering. There was standing room only on the porch itself and a large overflow crowd on the surrounding lawn.

By late afternoon, eleven chili teams were set up along the north side of the porch, preparing their recipes on gas grills. The crowd was growing steadily, and the outdoor booths were doing a brisk business in both food and drink as the crowd prepared themselves for the Chili Cook-off, to be followed by a night of music and dancing.

The three judges exited the cool of the restaurant's interior at seven p.m. with clipboards in hand for the preliminary round of tastings. The first judge was an impossibly wrinkled string-bean of a trail cook from Arizona that looked like beef jerky in blue jeans. He was followed by a muscular wildcatter with bad skin and thick, wavy hair. Last was a thick-set Chicano gentleman with nervous hands. The only common thread among the three was an expression of serious purpose and bolo ties with turquoise and silver slides.

With no delay the judges were immediately set to work assessing the line-up of contenders, moving from stand to stand at their own pace and giving careful consideration to each entrant.

Kingston watched the Chicano judge in amazement. He'd initially scoffed at the 'artist' on the business card of the make-up girl Clairice, but he was frankly flabbergasted by her expertise. He now placed her well above anyone calling crayon swirls a good representation of a starry night sky or trying to pass off the statue of an armless woman as a masterpiece, when even he knew the hands were the hard part. Turning his feckless pink nephew into a dusky and dignified Mexican, now there was something worthy of the label 'artist'. When he'd shaken hands with each of the three judges at the start of the competition, it had been difficult to imagine Senor Lopez as anything other than a chili expert of Mexican parentage hailing from the baked hinterlands of west Texas. The only clue that Julius was somewhere underneath Clairice's astonishing craftsmanship was the rabbit-like blinking of his watery eyes. Though Kingston's nerves were still on edge, his nephew's convincing appearance had done much to relax him, and with nothing to do until the first round of judging finished, he mused a bit on the past year.

He'd driven his team like never before, and their work, combined with an innovation from the Alberta branch of The Chili Collective, had resulted in a recipe so spectacular and so clearly better than his winner of the previous year that he'd almost cancelled bringing Julius down, leaving the fate of his spectacular new chili to honest judging. He'd assembled a group of independent taste experts to evaluate the new recipe against facsimiles of the previous year's entrants and that assessment was then handed to the Butterwort accounting department. The experts there estimated that the odds stood at 88.1 percent in favour of Butterwort's Bowl o' Bliss to take the win.

That result lent additional weight to his cancelling the impersonation ploy, but after long deliberation he'd decided that when statistical analysis is so clearly in one's favour it can hardly be considered dishonest to bend the outcome a bit more toward the proper arc of justice; he'd stick to the original plan.

Now, certainly in some cases (that perennial basement chili team, the Briland Hotheads, leapt to mind), inserting a fake judge to ensure victory shades into cheating; Kingston was fair-minded enough to admit that. In his case, though, as a front-runner and three-time winner, the impropriety was little more than an insurance policy to offset any shenanigans and a prudent hedge against the remote possibility that the Mutt'n'Fish boneheads would stumbled onto some improved recipe. After the untrammelled joy of winning two years in a row, the thought of losing to Scoonie and Billy, or horrors,

Maximillian and his damned fez and tassel; well, it was too devastating to contemplate.

Of course that was all moot at this point, and he turned his attention back to the matters at hand. The first round was wrapping up and Julius had put on a convincing show of giving each chili a fair tasting. Now the three judges would withdraw to the captain's table in the back of the Mutt'n'Fish and take fifteen minutes to consult their notes and mark their tally sheets. It was a simple system where each chili was awarded a score of from one to ten and the three teams with the highest scores advanced to the final. In the case of a tie, there would be a re-tasting between the contenders.

There was no tie today and the three judges handed in their tallies in half the allotted time. The officious head referee exited the restaurant and climbed up on a table with the first-round scores in his hand. His assistant handed him a bullhorn and after waiting for quiet, he announced the results; Butterwort's Bowl o' Bliss, the Abaco Afterburner, and The Mutt'n'Fish Miracle were the three finalists. Cheers went up from the various factions as each was announced. If anyone wanted to see the particular scores in detail, it was announced, they would be posted shortly on the cork board next to the door.

Kingston was almost disappointed. He'd hoped the Mutt'n'Fish would fail to make the final, but he wasn't going to let that tarnish this glorious day. No. Looking at it in another, more positive light, a loss at the finish line would be all the more crushing for the loathsome three. Yes indeed, this could shape up to be a more dramatic victory than either of the two previous years.

The competition was set to resume in ten minutes, with the final taking place inside the restaurant. In anticipation of this, the keener chili fans had already moved indoors, for there was only seating for a fraction of the burgeoning crowd. Lively discussion, disputation, and wagering had erupted on all sides.

The proceedings had reached a pivotal point in Kingston's scheme. Due to the fact that the final was a blind tasting, it was, of course, essential that Julius know which of the chilis in the white porcelain bowls belonged to which team. Kingston himself was the instrument through which this essential information was to flow. This was another case in which the task was too important to be delegated. He moved to the porch railing and positioned himself for an unobstructed view of the chili booths of the three finalists.

He made note of which chili went into which nondescript chili bowl. These were collected on a tray carried by the second assistant to the concierge, a very high honour for young Myron. He was mindful of the dignity due such trust and this accounted for his moving so painfully slow. Kingston's foot tapped impatiently, but finally the young man arrived at the last stop, the Mutt'n'Fish chili booth manned by Maximillian and Billy. Kingston laughed to himself at the care Maximillian took filling each bowl: Nothing you can do, old friend and nemesis, he thought to himself, will help your cause today. As the last bowl was placed, Billy added a spoonful of something and gave it a swirl. Last-minute additions of spice were an accepted chili competition practice, but not something Kingston had bothered with this year. No final-hour efforts were necessary for the ascendance of Bowl o' Bliss to its rightful place today. Billy's action, though, reassured Kingston of the rightness of using Julius to ensure a just outcome; the Mutt'n'Fish was pulling out the stops.

Confident he had the order down pat, Kingston slipped into the restaurant ahead of the slow-moving Chili Bearer and took his seat in the centre of a group of his friends and boat crew.

The tedious process of distributing the chili took some time with the inexperienced young man, but finally each of the tables up on the elevated stage had three bowls arrayed on it. The judges walked solemnly up the steps and each took a seat at a table.

Kingston chided himself for being unduly worried the past weeks. The anticipated difficulty of keeping the bowls straight during the transfer from porch to restaurant had been no such thing. It was a cakewalk.

Likewise, his concern with transmitting the information to Julius. Catching his nephew's attention, he signalled with a simple tug on his left ear and then two swipes of his finger along his nose and, presto, the layout was as clear as if it were broadcast in flashing neon.

As the bell announcing the start of the final sounded, the weight of worry that had accrued over the past year began to lift from his shoulders. It wasn't until this moment with his chili in the final and Julius sitting with the necessary knowledge to mete out justice, that he really allowed himself to relax and breathe easy. If he wasn't mistaken, the twitching he felt in his shoulders were the muscles anticipating the hoisting of the coveted black chili pot over his head in triumph. A rare generosity of spirit toward his nephew, his crack chili team, and his abused boat crew rose within him. He'd have to guard against letting such dangerous softness get the better of him.

The judges were again allotted fifteen minutes to make their evaluations, and in this final round they wrote the scores directly on the bowls; this packed a dramatic visual punch as the bowls were turned outward, revealing the score, and heightened the crowd's anticipation as they watched the head referee identify each bowl by hanging the corresponding team's name below it.

Though Kingston was finding the final to be reassuringly anticlimactic, Scoonie and Maximillian were in quite another state of mind. Scoonie was far the more excitable of the two men and during any other fifteen-minute period of the year, this was an inarguable fact. During the final judging of the Cook-off, however, upon whose pointy end pivoted twelve months of unstinting effort, the fragility of Maximillian's nervous system approximated that of his emotional friend.

Kingston's confidence, with his ace in the hole, remained high as the bowls were turned to reveal their scores, yet they weren't lining up quite as favourably as he'd expected. It was nothing catastrophic, of course. With Julius on the panel he was guaranteed first place, but he'd hoped the scores in the final would not just beat, but humiliate, the Mutt'n'Fish. Instead the Mutt'n'Fish Miracle had edged out Bowl o' Bliss by a small but painful margin with both the old trail cook and the wildcatter.

The scores read, reading left to right at the trail cook's table: Miracle—9; Bowl o' Bliss—8; Afterburner—6.

The old fossil always had been tough grader, but he must be getting senile to put the Mutt'n'Fish above the Bliss.

The wildcatter's scores read: Miracle---10; Bowl o' Bliss---9; Afterburner---7.

See, this was precisely why he'd had to resort to bringing his nephew into the thing. He'd known that such a result was possible. Improbable of course, but still within the realm of the possible. And the Mutt'n'Fish bunch had indeed stumbled on an improvement—likely by some nefarious spying—and that possibility was precisely what had prompted him to insert a ringer. He despaired of the deceit required to ensure a just outcome in this modern day.

Thankfully, 'Fernando' would set things in order. He was somewhat behind his fellow judges with only one bowl marked—a seven—and because he'd been instructed not to give the Mutt'n'Fish higher than a five, this would have to be the Abaco Afterburners. This was officially confirmed a moment later when the referee posted the Afterburner placard beneath it.

Julius quickly followed this by awarding the next bowl a perfect ten. This was, of course, the Bowl o' Bliss.

The crowd held its breath for the final score, but the Chicano gentleman stalled, apparently suffering some discomfort.

Kingston shut his eyes and prayed that his boneheaded nephew had the sense to remember that under no circumstances was he to award the Mutt'n'Fish a score of more than five. That had been dubbed the 'safety number' by the statisticians in the Butterwort accounting department. It was the Mutt'n'Fish score certain to ensure Kingston a victory under almost any imaginable circumstances. Julius seemed about to mark the bowl when a vigorous quiver passed through him and he shut his eyes in an apparent attempt to regroup. He followed this by opening his mouth and sticking his tongue out, frantically fanning it. This delighted the younger members of the audience and resulted in much high-pitched laughter.

Kingston's suspicions were now confirmed. Being an old hand at this game, he'd suspected Julius of suffering from an overdose of capsaicin, the component in chili peppers that accounts for their heat. They'd prepared for this in the training sessions, but apparently not rigorously enough.

The devilish stuff sometimes had a cumulative effect and Kingston had seen it build up during the course of a competition to the point of a judge having to withdraw. They were so tantalizingly close now. A single mark on the chili bowl was all that was required to close out the competition. Kingston's heart quavered. He focused on Julius's hand, willing it to move…

And incredibly, miraculously, it did. He raised the marker to the porcelain and made a…what? It was impossible to tell. The hand dropped, and instead of turning the bowl to reveal the score, Julius resumed fanning his mouth. It took all the restraint at Kingston's command to not rush the stage and rotate it himself, when suddenly his nephew leaned forward and, in a pained effort to turn it around, pushed it off the edge of the table. The bowl fell, bouncing once and spinning on the plywood stage. It came to rest with the score hidden.

Despite the many people intently watching the drama unfold in front of them, only three pairs of eyes were focused with the intensity necessary to make out the number on the bowl as it fell end over end. One pair of eyes belonged to Kingston and the other two pairs to Maximillian and Scoonie. Not even Billy, watching closely over the shoulders of his teammates, had been able to make it out.

It was curious that the three of them, despite all having correctly identified it as a seven, had essentially the same reaction: Bottomless despair. The three men had been standing and now all three sat, each one the very image of wretched dejection.

Kingston buried his face in his hands. To understand this reaction, one must realize that the tension of the last few minutes had caused him to add the scores incorrectly; he thought that he had lost.

Maximillian and Scoonie, on their side, were in equally poor shape from having done the reverse: They'd added the scores correctly; they knew that they had lost.

A referee walked stiffly out and returned the bowl to the table. He then turned to face the crowd, and, stentoriously clearing his throat, announced the results: 'The Final Tally is: Abaco Afterburner—20 points, Mutt'n'Fish Miracle—26 points, and this year's Porgy Island Chili Cook-off Champion, Butterwort's Bowl o' Bliss with 27 points!'

Thinking he'd lost, Kingston's state was so deeply distressing, so heartrending and absolutely crushing, that the announcement failed to register for some seconds. As it did, the fear of having misheard, of having his hopes raised and then dashed yet again, gave him pause. He wasn't sure he could endure a reversal. On the other hand, the shouts of his friends and crew surrounding him were unreservedly jubilant.

There was one way to be indisputably certain: He opened his eyes and slowly turned his head until he could see Scoonie and Maximillian: Sure enough, the two of them sat ramrod straight, expressionless. This was the third year running that he was witness to the blessed sight of those two sitting in shock at being bested by the Butterwort chili! He leaped up with a rude bellow, waving his arms in the air.

He'd won a fourth Chili Pot, and was the first to ever take three consecutive wins!

He tilted his head back and closed his eyes as if giving thanks to his maker. Actually, he was taking a few moments to congratulate himself for his brilliance in bringing his nephew into the thing. It had been a risk, but it turned out, a necessary one. His judgement that the lad had a bit of the old Butterwort spirit hidden in him had been sound.

Opening his eyes, he saw that Julius remained seated on the stage. The other two judges had already stepped down and were making their way to the bar. Senor Fernando Lopez had been explicitly instructed to also leave at the first opportunity and return to his room, as every second spent in the Mutt'n'Fish added to the risk of discovery.

Studying his nephew's pie-eyed expression and heavy breathing, he realized that his lingering was due to the continuing effect of the chili peppers. Didn't he realize that with his work done, all that remained was to wipe the tears from his eyes and make his way back to the cottage, where he could recover without making a spectacle of himself?

Kingston nodded subtly, motioning toward the door for Julius to scram, but the young blot wasn't paying attention to anything beyond the sizzling nerve endings in his mouth. The initial fiery blast hadn't dissipated as he'd been told to expect. Rather, it had acted as a detonator, setting off yet a bigger explosion of heat. Clinging to consciousness, his eyes rolled back and he managed a muffled cry while motioning for water.

Every eye in the restaurant now watched in fascination at the escalating drama on the stage. The laughter had alerted even the most distracted in the audience to the judge's anguish. There's no doubt that this wouldn't have been more than a lightly remarked instance in an eventful day if the unthinkable hadn't followed: The suffering fellow grasped a handful of his own flesh and peeled it from his face, exposing a pink and spotted layer underneath. There were shrieks in the crowd as the skin fell from his hands, and when he pulled off another strip of jowl, a woman in the front row swayed and fainted. He appeared to be turning into the figure of raw musculature often illustrated on posters in science classrooms.

Someone appeared with ice water and Julius stopped pulling at his face long enough to take the pitcher in both hands and drink deeply. The relief this provided brought a momentary smile to his gruesome features, hanging in tatters. This heightened the macabre aspect of the scene and another woman collapsed.

At this point everyone in the audience still conscious was on their feet. Only Kingston had resumed his seat, staring lifelessly.

In the row behind Kingston and company was Missy's young niece, Patsy, and her state of mind couldn't have been more at odds with the general sentiment of the crowd. Having gotten time off from Waltanique's stand (doing, incidentally, a record fritter business at a booth just outside), she'd been following the chili competition with the keenest interest. Something about the Chicano judge had held her attention for the past half hour, though she was at a loss as to why a middle-aged Hispanic man should captivate her. Her fascination with this man was no longer a mystery. Now all was being revealed, or rather, enough to put a song of hope in her heart. She had no idea what lay behind what was unfolding in front of her, but the sight of the young man she hadn't been able to keep from her thoughts raised a lump in her throat, and without conscious effort, her feet began carrying her to the stage.

From behind Maximillian and Scoonie, Billy observed the proceedings calmly. He listened to the two men as they pieced together the events unfolding before them and even directed their attention to key points: The rubbery nature of the flesh lying around Julius's feet; a broken Butterwort rising from his seat and trudging out the door without a look back; and most particularly, the chili judge's peculiar resemblance to a youthful Kingston. What puzzled Billy himself was Missy's niece tenderly ministering to the defrocked judge with an unmistakable love-light in her eyes. He tried to catch Missy's eye, but she wasn't having it. She sat with a knowing and satisfied expression, gazing at the stage.

'You realize that this means we've won,' Billy said, turning his attention back to his two puzzled teammates and nodding at the scores posted by the other two judges.

'That's right, we have,' Maximillian said. 'We're leading now that his scores will be disallowed.'

'Disallowed!' a confused Scoonie whined. 'Whose scores?'

'The fake Fernando, whoever he is.'

'Yes, he is certainly, disturbingly, fake,' Scoonie agreed. 'But what...'

'I expect we'll find,' Maximillian said, putting his arm around Scoonie's shoulder, 'that our friend Kingston has been up to his old tricks.'

'I hope you two are prepared to accept our tenth Chili Pot.' Billy said.

'You're coming with us, aren't you?'

'There's nothing I'd like more, if only I could. However, other duties call. I'll celebrate with you shortly. Right now, it's deadly important I speak to someone.'

The two men stared at him in disbelief. 'What can be more important than accepting a Chili Pot?' Scoonie said, speaking for both of them. 'And where is the girl Natalie?'

'Yes,' Maximillian agreed. 'She ought to be the one accepting the pot.'

'She left the building earlier for some reason,' Billy said. 'But she'll be back soon. Don't neglect her, or me, in the speech. We'll be watching.'

Down on the stage the head referee and his assistant were waiting for Patsy to grant them access to Julius; she was guarding him with the ferocity of a tigress.

Billy walked back, smiling at Gladys as he passed the bar on his way to join Ginger, Leonard, The Baron and The Countess. Leonard and Ginger were seated to The Baron's immediate right and his mother was hunched on the opposite side with an aristocratic scowl on her face. Billy pardoned himself as he squeezed past the crusty dowager and she acknowledged him with a dismissive nod.

'This must be Natalie's seat,' he said, settling into the space between Ginger and The Baron. 'May I take it for a few minutes?'

'Of course,' Ginger drawled while The Baron gave a curt nod.

'We've won!' Billy said. 'A tenth chili pot after a hard-fought battle.' Ginger and Leonard joined him in celebrating, but The Baron and his mother looked on unimpressed. Billy noted the near empty roundhouse mug in The Baron's hand.

'You like those, don't you?' Billy said.

'It was given to me,' he said, shrugging. 'It helps to pass the time.'

'I hope all this isn't boring you,' Billy said.

'No, it's fine,' the Frenchman answered, 'these island celebrations have a certain appeal to me. I find the primitive charm entertaining.'

'Where did Natalie go?' Billy asked.

'To the ladies' room,' The Baron said.

Billy looked puzzled. 'That's odd. The reason I asked is, I thought I saw her leave with Stewart a few minutes ago.'

The Baron tilted his head back and looked down his nose at Billy. 'No, I'm afraid you're mistaken. She will return shortly.'

'Yes, I'm sure you're right. It was probably someone that resembled her.'

The Countess peered around her son at Billy. 'What is the point of that tasteless exhibition onstage?' she said. 'Was it intended as humour?'

'I can't say, but it didn't seem to get many laughs, did it?'

'It was ghastly,' she said. 'Can we expect more of that kind of thing this evening?'

'If not worse,' Billy said blithely, and turning, he cried 'Drinks!' as Gladys stopped in front of them weighed down with a tray of heavy mugs brimming with dark liquid. 'Let me help you, dear,' he said, standing to help hand out the Rum Roundhouses.

When they'd been distributed up and down the line, Billy raised his mug and announced, 'To The Countess, and to a more tasteful evening to come.' She gave a grudging smile and they all toasted.

After a few sips, he stood to go, putting his mug down next to The Baron.

'Excuse me, I'm being called away. Feel free to drink that if I don't return.' The Baron gave another curt nod, happy to see him go. There was something about these Moxeys that irritated him no end.

It was a full ten minutes later that Ginger innocently asked The Baron where his fiancé was, and another ten minutes passed before Natalie finally returned to her seat. In the interim The Baron's blood pressure had climbed steadily and he was halfway into Billy's drink. As Natalie sat down it took all the restraint at his command not to explode in a temper. He only just managed by turning and engaging his mother in conversation. Natalie waited for him to stop speaking before squeezing his knee. He turned and gazed at her, expressionless. She was giddy.

'Everyone's saying the Mutt'n'Fish won! Can you believe it!' She turned to Ginger, beaming.

'They haven't made the official announcement reversing it yet,' Ginger said, 'but Billy said that they have, in fact, won. You should have seen what happened with one of the judges,' she said, pointing to where Julius was being helped off the stage, supported on each side by Patsy and the referee. 'It was bizarre, like some sort of performance art or something--'

Natalie stopped her with a raised finger.

'Excuse me for a moment,' she said and turned to her stone-faced fiancé. 'I hope I didn't worry you.'

'Not at all,' The Baron said. 'In what way?'

'Didn't you wonder what happened to me?'

'I understood you to say you were going to the ladies' room.'

'Yes, but I've been gone half an hour. Didn't you miss me?' she said brightly.

'I hadn't noticed. Was there a problem?'

'I ran into Missy, the woman that manages the Arms and she asked me if I'd help her. She'd gotten a call that her mother had fallen down the stairs and she asked me to go with her to lend a hand. Her mother lives down by the harbour and by the time we got there she seemed fine and we chatted a bit and came back. She was a darling old woman, as thin and stately as Missy is short and sturdy.'

'Why didn't you call?'

'I only had my make-up kit and my phone was in my purse,' she said, pointing under her chair. 'Here with you.'

'The woman Missy had no phone?' he said, his eyes wide with sarcasm.

'It wasn't working, and strangely enough, neither was her mother's.'

'That is strange. Very strange,' he said. 'I thought that perhaps you'd run into your friend Stewart Moxey and that accounted for your long absence.'

His eyes were as cold and glassy as a shark's.

'I'm not sure what you mean by that.'

He shook his head dismissively.

'Anyway, I'm back now,' she said, eyeing him curiously before pasting on a smile.

'You left with Stewart Moxey,' he said.

'No...' she said, 'I didn't.'

The Countess leaned around her son, looking particularly toadish as she stared wide-eyed at Natalie. 'You were seen leaving together. The little one said so.'

'But I didn't...' Natalie said, thoroughly confused. 'The little what, what does she mean?'

'William, the smaller brother, saw you leaving,' The Baron explained. 'It's fine, of course. We have perfect trust, you and I. I have full trust in you. That is why it is so puzzling when you are less than truthful.'

'Of course you trust me,' Natalie said. 'That's why I don't need to explain.'

The two glared at each other.

Billy was waiting at the end of the bar near the front door when Stewart entered. Billy grabbed his brother's arm and pulled him aside.

'Stew, we won!'

'Yeah, I just heard! Great news. I'm sorry I missed it, I got a call about--'

'Yes, yes,' Billy interrupted. 'A false fire report. I know.'

Stewart nodded. 'Max and Dad must be over the moon.'

'In celebration,' Billy said, picking up two tumblers on the bar filled with a dark liquid and handing one to his brother.

'To a tenth chili pot!'

Stewart eyed it suspiciously but joined in the toast. 'To the tenth!' Stewart said, throwing it back. He choked a bit but got it down.

'Was that...'

Billy nodded.

'You might've warned me, I thought it was Meyers.'

'Don't complain. Nothing better to get you in the proper frame of mind.'

'Frame for what?' he said, laughing. 'I thought Missy confiscated it? What happened?'

'I think she discovered she has a heart after all,' Billy said. 'Come with me for a minute. I have something to show you.'

He took Stewart by the arm and led him down one of the crowded rows of celebrating party-goers. They found themselves squeezing behind Leonard and Ginger, when Ginger turned.

'Hey there, Stewart!' she said in an excited falsetto.

Billy pushed the hesitating Stewart forward between them.

'Ginger, Leonard.' Stewart nodded in greeting. He shot Billy a puzzled look as his brother continued on his way down the row.

'I'll catch up later,' Billy called back.

Ginger took Stewart's arm and pulled him forward.

'What can I do for you?' Stewart said awkwardly. He could see Natalie and The Baron out of the corner of his eye and it was distinctly uncomfortable with the two only a few feet away.

'I think The Baron has a question for you,' Ginger said.

'Oh?' Stewart said, turning and feigning surprise that The Baron was there. 'How are you? Enjoying yourself, I hope.' His own discomfort blinded him to the tension sparking the air between the couple.

Ginger sat down as Leonard took Stewart's elbow, easing him forward past her. Before he could voice his annoyance to his cousin, he was almost bumping into Natalie and his awkwardness couldn't have been more obvious. He nodded, apologizing, and looked past her to The Baron. As much as he disliked the Frenchman, it was less painful than engaging with Natalie.

'Something you wanted to ask me?' he said. The strain in the air between Natalie and The Baron was apparent even to Stewart now. In the eyes of The Baron, Stewart's discomfort was as good as an open admission of guilt and his refusal to look at Natalie only further confirmation.

'Did you and I leave the building together,' Natalie asked, demanding Stewart's attention. She spoke matter-of-factly.

'No,' Stewart said, stiffly acknowledging her. 'But why are you asking me, wouldn't you remember?'

'Of course she remembers,' The Baron said. 'Pardon me,' he said to Natalie and, taking her by the shoulders, pressed her firmly down in her seat, enabling him to step closer to Stewart.

'Where were you the last half of an hour, my friend?'

'I got a call to check on a bush fire down on the south point. Luckily, it turned out to be a false report.'

'You dealt with a wildfire in half of an hour? Impressive,' The Baron said.

'Like I said, it turned out to be nothing. A false alarm.'

'I see,' he said. 'Not impressive then, but rather, very convenient.'

'Well, it was a relief, if that's what you mean,' Stewart said, trying to maintain a level of civility. The reason for the Frenchman's vitriol escaped him.

Natalie looked up at The Baron, vindicated. He was reddening rapidly, which made him very red indeed.

'How very fortunate for you, my friend,' he said acidly to Stewart before looking down at Natalie. 'You expect me to believe him?!'

Natalie's temper was also rising. She pushed The Baron's hand off her shoulder and stood defiantly. 'No. I expect you to believe me!'

'You silly woman. You…' The Baron's English trailed off at this point, replaced by a stream of profanity in his native tongue. Stewart's meagre high school French couldn't keep up with The Baron's slurred torrent of invective, but the shock registered on Natalie's face indicated it was some vile stuff. Stewart pushed towards him and Natalie raised her arms between the two of them.

'What did he say?' Stewart said.

'Nothing. It doesn't matter. He's just drunk.'

'But what was that he called you?'

Ginger stood and, leaning forward, whispered in Stewart's ear.

'Gin--!' Natalie cried, but before the syllable died on her lips, Stewart's fist was on its way around her in an arc calculated to meet The Baron's jaw. The men's eyes locked and The Baron smiled smugly as if he'd expected, and—Stewart realized with a shock—possibly even provoked this response. It was obvious that The Baron had complete confidence in his ability to deal with Stewart's fist, and but for two factors it was sound judgement: The first was the effect that two and a half Rum Roundhouses made with William's Unblended have on a man's reflexes; the other was the pent-up passion behind Stewart's arm. Ten days of simmering frustration invested the punch with more power and speed than anyone would have credited to even such a world-class athlete.

A freeze-frame photograph of The Baron a split-second after Stewart's fist met his jaw would have revealed not pain or regret or even anger (though these followed soon enough after The Baron regained consciousness): Each of the facial muscles on the illustrated chart mentioned earlier registered astonishment. On Stewart's side there was also surprise, mainly that his fist had taken the initiative with no conscious prompting. It had been an entirely reflexive response.

He watched The Baron fall to the floor in a heap and turned to see Natalie flash him a sharp look of—what? Shock? Anger? Confirmation? As he stood wondering, a designer handbag slammed into the side of his head driven by the righteous fury of a fifty-eight year-old countess. Though it caught him squarely, it hurt less than the slap from Natalie that followed from the other direction. Each woman having made her point, they turned without a word and sank down to minister to the man sprawled at their feet.

The Baron had fallen with the special dispensation granted to infants and drunks, and he was fundamentally sound. His head had just missed the corner of a chair, though it had met the hardwood floor with a loud thump.

'I'll get a doctor,' was all Stewart could think to say and neither women deigned to acknowledge him.

The news of the altercation was spreading the length of the building and being relayed to the sizable crowd outside on the porch and grounds. In no time at all, murmurs and hushed speculation replaced the bright chatter and laughter both inside and outside the restaurant.

With Leonard's help, the quick-thinking Ginger had already located a doctor, and Stewart, seeing the situation was well in hand, made his way to the door. He pushed outside and the crush of people crowding in to witness the drama parted like the Red Sea when they saw who it was and the grim set of his jaw. Stewart strode forth like Moses, oblivious to the stares and whispers around him. Yet again, the news spread that Stewart was responsible for flattening The Baron and this time it was true.

When the fresh night air met his face his mind cleared and any momentary satisfaction he may have felt from administering a well-deserved blow to The Baron faded. What he'd done on Natalie's behalf he'd have done for any female and if she failed to appreciate it, as she so obviously did, fine. It wasn't any less a man's duty, appreciated or not. If the blister's attitude was sympathy for the money-grubbing baron, good for her. It was a deflated and fitting end to his involvement with Natalie Jones and her husband-to-be.

Unthinking, he made his way down to the beach. There were a few scattered groups of people there and they began migrating up to the Mutt'n'Fish as sounds of the band tuning up were heard. This suited Stewart for he was in no mood for company. There was a light offshore breeze and the large moon had drawn out the tide until the broad expanse of wet sand resembled nothing more than a vast, rain-slick wasteland. What he'd formerly considered one of the more beautiful vistas of his home, low tide in moonlight, now struck him as the most bleak and forlorn sight imaginable.

Skirting the foam wash, he watched as the water drew out and the moon cast his shadow on the glistening sand. With a start he saw another shadowy form appear at his feet. Turning, he saw the dark outline of a diminutive figure standing a few steps behind him.

The face was hidden in shadow, but the body posture indicated someone preparing to express disapproval in the strongest terms. Breaking the silence, the voice contained just the note of condemnation he'd expected.

'Mr. Moxey, that was a horrible, brutish thing to do.'

Stewart was in no mood to argue. 'Is he all right?'

'Antoine will be fine. You, I'm not so sure.'

'What?'

'You seem ignorant of the most elementary things.'

He nodded without speaking. A response would only prolong this.

'Don't you know the least little thing about romantic drama?'

What? Stewart thought. He shook his head in disbelief as the voice continued.

'One of the fundamentals of a good romantic drama is that when the antagonist, let's say a lying, really despicable villain, hopes to win the heart of the girl loyal to the protagonist, it is absolutely fatal for the villain to attack the hero. Can't you see how that only reinforces the girl's devotion to the protagonist?'

Stewart nodded slowly, working through the literary terminology.

'And yet you did what you did,' she said.

He nodded again.

'Did you think,' she said, turning slightly, 'that in spite of the fact that the villain knocked her beloved to the ground, the mutton-headed girl could in fact find herself in love with the villain? Was that the plan?'

Illuminating her features as she looked vaguely skyward, the moon was once again perversely working to set off Natalie's astonishing beauty. It was as if the heavens themselves were determined to break his heart. He turned his attention to her last statement.

'What do you think?' she pressed.

He shook his head, not trusting his conclusion.

'Is that a no, or you don't know?'

'Is this a tragedy?' he asked.

'You are hopeless, do you know that?'

Though he would have agreed with her just two minutes earlier, something led him to doubt it now.

'Repeat that bit about the girl and the villain.'

'How about this?' she said. 'Suppose it turns out he isn't a villain at all. What if the mutton-headed girl finally figures out that he's the only man for her?'

She turned and looked at him severely. Despite the fact that he seemed to be losing the feeling in his legs, he managed to remain standing.

'I have a problem with that,' he heard himself say.

Natalie was taken aback.

'With my criticism?'

'Yes.'

'Well,' she said stiffly. 'Let's hear it.'

'I don't like you calling the girl mutton-headed.'

She lowered her face, and even hidden in the shadows her smile shown clearly.

'Oh Stewart, but she was!' she said, suddenly laughing.

She ran to him and he folded her in his arms.

245

2ND MONDAY

The Butterchurn VIII left as the sun was rising, but not before Kingston posted a public declaration maintaining that he'd been framed by the powers that be and Porgy Island would be lucky to see the likes of him ever again. Before the two mustard yellow vessels had cleared the point, the enormous Papillion began tediously nosing out of its berth, yearning for salt spray and the open sea. It carried an aristocrat nursing a sore jaw and an unprecedented hangover, one who was being subjected to what was likely the most relentless haranguing that the son of an unhappy countess has ever endured.

Julius had defied his uncle's orders that he return home with him and he and Patsy were seated on the front porch of the Mutt'n'Fish having coffee and gazing into one another's eyes. Clairice also sat at the table, amused and ignored by them. Julius pointed out that he'd added just enough cream to his coffee to duplicate Patsy's incomparable skin tone. She giggled and told him not to be silly. Not six feet from their table, Natalie had cornered Billy, but neither of the two entranced lovebirds noticed them either.

'Good Morning, Billy."

'Good morning to you, young Natalie. What have you done with my big brother?'

'He's probably in his room sleeping. We sat up all night talking on the front-desk couch and we were there until Missy opened this morning and shooed us off. The poor guy was bushed.'

'What about you?'

'I know I should be, but I'm too excited to lie down, much less sleep.'

'In Stewart's defence, he hasn't had a good night's sleep in some time, you know.'

'So he told me.'

'Tortured by some female.'

'Yes, they'll do that.'

Billy snorted. 'He is such a hopeless rube.'

'You say things like that, but I don't buy it for a minute.'

'What are you talking about?'

'Well, how much of yesterday was happenstance?'

'Happenstance?'

'Yes. Happenstance.'

'That's one of those archaic words, isn't it?' He patted his pockets. 'I'm afraid you caught me without ye olde dictionary this morning.'

'Billy.' Her eyes bored into him.

'You think yesterday was planned? Scripted? You must think a lot of me to imagine I could put together something like that.'

Natalie tilted her head back, eyeing him narrowly. 'Well, not just you. Missy. Ginger. Maybe even Leonard. I'm still working it out.'

'Missy working with me? We can't even agree on the day of the week.'

Natalie turned and nodded at Patsy. 'That's her niece, isn't it?'

'Well, yes. Yes, it is, coincidentally.'

'Yes, coincidentally. And Stewart getting a call about a non-existent fire. Missy needing my help and her cell-phone not working. And then Leonard practically pushing Stewart in Antoine's face.'

Billy shook his head incredulously. 'Mysterious false alarms, Missy's dead phone, Leonard manhandling Stewart! How would I know anything about any of that?'

'That's just what I'm wondering. What about those Rum Roundhouses served to The Baron? Positively toxic! Did you order those?'

'Do I remember ordering drinks yesterday? Yesterday! Of all the mad, merry days of the year of which to demand an accounting! A day we celebrated winning a Chili Pot after a four-year drought. Our nemesis publicly humiliated and exposed for the squalid cheat that he is. All-in-all, surely the most significant Awards Day in this island's storied history. Yes, I celebrated. I imbibed. Guilty as charged. And in the course of that, I'm sure I must have ordered drinks: But when? What drinks? For whom? These specifics are not at hand, I'm afraid. If I may be forgiven a certain fogginess concerning one day out of the year, let it be yesterday's Awards Sunday.'

Natalie shook her head. 'That was a good speech. I'm taking it as a yes. And for all of it, thanks ever so much.' She kissed him and turned to walk to the back.

Billy shook his head and staggered a step or two as he followed her.

Maximillian and Scoonie were in their customary places at the captain's table and next to them sat a smiling Ginger and Leonard. They raised their coffee cups as Natalie approached and Scoonie stood and pulled out a chair for her. In the centre of the table sat as cast-iron pot with a bright copper rim and a bronze plate reading, 'First place, 32nd Porgy Island Chili Cook-off.'

'This is a happy group,' Natalie said, beaming.

'None happier anywhere,' Scoonie said as she sat. 'This celebration is liable to run for weeks.'

'Did I hear right that Kingston said he's not ever coming back?' Leonard said in his straightforward way. The table was quiet for a few moments.

'Well,' Maximillian said, clearing his throat. 'I'm afraid that was typical Butterwortian dissimulation. The harbourmaster was by for coffee earlier and he said he found a note marked 'Confidential' pinned to his door; a reservation for Kingston's spot at the wharf next year.'

Scoonie and Billy both looked at Maximillian, and Natalie couldn't help noticing that all three were smiling.

Made in the USA
Lexington, KY
24 September 2019